To Liz

THE CIRCLE

A contemporary psychological novel with a twist

Marion Macdonald

Thank you for all your input.

Marion Macdonald.
x

Copyright © The Circle 2020 Marion Macdonald

All rights reserved

The characters and events portrayed in this book are fictitious. Any similarity to real persons, living or dead, is coincidental and not intended by the author.

No part of this book may be reproduced, or stored in a retrieval system, or transmitted in any form or by any means, electronic, mechanical, photocopying, recording, or otherwise, without express written permission of the publisher.

Independently Published

ISBN - 9798660014260

For our dear friend Jeanne. We miss you.

'Be careful how you treat people. What you do to others has a funny way of coming back to you.'

ANON.

PROLOGUE

I'm freezing. Large flakes of snow are falling, silently covering the roads and pavements. Wearing only a skimpy dress, high heels and a coat that doesn't cover my bare legs, I'm waiting for the bus and wonder if it will come in this weather. There's no mum or dad waiting to pick me up like the other kids after tonight's Christmas dance. Mine are partial to a little drink, so they don't have a car. It's either the bus or walk home for me but in these heels that isn't a choice tonight. No-one else is at the bus stop and the lights in the school where the dance was held are off now. I gnaw the peeling nail varnish from my nails, mirroring the gnawing feeling of fear in my belly. The bus shelter is now thick with snow and I peer out to see if the bus is coming. Headlights bring hope. *Please, please, let it come* I pray, but my prayer isn't answered as it's a car that's approaching.

The car stops and the passenger window slides down slowly, but I can't see who the driver is. I step back deeper into the shelter. We've been warned at school about getting into cars with strangers. I don't know what to do. What if he gets out and pulls me into the car? What if he rapes me? All these scenarios screech through my mind as I stand rigid against the cold Perspex shelter. I hear the clunk of the door as the driver leaves the car and open my mouth to scream but nothing comes out.

'Debbie?'

It's Mr Fraser, my English teacher and I almost pee myself with relief.

'Hi Debbie, are you alright? You look really cold. Can I give you a lift?'

I don't hesitate. Mr Fraser isn't a stranger. He's been giving me extra tuition for the last four months.

'Oh yes please, Mr Fraser, if it's not out of your way. I don't think the bus is coming and I can't walk home in these shoes.'

His eyes move over my bare legs and sparkling shoes.

'Yes, not the most sensible of choices on a night like this,' he says, smiling.

He opens the car door and takes my hand as I teeter out of the shelter. I climb in all legs and arms and he closes the door gently before moving round to the driver's side. The warmth is lovely. I pull out the seatbelt which he takes from me and clicks into place. The brief touch of his hand is like an electric shock and my stomach fills with butterflies fluttering away happily.

'Right, let's get you home Debbie. This is no night to be out on your own.'

'Thank you sir.'

The journey takes five minutes and we chat about Christmas and what Santa is going to bring me. I lie. There's no way I'm telling him that Christmas will be like any other day. Mum and Dad will get drunk and dinner will be a carry out from the Chinese takeaway. There will be no Christmas tree and no presents for me to open. When we arrive in front of my house it's dark and dingy in comparison with the other houses in the street with their festive lights and decorations.

'Thanks Mr Fraser. You're my knight in shining armour,' I say, unclicking my seatbelt and opening the car door.

'Wait Debbie. Let me help you. You'll have difficulty walking in this snow.'

The cold stings my bare legs but I'm thrilled that he's going to walk me to my door. He takes my hand and the butterflies flutter happily again as he helps me out. I fall against him when my heels dig into the snow and we laugh. His laugh is warm like his car, and I wish I could hold his hand forever.

Too soon we reach my front door and I rummage in my bag for the key. I look up when I find it and see him looking at me with such tenderness that my breath catches in my throat. In his hand is a small silver parcel tied with a red ribbon and he is holding it out to me.

'Merry Christmas Debbie, I hope you have a lovely time.'

'Thanks Mr Fraser. This is so kind of you.'

Tears blur my eyes and I give him a wobbly smile. Then, before I know what's happening, my lips are reaching up to meet his.

PART ONE
KNITTING

'Properly practiced, knitting soothes the troubled spirit.'
Elizabeth Zimmerman

1

Jessica

I filled the kettle, opened the shutters, and peered out into the garden. It was bright with winter sun and there was a slight frost on the ground. I live in Kirklee, an affluent area of Glasgow full of beautiful old houses and close to the Botanic Gardens. I'm lucky and I know it. Last year, I bought an apartment in one of those beautiful old houses. It had been converted as there was no longer any demand for the ostentatious dwellings of the wealthy that had been built there in the nineteenth century.

That's how I met John. He was the estate agent in charge of marketing the apartments. He was smart and a good salesman, but I already knew it was perfect for me. It had its own private entrance, so I didn't need to socialise with the neighbours unless I wanted to, and it had a garage with one of those automatic doors that glide up at the touch of a button - quite a plus in congested Glasgow. In fact it had everything I wanted, so I didn't need much sales pressure from John.

When shortly after moving in I held a small housewarming for my publisher and others in the literary world, I sent him an invitation. At that time, I didn't realise he was married, or I wouldn't have got involved. So I was surprised to find that I enjoyed the illicit meetings and didn't believe him when he said he would leave his wife for me. It's what most married men say to their mistresses isn't it? So, when he told me he was leaving Pam and his two kids, I was gobsmacked and tried to get him to change his mind, but the man was not for turning.

Cathy, my cleaner, was due in at ten, so I was making a pot of tea for our morning ritual. The kettle clicked, I heated the pot and dropped in a couple of tea bags. Scottish breakfast tea with milk and one sugar for Cathy and black with no sugar for me. I wondered what Cathy would make of the broken glass and the whisky stain on the lounge wall. I would need to tell her what had happened last night as John had texted to say he was coming round for his things today. I didn't want to see him so would ask Cathy to do it.

My thoughts went back to last night and I shivered. It hadn't gone as well as I'd hoped, and I could understand why. He had given up his wife and family for me not to mention the matrimonial home so it must have come as a shock when I told him it was over. He cried and pleaded with me to let him have another chance but as I explained it wasn't him it was me.

'I'm sorry John, I can't help how I feel. Being abused when I was a kid has had a big effect on me and sometimes I just sink into a pit of depression. When I'm like that, I'm no good to anyone. I can't write, I can hardly speak. Maybe you should think about going back to your wife and children.'

That was when he lost it.

'Go back to my wife and kids. You've got to be fucking joking. I gave up everything for you. I thought this was for ever and you tell me to go back to them. Even if I wanted to Pam wouldn't have me and the kids hate me for leaving them and their mum.'

He poured himself a large glass of Macallan, his favourite malt, but threw it at the wall before finishing it, leaving the stink of whisky and an amber stain on my white wall. He was tearing at his hair and his eyes were ablaze with fury. I felt slightly scared. No-one had ever reacted like that when I wanted to finish with them. In fact I always thought there was relief in their eyes but not John. Perhaps he genuinely did love me, but I knew I wasn't made for love and would be doing him a favour in the long run. I decided it was time for tears. It had always worked in the past but with John it set him off again.

'Don't pretend you're upset Jessica. I've lived with you for six months remember. I know when you're putting on a face. I could kill you, you bitch,' he said, grabbing me by the arms and shaking me like a rag doll. Now I really was scared. Before he knew what was happening, I kneed him in the groin. He whimpered in pain and dropped to his knees.

'Get out,' I screamed, 'before I call the police. I can't believe you're treating me like this John.'

And I burst into tears, for real this time. As quickly as his anger erupted, it began to subside. His body sagged like a burst paper bag and he sank into the easy chair that he had claimed as his own when he moved in. He put his head in his hands and sobbed like a baby.

'I'm sorry Jessica. I don't know what came over me. Please forgive me.'

'I forgive you John, but you really need to leave. I can't cope with all this drama.'

He looked up at me then and I saw the dislike shining out of his eyes.

'You really don't give a damn about me, do you?' he said, as he rose wearily from the chair and went to pack a bag.

I had breathed a sigh of relief as I closed the door behind him and there was no way I wanted to see him again.

Hearing Cathy's key in the door brought me back to the present and I poured her tea out and got a couple of ginger nuts from the tin.

'Morning Cathy. How are you today?'

'I'm good thanks Jessica. What about you? You look a bit washed out if you don't mind me saying. And what's all that stuff doing in the hallway? Are you decluttering again?'

'John and I had a fight last night and we've decided to split up. I'm afraid there's some extra cleaning up to do in the lounge. The stuff in the hall is John's so if you don't mind will you give it to him when he comes round at lunchtime. I've got some shopping to do so I won't be in.'

'That's no bother Jessica. You do what you've got to do, and I'll deal with him.'

I knew I could rely on Cathy. She was more than my cleaner. I had known her for years. She was our next door neighbour when I lived in Knightswood with Mum and Dad and had looked after me on many occasions when they couldn't. When I moved in here and heard that she had been made redundant from the cleaning company she worked for, I had offered her the job as my housekeeper. I was delighted when she accepted although her dedication to keeping my house nice and clean was almost my undoing.

Greer

Greer Gibson popped into Waitrose as she was wont to do when she finished her work on a Friday night. She worked with a charity that helped young people set up home once they had been provided with a flat by a local Housing Association. She also taught them how to manage their budget and housekeeping. Mostly the youngsters she dealt with were care leavers but there were also kids who had gone off the rails and been thrown out by their parents. Greer's children had long ago moved away from home, so the work kept her busy and made her feel grateful for what she had. Although she enjoyed her job, she liked that Friday feeling she got when she finished and always bought herself a pizza from the freezer and a bottle of white wine if she wasn't meeting her friend, Marie. Tonight, Marie had a hot date, so she was relegated to the shelf and her own devices.

Picking up a bottle of wine to check how strong it was, she was unaware of a woman pushing past her until she almost made her drop the bottle she was holding. The woman didn't apologise but continued on her way as if Greer were invisible. She didn't take offence preferring to be invisible rather than in the limelight. When she looked after the woman, she thought there was something familiar about her but she couldn't quite put her finger on what it was.

When she came out with her wine and pizza secreted in her bag for life, Greer noticed the woman again. She was placing her utilitarian purchases of bread and milk into a basket sitting on the front of her bike and it was then that it struck Greer who the woman was. Her heart missed a beat as she recognised Jessica Aitken the popular crime writer. Before she could stop herself, she moved towards her.

'Excuse me. Are you Jessica Aitken the novelist?'

The woman stopped what she was doing and looked at Greer. She didn't smile, just stared, her eyes slightly screwed up as she did so.

'I'm sorry to disturb you but I just wanted to tell you I'm a fan. I love your writing.'

The woman then came to life and smiled the smile that lit

up the face that sat on the back cover of all her novels.

'I'm sorry for staring. I was wondering if I knew you. You look like someone from my knitting circle.'

'You knit?' Greer asked, astonished that this woman would be into something so mundane. She thought it was only women of her age who got any pleasure from stitching plain and purl. 'So do I! I'm in my local U3A Stitch and Bitch Group. Which one are you in?'

The writer's nose wrinkled a little as if she had just noticed a bad smell.

'Not quite the age for that yet,' she said, with a smile that was more like a grimace.

'No, sorry, I didn't mean that,' said Greer, realising that she had bruised the other woman's ego by inferring that she was of an age to be part of the growing band of mature women and men who made up the University of the Third Age. The woman must only be in her thirties and had a long way to go before she would be eligible to join.

'I'll let you get on then. Sorry to have disturbed you.'

'Don't worry about it,' the author called out, swinging her slim Lycra-clad legs over her bike. 'Perhaps I'll see you at my knitting circle.'

Chance would be a fine thing thought Greer, imagining what it might be like to be part of an elite knitting circle like the one that the author probably belonged to.

2

Barbara

As Barbara King set out the seats for her therapeutic knitting circle, she wondered how things would go that day. She had set up the group to help women who had been through historical sexual abuse, rape, or domestic violence trauma. The women could choose to talk about what had happened to them or not but sometimes just realising that they were not alone was helpful. Barbara had found that having something mindful to do such as knitting, was helpful to the women too.

The meetings were held in a pleasant room in a local community hall near Partick station. It had lots of natural light with full length windows on three sides of the room and swing doors out into the communal hall. The floor was covered with standard issue oak laminate flooring and was painted in peaceful pastel shades of lemon and duck egg. There was also a faint fragrance of patchouli and lavender lingering from the aromatherapy treatment rooms provided by the centre which Barbara believed helped the women to relax and feel less upset if they did decide to share their story.

Barbara was a little upset today. She and her husband Rory had had words because he was going to be working late yet again. He was a lawyer and always seemed to have too much work on. Now he had been nominated to head up the Law Society of Scotland which would entail extra work for the next few years.

'I'm the head partner, Babs. I've got to show a good example to the others.'

'What about showing a good example to your family? You've not been in for dinner all week. I'm busy too running my own practice, but I can still manage to be in for dinner.'

'Look I've got to go. Let's have a chat tonight and see if we can agree something.'

It annoyed Barbara the way he always managed to escape any conflict between them. Sometimes she would love to have a stand-up argument, but it wasn't their way. She felt she was to blame for that. She practised mindfulness meditation every day and that coupled with the training in self-awareness undertaken as part of her psychology and counselling degree meant that she always tried to be conscious of what she was saying and the effect that it had. She knew it provided a good stable environment for her children, but just sometimes she wished she were more like her clients and could rant and rave.

She had a new group starting today and wondered how they would get on. She never knew how things would work out between the women who came to the group. Sometimes they gelled really well and at other times there were tensions which created an atmosphere where therapeutic work was difficult. As there were only three women this time, she hoped that she would be able to facilitate whatever happened between them.

She looked at her paperwork and saw that the only person she had already worked with was Jessica Aitken. Jessica had come to her a couple of years ago after her father died as she was finding it difficult to cope and had attended last year's Autumn circle sessions when their one to one counselling had ended. It was Barbara who had suggested that the circle might be good for Jessica. First of all because she felt Jessica was becoming too attached to her and moving on to group therapy would help with that but also although she had talked a lot about her childhood, she had never really said much about what had happened to her when she was fourteen. Unfortunately, Jessica hadn't formed any friendships with members of the last group, always keeping slightly apart from the others which Barbara thought was a pity. She needed love and support but did her best to push people away.

She was a huge contradiction. The image she portrayed to the media and her fans was completely different to how she was in the group. In front of her adoring public, she was always bright and smiling; always had time to chat and give autographs while in the group she tended just to sit, knit, and listen to the others. Barbara couldn't help feeling she was a bit like the *Tricoteuses*, the knitters who used to sit at the guillotine during the French Revolution watching people getting their heads chopped off.

The other two were being referred by agencies who were supporting them and first to arrive was Evie, but she had someone with her.

'Hello, my name's Evie Boyle and this is my support worker, Mrs Gibson. I felt a bit shy about coming on my own so asked Mrs Gibson to come as well. I hope that's okay.'

The girl looked much younger than her eighteen years and constantly shrugged her shoulders and swung her high brown ponytail as she spoke. The skin on her hands was red with eczema and Barbara hoped she would be able to hold the knitting needles without too much pain. She felt her heart melt as she looked at the girl and hoped that she would get something out of the knitting circle.

'That's fine Evie.'

'She's gonna show me how to knit as well. She's a great knitter. She showed me a cushion she'd made. I want one for my house when I get it.'

'So, you're a knitter, Mrs Gibson,' Barbara said, holding out her hand. She didn't normally offer clients her hand as some people couldn't tolerate touch, but she made an exception as the woman was there to support a client, not a client herself.

'For my sins but call me Greer please. I feel like a teacher when I'm called Mrs Gibson.'

Barbara noticed a slight frown cross Greer's face as she said the word 'teacher' and wondered what she was thinking about. However, she quickly recovered herself and sat down next to Evie with a smile.

Next to arrive was Charlotte. She could see Greer's eyes widen as she took in the woman's blue hair, pencilled eyebrows, and tattoos. Barbara was having a similar reaction but was trained not to show it.

'Good morning Mrs King, I'm Charlotte MacGregor, I'm here for the knitting circle,' she said, in a quiet, polite voice which belied her appearance.

'Good morning Charlotte, welcome. Take a seat wherever you wish.'

Charlotte sat beside Barbara which left a seat next to Greer for Jessica.

'If you don't mind I prefer Lottie to Charlotte,'
'Of course. Lottie it is.'

They were just waiting for Jessica to arrive now. At that moment, the door burst open and in came Jessica, pink from her cycle down from Kirklee. She looked the picture of health in her black and pink cycling gear, her blonde curls springing loose as she removed her helmet. She plonked herself down on the seat next to Greer and Barbara saw the look of shock on Greer's face as recognition dawned. She must be a fan.

'That's us all here now. I'll just run over why I've set up this group and what the ground rules are. So I'm Barbara King and I work in private practice as a counsellor/psychotherapist. I set up this group as, from my own personal experience and my knowledge of working with vulnerable women, I know they can benefit greatly from sharing their stories with others who have been through similar trauma. I should say that if you don't wish to share that is fine. Knitting is the other thing we do, and it can be very therapeutic in its own right.'

She smiled round the group and took out her knitting.

'What do you mean from your own personal experience Mrs King?' asked Lottie.

Barbara had hoped someone would ask her that question. She always liked to share her own story as she felt it encouraged the women to see her as one of them, a survivor, which in turn meant they were more likely to share their own experiences.

'Well, when I was eighteen I was raped while I was on holiday. I had been drinking and for a long time I blamed myself for what happened. Back then, most people, including me, thought that if a girl was drunk then she was asking for it. I didn't tell anyone about it and began to self-harm. But with the help of my mum, a counsellor, and a group of good friends, I came to realise that I wasn't to blame. The man who did it took advantage and he was the one to blame for what happened, not me.'

There was silence after Barbara stopped talking but she could see the compassion on their faces and knew that she had achieved what she had set out to do. She then went on to set out the ground rules of mutual respect, confidentiality, touching etc and then explained that meetings would be held every two weeks and would run until the end of May. At the start of every meeting, each person would say how they were feeling that day just to break the ice. The first to speak was Greer.

'Hello, I'm Greer. I'm here to support Evie. I'm feeling good and happy to be here today.'

Barbara thought she was going to say something else, but when she looked round at Jessica she seemed to change her mind.

'I'll go next if that's okay,' said Jessica. 'I'm feeling a little sad this morning. My boyfriend John finished with me last week.'

'Oh that's a shame for you,' said Evie.

'Well it's what always happens. I seem to be able to start relationships but they never last because of my past.'

Barbara wasn't sure if Jessica was going to continue but if she was, she didn't get the chance as Lottie spoke next.

'I'm feeling quite good today. I auditioned for the choir at my church last night and was accepted. They said I had an exceptional voice.'

Barbara smiled encouragingly at Lottie and hoped she hadn't noticed the surprise on Evie and Greer's faces. With her 5ft 6in body covered in tattoos, it was hard to imagine her being part of a choir singing hymns.

'Good for you Lottie,' smiled Jessica. 'You'll need to give us a wee performance sometime.'

'Thanks, Jessica,' said Lottie.

A silence fell on the group again as Evie tried to pluck up courage to check-in. Barbara decided to help her out.

'So, what about you Evie? How are you feeling today?'

Evie's face went pink and she swung her ponytail and pulled her shoulders up to her neck before replying.

'I'm glad to be here thanks Mrs King. I've never knitted before or talked much about myself, so I feel kind of nervous and excited at the same time. Thanks for letting Mrs Gibson come along.'

'Please call me Barbara, Evie. We're all in this together and

it's nice to be on first name terms.'
    'Thanks Mrs ... eh Barbara.'

Greer

When she picked Evie up from her supported accommodation in Maryhill that morning to take her to the knitting circle, she never dreamed who she would be sitting next to. She became a fan of Jessica Aitken after seeing her at *Aye Write,* Glasgow's prestigious book festival, last year and was hoping she would be on again this year. Jessica had been very entertaining when she gave a presentation on her latest book and afterwards she had taken time to talk to Greer and her other fans when she was signing her book for them.

She did wonder why Jessica was attending a therapy group though and found herself becoming excited at the prospect of finding out. She couldn't believe that only last week Jessica had literally bumped into her in Waitrose and now here she was sitting next to her. She had been going to tell everyone what a big fan of Jessica's she was and about meeting her, but she thought better of it when she saw the look Jessica was giving her. She had obviously just recognised her.

Barbara brought out wool and needles for Evie and suggested a baby hat might be good to get her started. Greer showed her how to cast on and helped her get the hang of plain and purl. Evie was delighted that she was able to do it although the hat was still lying unfinished by the end of the session. Despite a shaky start where everyone had to check-in, Evie began to relax and decided to tell the group her story. But talking and knitting at the same time was not within her grasp nor Jessica's either by the look of things. She could see that Jessica was a proficient knitter as she was knitting an elaborate cardigan in a beautiful shade of blue, but she didn't get much done by the end of the session as she took a real interest in what was being said. Greer thought having knitting as a prop was a good idea as it gave the women something to do when they didn't want to talk.

'My name is Evie and I'm eighteen,' Evie had begun, hunching up her shoulders. 'I was given up by my mum when I was five as the social workers took me off her and she thought I would be better off with foster parents. She got that dead wrong though cause I could never settle with them. I just wanted to be with her. I've been in and out of foster homes and children's homes ever since so was glad when I turned sixteen and could leave.'

'Did your mum keep in touch with you?' asked Lottie.

'No, she died of an overdose.'

'Did she kill herself because of the guilt?' asked Jessica.

'No, she injected too much heroine.'

Evie's eyes were bright with unshed tears and there was another silence for a short time until Lottie spoke up.

'Can I ask why you're here?' she asked, in her quiet voice.

'Well, when I left care, I was put up with a family who give support to people like me. It was great at first and I thought I was lucky to find such a caring couple.'

'What happened to shatter your dream?' Jessica asked.

'I fell in love with the husband,' answered Evie. 'He made such a big deal of me, always complimented me on how I looked and bought me wee presents every now and then.'

'What kind of presents?' asked Jessica, getting interested in the story.

'Lipstick, nail polish, stuff like that and one time he even got me a gold chain with my initial on it for my birthday.'

Greer could see Evie smile at the memory and wondered if she was still in love with the man who had taken advantage of her.

'So, when did he begin to ask for sex in return?' asked Jessica, putting her knitting down. 'They lead you on these men, making you think they love you and then when you give them what they want they dump you.'

'Is that what happened to you Jessica?' asked Evie, her big eyes looking at Jessica with sympathy.

Jessica nodded but didn't elaborate.

'Everything changed when his wife went to stay with her mum who was ill. He began to buy me underwear, you know thongs and stuff like that. I didn't mind at first as I thought they were dead pretty but then he asked if he could photograph me in them. I was a bit unsure but flattered at the same time. I wondered if he loved me, so I asked him.'

'And I'll bet he told you his wife didn't understand him and that you were the best thing that had ever happened to him,' said Jessica.

'That's right,' said Evie, and Greer could see the look of surprise on her face. She was so naïve she thought Jessica was a mind reader.

'He told me he loved me and wanted to show me how much. He began to come into bed beside me at night. Made me late for work a lot and I got into trouble from my boss.'

She said this in a kind of flirty voice and smiled at the memory.

'It started off with just kissing at first. I'd never been kissed before and I loved it and wanted more. I mean he never raped me or anything Barbara. I did it willingly because I loved him and thought he loved me. The result is that I'm now having a baby,' she said, looking down at her stomach.

'I think you're still in love with him Evie,' Jessica laughed.

'Remember our ground rules Jessica,' interrupted Barbara for the first time.

'Yeh, no worries. Sorry Evie.'

When Greer got home that night, her head was full of the meeting. She still couldn't believe she was in a group with an author and especially one that she liked so much. It had been a new experience for her being involved in group therapy. She thought Barbara had been very brave to put herself and her experience out there but she was glad she had as it had got Evie to talk about herself. Poor Evie was obviously still in love with the man who was supposed to look after her. She didn't even seem to know that she had been taken advantage of.

She thought about her own daughter and remembered how she had changed so much when she was fifteen, just a couple of years younger than Evie. Sophie had been devastated by what had happened to her dad and she had begun to take alcohol and drugs. She had refused to listen to her when she tried to talk to her about it. The school had even referred her to a psychologist as she had changed so much but it hadn't improved anything. She had failed her exams and thus lost any chance she had of making it to university as they had always planned for her. Her behaviour towards Greer became aggressive and there had been several loud arguments generally leading to Sophie stomping out of the house. She was ashamed to admit that it had been a big relief when Sophie had got together with a guy who was going travelling. She had never come home.

Jessica

I welcomed the silence of my home knowing that John wouldn't be sitting half pissed waiting for me but did wish that things had gone better than they had. I always thought of my public when I was beginning and ending relationships. I tried to make sure I was never involved with another man when I was finishing with my current lover. No point in making the partings worse than they needed to be and it was important not to have a vengeful ex who might blab to the papers. After how John had reacted, I didn't know if he would be vengeful or not. I knew I was just a minor celebrity, but I felt it was important that people didn't see the negative side of me. I had worked hard over the years to present a confident and successful image and I wasn't going to let anyone spoil that. People might stop buying my books and then where would I be.

I wished I could stop worrying about what people thought of me and get over my constant insecurity about money. I was doing well as I was a prolific writer. I churned out books every year and Dorothy, my publisher, was now talking about the possibility of one of my books being made into a TV drama. If that happened, I would be well set. I had made good investments and my mortgage on this apartment wasn't too onerous so really I had nothing to worry about in terms of financial security.

But I could never forget my early life as a child when most of the money that my parents had went on alcohol. There wasn't much left over for food and other things that a little girl needed. I hated going to school with second-hand clothes from the charity shop that my mum loved going to. I could smell that damp, death, already-used smell that permeates charity shops and felt infected by them in some way. I frequently went to school hungry and it was school dinners and sometimes Cathy that kept me going. It wasn't unusual for my mum to forget about washing my hair or giving me a bath. I was probably a smelly little thing. I could have been bullied at school because of the state I was in, but I had learned to stand up for myself from an early age so was given a wide berth by the bullies. But I remember how I constantly simmered inside and, in some ways, would have liked the excuse to give someone a good beating.

By the time I reached secondary school, I had begun to take care of myself and my parents. By that time, they were full blown alcoholics who no longer worked, and I became their unofficial carer. Alcoholism was a lucrative illness to have and I found that the benefits they received from the government gave them quite a substantial monthly income. I could feed and clothe myself as well as control the amount of alcohol they drank. But I was a teenager and teenagers like to experiment. I was no different. I tried cigarettes, booze and hash and wore clothes that were way too revealing but I ignored anything my mum and dad said. What right did they have to tell me what to do, the booze bags. How easy it would have been for me to go off the rails, but fate had intervened when a new teacher, Mr Fraser, had come to Knightswood Secondary.

That made me think of the last circle meeting. It had wound me up for some reason and I wasn't sure why. Perhaps it was because I had to share Barbara. She and I had done a lot of work together over the last couple of years and I have to admit I had come to love those sessions. It's not often that you get to talk about whatever you want and not be judged. I had been shocked when Barbara revealed her story to the group. She had never confided that to me despite how much time we had spent together nor had she mentioned it in the Autumn session of the circle. Also hearing that young girl Evie talk about what had happened to her had brought back everything that had gone on between me and Mr Fraser. There was also something about the Greer woman who was supporting Evie that made me uneasy. She was a social worker type with her cropped salt and pepper hair and dangly earrings and I didn't like the way she looked at me. I nearly freaked when I saw her sitting next to me and recognised that she was the same woman who had come up to me outside Waitrose.

I hadn't even managed to make much progress with the cardigan I was knitting my mum for her birthday. The pattern for the cardigan was a complex one using thin needles and 4ply wool and I knew I had only chosen it to impress her. My dad had died of alcohol related dementia two years ago and my mum had given up the drink. She had managed to turn her life around, but instead of trying to atone for all the harsh years she had put me through, she continued to be dismissive of my achievements and took every chance she got to make me feel small. I let out a sigh as I thought about Mum and wondered why I continued to seek her approval. I was like one of those women you read about in the papers whose partners treat them like dirt, but they keep going back for more.

To cheer myself up I made myself a latte on the fancy coffee machine that had been fitted as part of my kitchen and checked the email that I used for fans. I got a kick from corresponding with my fans. At least they loved me. I scanned my messages and spotted one from Magnus Nelson. My mood immediately lifted. He had been writing to me for the last three months and I had gradually come to look forward to his emails. Not only was he handsome, he was funny. I liked people who could make me laugh. He was telling me that he was coming to Glasgow and would it be possible to meet up. I hesitated wondering if it was a good idea but in the end decided to meet him. If I didn't like him I didn't need to meet him again. As things turned out, I did like him.

3

Barbara

Despite her argument with Rory, Barbara felt things had gone well at the first meeting of the circle. Jessica had seemed to accept that she was part of a group and didn't try to get her attention all the time. She thought that Greer would be a good addition although she was only there to support Evie, but she was an experienced knitter and seemed to have a sensible head on her. She thought Evie had done well telling her story, but the poor girl was still deluded and probably had fantasies that the father of her child would come in like an enchanted prince and save the day. She wondered what happened to these men who betrayed the trust of young girls. In this case, because Evie was eighteen at the time that sexual intercourse took place and she was adamant that he hadn't forced her, he wasn't going to be charged but Barbara had no doubt that his family life was over for good.

The rest of her day went smoothly. She had her Barlinnie surgery in the afternoon and after that caught up with paperwork. When she got home, she could hear raised voices. The kids bickering about something, probably whose turn it was on the Xbox. She wished they had got them one each sometimes, but she felt that was over-indulgent.

'Hi kids, I'm home.'

'Hi Mum,' called her thirteen-year-old daughter Ella, coming through straight away to give her a hug. She thought how beautiful her girl looked with her long red hair and brown eyes. She gave her a warm hug back.

'What's for dinner? Is dad in tonight or is he working late again?' Ella said, with a toss of her high pony.

Pouring herself a glass of water from the tap, she answered, 'Salmon and pasta is the answer to your first question, and I don't know is the answer to your second question.'

'I heard you and Dad arguing this morning about him always working late Mum. You're not going to split up about it are you? My friend June's dad left her mum for that author Jessica Aitken.'

Barbara almost choked on the water she had begun to sip. Hearing the name of her most famous client in her house was a shock. She never brought paperwork home or talked about clients to the family not even in a casual way. She looked at Ella to see if she had noticed her reaction to Jessica's name but her next words made her realise she thought she had choked because of her question.

'Sorry Mum. Are you alright? I didn't mean to upset you asking that about Dad.'

'It's alright sweetie. I had no idea you were thinking like that. Dad and I aren't going to split up. We both just need to get a better work/life balance. Come here my silly bunny.'

Ella went willingly into her mum's arms.

'I'm so glad Mum that I'm not going to end up like June. Do you know her dad turned up at their house the other night begging to be let back in because he had come to his senses and finished with Jessica Aitken? But her mum refused point blank to let him. June had kind of wanted her mum and dad to get back together again as she felt sorry for him looking so lost but in the end, he had made the choice to leave them, so he deserved everything he got. But Mum, I could see that she was really, really, sad about it all.'

'What's going on here? Can anyone join the love-in?' said a deep voice, and Barbara looked up to see her sixteen-year-old son Ben coming through the door, his brown eyes filled with laughter at the two of them. He was tall and gangly, but his body was starting to fill out and she could see a dark shadow starting to form on his chin.

'Yes,' she said, letting go of her daughter and grabbing him. 'Give your mum a hug big boy.'

As she tidied up the kitchen after dinner, her thoughts went back to what her daughter had told her about June's dad trying to get her mum to take him back. Jessica had never mentioned that her boyfriend had left his wife for her but what she had told them about the end of their relationship tied in with what Ella had told her. He must have finished with Jessica as he realised he had made a mistake and was trying to get back with his wife and family.

She worried about June and about Ella. They were best

friends and if June went off the rails because her dad had left home, then it could affect her own daughter. The girls were at a difficult age even when family life was going well because of hormones raging through their bodies so she would need to keep an eye on things just in case. Young lives could be ruined as she knew only too well.

Rory hadn't come home for dinner, but he had at least texted to let her know. She felt a small flurry of anxiety about what Ella had said. Could it mean that her and Rory would split up? No, she was becoming paranoid. They were solid. Always had been. But why was he constantly at the office. He had built up his career over the last ten years and was secure given that he was now head partner, yet he seemed unable to relax and accept the fruits of his hard work. It was like he had to keep proving he was good enough.

She heard the key in the door and went out to greet her husband. He looked tired and gave her a little hug. He was distracted so his kiss was automatic rather than warm. He poured himself a glass of wine as she heated his dinner in the microwave.

'Sorry I'm late again darling. Things are so busy just now. I know you're upset about it and want to talk but not tonight please. I just want to have a couple of glasses of wine and stare at the telly.'

'Okay but why don't we get my mum to come over and sit with the kids on Saturday. We could go out on a date and really talk.'

'That sounds good. Let's do that,' he said, tucking into his pasta and salmon.

'You'll never guess what happened today. Ella heard us arguing this morning and was worried that we were going to split up,' Barbara told him with a slight laugh, but she wasn't prepared for his reaction.

'For fuck sake Babs, do you need to keep going on and on. I thought we had agreed to talk at the week-end.'

'Well I thought you would want to know that your daughter was upset and worrying that we would split up.'

'We're not going to split up. Stop making a mountain out of a molehill,' he said, and went through to the TV room closing the door firmly behind him.

Barbara was distressed. She had never known Rory to be like this. He had always matched her temperament and they had managed to find their way through relationship difficulties by showing compassion for each other sprinkled with humour. But his humour seemed to have deserted him now. What was going on she wondered? Was he having an affair? She couldn't imagine that he would be, but what else could it be?

Greer

It was Friday night and she had arranged to meet her friend Marie Grant in the *Oran Mor*. The converted Nineteenth century church at the corner of Byres Road and Great Western Road in the heart of Glasgow's west end was their favourite place to meet for a drink. They both agreed that the cosy bar was a great venue with the artwork by Alasdair Gray and others adorning the walls and you never knew who you might bump into as the bar attracted visitors from all over the world as well as actors, writers and artists.

Marie was a support worker in the same place as Greer and they had been friends for a couple of years now. They were like chalk and cheese both in looks and outlook but for some reason they got on well together. Greer was petite and had strong moral views on climate change and sexual politics. Marie, on the other hand was plump and curvaceous, didn't believe in climate change and had no sense of morality in her dealings with members of the opposite sex. The only things they had in common were their age and the fact that they were no longer married. They were both in their sixties and if the government hadn't changed the pension age they would probably have been retired by now.

She was more than ready for a good night out. The circle meeting last Monday had been an eye opener. She thought of Evie and wondered how it had felt for her to tell her story in front of strangers. She knew she would hate to be put in the spotlight like that and wondered what helpful purpose it served. She much preferred to write down her thoughts and had kept a journal for over twenty years. She worried sometimes what would happen if she died and it became public; her innermost thoughts and feelings being read by strangers. But, she consoled herself with the thought that she would be dead and wouldn't know anything about it.

The phone rang, and she hoped it wasn't Marie phoning to cancel because she had got a better offer. She hadn't bought her usual Friday night bottle of wine and pizza on the way home because she was going out so would need to sit and watch television with beans on toast and a cup of tea if it were. She was therefore somewhat relieved and delighted when she heard her son's voice.

'Hello Sean,' she said, her pleasure making her voice rise slightly. 'It's lovely to hear from you. How are you?'

Sean was a GP and lived in Manchester. He had done well for himself, but he had never married, and she wondered if it was because of what had happened with his dad. She longed for grandchildren, but it didn't look as if she would ever be a granny.

'I'm good Mum. I'm just about to watch the footie but thought I would give you a quick call before it started.'

'Who is playing?'

'City and United. I know you're not interested in football Mum, so you don't need to pretend. What have you been up to then? Not going out with Marie tonight?'

'As it happens, I am. I'm just about to go and get ready. But you'll never guess what?'

'What?' Sean laughed, no doubt at the excitement he could hear in her voice.

'Well you know that part of my job is to help people who are getting a house to set up home and budget and so on.'

'Yes,'

'Well as part of the support I'm giving my current client, I have to go along to a knitting circle.'

'A knitting circle. Aren't you already in one of them?'

'Yes, but this is different. It's a therapeutic knitting circle with a counsellor to lead it. Knitting is just a side-line. The women are there to talk about what happened to them in the hope that it will help them get over it.'

'Interesting.'

She noticed that the tone of her son's voice had changed as he continued.

'Did you have to tell them about what happened to you?'

'No, don't be silly. I'm only there to support my client.'

She could feel a flutter of anxiety as she sensed his discomfort at the thought of her sharing information about herself.

'Well it sounds as if you've had an interesting week Mum.'

'But I haven't told you the exciting part. You'll never guess who I met there?'

'Who?'

'Jessica Aitken, the author. Oh sorry love, I've just remembered everything in the circle is confidential, so please don't tell anyone that I told you.'

'No need to worry Mum. I've never heard of her. Look I'll need to go, the game's coming on in a minute and I want to get a beer and settle down.'

'Alright son. Speak to you next week.'

She felt a lump in her throat as she hung up the phone and grabbed a tissue to blow her nose. Then she smiled. At least one of her children kept in touch with her.

As she got changed, she began to think about what had happened to her. It had been life-changing that was for sure. She had lost her husband, her daughter, her home and all her friends. Her son had never returned from university preferring to stay in Manchester where he had studied medicine but at least he had kept in touch with her and she was able to go and visit him every six months. She wished he would come home. It was all so long ago; no-one would know him or probably care any longer. No-one knew who she was, not even Marie. She had met Marie after it had all happened and had never told her. She often wondered whether she would still want to be her friend if she knew.

When she reached the *Oran Mor*, it was busy as usual, and she hoped that Marie was already in and had a seat for them. As she walked up towards the back looking for her, she couldn't believe her eyes. Jessica Aitken was sitting on the bench at the top end of the bar, just in front of the ladies' toilet looking very cosy with a good-looking man. She was all over him and he seemed delighted at her interest. She wondered if Jessica was on the rebound as she had told them at the circle that she was upset because her boyfriend had finished with her, but she didn't look upset tonight. She was positively glowing. Greer wondered if she should say hello but then thought about the ground rules of the circle. Membership was confidential, and it had been agreed that no-one should acknowledge each other if they met outwith the circle.

So, that was three times within a week that she had seen

Jessica; that definitely meant something and she wished she could tell Marie. As she made her way around the top end of the bar, she spotted her friend sitting at a long table with a bottle of white and two glasses half filled. She had squeezed herself in beside a group of men sitting drinking pints and was in animated conversation with them. She smiled to herself. Trust Marie to find a seat next to a group of men. She never gave up trying.

Jessica

What on earth is she doing here I thought as I saw Greer walking up the side of the bar towards me. I quickly turned my attention to Magnus staring into his eyes so that I wouldn't need to acknowledge that strange wee woman as I thought of her. That was three times this week that I had met her, and I wondered briefly if she was a stalker. I could see Magnus couldn't believe his luck when I came onto him like that, but I quickly pulled back once Greer was out of sight. No point in raising his hopes too soon. The pleasure of a new romance was the chase, the game. Now that I had finished with John, I was free to start up with someone new. This was our first date if you could call it that. It was somewhere public and therefore safe. Although I felt I knew him because of our online chats, I never took chances with men when I first met them and always took my time before inviting them home and sleeping with them. It was inevitable that I would sleep with them if I fancied them, but I didn't want to appear too eager. I wanted them to think I was a nice girl.

Magnus was a bit of snazzy dresser. Although he wore a navy blue suit and light blue shirt, they were clearly expensive and his tie was a mix of bright blues, pinks and yellows. He was also as handsome as his picture on Facebook. He wore his black hair longish, was clean shaven and his eyes were like chocolate buttons. He had a slight accent and when I asked he told me he had been brought up in Belfast but that he was now based in Manchester. He was a sales rep for a pharmaceutical company and did a lot of travelling. He had been married but it hadn't worked out because of that, so he was looking for love again. I doubted that he would find it with me. I had had so many relationships because I was looking for love too, looking for someone to fill the void, but they never did. Barbara told me I might be self-sabotaging, deliberately picking men who weren't good for me. I didn't believe her psychobabble although I did sometimes wonder why things never worked out. Perhaps Magnus would be different. But if not, he would provide me with some entertainment for a while. I was glad that he was getting divorced though, as I didn't want the same problems I'd had with John.

'So, tell me about your writing, Magnus. What's your genre?' I said, giving him my winning smile.

'I wouldn't say I have a genre yet. I've only just finished my creative writing course so I'm finding my way. Tell me how you got into writing Jessica.'

As I looked at his eager eyes, I felt myself entering a different zone and wondered if I should tell him about my little memoir which had come out just at the right time. My initial genre had been 'misery lit' as *The Times* daubed it, and it had given me a good springboard to launch my crime novels from. Mr Fraser would have been proud of me. But men were sometimes frightened off when I told them about it; made them feel vulnerable or something as if they might be contaminated. Others were overcome with sympathy for me and wanted to make it all better. I looked at Magnus and decided I couldn't be bothered going into it tonight.

'I've written stories all my life, Magnus,' I lied. 'I just knew that I was born to be a writer and my teachers at Knightswood Secondary saw my potential and helped me get the grades I needed to go to university. I studied English Literature and Creative Writing and came out with a first-class honours degree.'

'Wow, you must have been good. I only got a 2.2 in Science and Biology, but it was enough to get me into the job I'm doing now. I love my job but need to travel a lot and it can be lonely. Writing has been my way of filling the empty hours in hotel rooms in different parts of the country. I'm so glad you agreed to meet up while I'm in Glasgow. It makes all the difference having someone to talk to who's not a potential buyer of pharmaceuticals.'

'I'd love to see something you've written sometime. I found it incredibly helpful to have writer friends look at my work before I sent it off to my publisher.'

'Was it easy to find a publisher? I hear it can take lots of rejection letters before you find someone.'

'I've heard that too, but I was lucky enough to get someone straight away. I'm still with them. Maybe if your writing's good enough I could introduce you.'

I knew this would be the bait that would draw him in closer even if he didn't fancy me, but I had the feeling that he did as he was all eyes and ears as I was talking. I decided I might not wait too long before getting up close and personal with him. Afterall, I had known him for three months online. I moved in closer letting my leg brush against his. He didn't move it away. As we continued our chat, there was a raucous burst of laughter from a table just round from where we were sitting.

'They're getting noisy round there,' Magnus said, taking my hand. 'Do you fancy moving onto somewhere quieter. I'm in the Grosvenor Hotel across the road and there's a nice intimate bar where we can chat without having to shout.'

I hesitated. If I moved across the road to his hotel, he might expect me to go up to his room and I wasn't about to do that. I had some scruples. But then I noticed Greer weaving her way towards the toilet and could hear a female voice shouting something suggestive at the back of her. I realised they must be part of that noisy table and if that woman was getting pissed then she might pluck up the courage to come and talk to me as the night went on. I couldn't bear the thought of having to pretend to be nice to her again so squeezed Magnus's hand.

'That would be lovely. Thanks.

4

Greer

She lay in bed waiting for her alarm to go off. She always woke up before it but was convinced that if she didn't put it on, she would sleep in. It was Monday again and she would be going to the circle meeting with Evie this morning. She wondered how it would go this week. They had been going for nearly a month now and she was finding it interesting watching how they all interacted. Evie, Lottie, and Barbara were all kind and supportive, but she wasn't sure about Jessica. She got the sense that she didn't like her and sometimes she couldn't decide if the comments she made were sarcastic or for real. Disappointingly, Jessica hadn't mentioned anything about the man that she had seen her with. She realised that she was curious about this woman that she had admired from afar since last year.

She thought about that night in the Oran Mor. The group of men they had met were out for a good time and Marie made sure they got it. She was always the life and soul and inevitably the men were attracted to her. Last time, one of the guys had been interested in Greer too. His name was David. He lived in the south side with his wife and two kids and was a good twenty years younger than Greer. Perhaps she should have been flattered, but for a start she would never go with a married man and for a second, she would never go with someone so much younger than her. She would feel like a cougar exploiting someone young and vulnerable. None of those things mattered to Marie and she had invited one of the men home with her. She had no sense of morality or health and safety.

Greer began to think about exploiting someone young and vulnerable. She tried to stop the thoughts coming but sometimes they just overwhelmed her, and she was back in the past. She would never forget the day she returned from her job as a Social Worker with East Dunbartonshire Council to find her husband sitting with his head in his hands. When he looked up as she came through the door, she could see his face was ashen and that he had been crying. His eyes were red and swollen and there was a pile of tissues on the coffee table in front of the couch where he was sitting. She felt herself go cold. Something bad must have happened for him to be in such a state.

'Paul what's happened?' she'd shouted, moving over quickly towards him. 'Has something happened to Sophie or Sean?' she'd said, sitting down beside him.

He shook his head, not speaking. She felt some relief that her children hadn't been involved in an accident or were lying dead somewhere. Nothing could be worse than that.

'What's happened love?' she said, quieter now that her initial panic was over.

He looked at her and the tears began to fall again.

'Greer, I've been suspended,' he said. 'I can't believe she's done this. I've only ever shown her kindness. Why would she do this?'

'Who? Do what? What's going on Paul. You're making no sense.'

She was still talking quietly trying to help him calm down so that he could explain but all that came out were loud gulping sobs. He was obviously in a state of shock. Had *he* been involved in an accident?

Her memories were interrupted by the alarm going off and she was grateful that she had to get up and meet Evie otherwise she would have spent the morning going over and over it all like a hamster on a wheel.

Barbara

Rory was home early for a change and Barbara was relieved. They all had a family meal together and then he played some games on the Xbox with Ben and Ella. Despite agreeing to go out and talk things over, it had taken a few weeks to agree a date when her mum could watch the kids. She was determined not to bring up anything tonight as they had at last booked to go out on Saturday for dinner and to talk things through then. She felt like she was treading on eggshells and she didn't want an omelette for dinner.

While Rory was playing with Ben, Ella came through, sat down beside her, and puffed out a sigh. Barbara turned the sound down on the TV knowing that her daughter was looking for something.

'That was a loud sigh. Anything wrong?'

'Not really. I'm bored.'

'I thought you would be pleased that Dad was home tonight to have a meal with us and play some games.'

'I am Mum. It's lovely having him here and I'm so relieved that the two of you seem to be getting on better but you know how you've asked Gran to babysit on Saturday, well I was hoping to go to a party at June's house, but it would be rude to go out and leave Gran here on her own.'

Barbara smiled to herself at her daughter's attempt to get her to agree to her attending the party.

'You know we talked about this Ella. Dad and I need a night out together and we can't be worrying about how you'll get home. You're the one who was worried about us, so you should be happy that we are going out on a date.'

She tucked her daughter's hair behind her ear and gave her a little peck on the cheek signalling that the discussion was ended. However, Ella didn't receive the signal and continued with her negotiations.

'Mum, you know how upset June is just now and I'm her bestie. It wouldn't be right if I weren't there would it?'

'I'm sorry Ella, but I'm not discussing this anymore.'

'I'll go and ask Dad then,' she said, swinging her hair rebelliously, reminding Barbara of the red haired warrior princess in *Brave*. The door slammed shut behind her. This is all I need, she thought. If Rory agreed, then their date would be off. There was no way they could go out and let her go to a party without dropping her off and picking her back up. Ella was only thirteen. Barbara had been so looking forward to going out. They seemed to do it very seldom these days, but she supposed they could still have their talk if the kids were out.

She could hear voices arguing in the next room and raised her eyes. Why was life never simple? Another door banged, and she could hear Ben shouting at his sister. She must have interrupted their game and he wasn't happy. Barbara was just about to increase the volume on the TV again, when the door opened. Rory walked in looking sheepish.

'I've said she can go to the party. Sorry. I know you were looking forward to going out, but we can talk here, can't we?'

'Well not in front of my mum. I better phone her and cancel.'

Jessica

The pale morning light glinted through a slight parting in my bedroom shutters. In the winter I always left them slightly open so that the natural light would waken me as it dawned on a new day. But today I didn't need it to wake me up. I was already awake. It was Monday, the day of the circle meeting. I wondered briefly how things would go today. Luckily that awful Greer woman hadn't said anything about seeing me in the *Oran Mor* with Magnus that first night we had met up. For some reason, I didn't want the others to know that I had begun going out with Magnus so soon after finishing with John. But a month had passed so I thought it would be reasonable to tell them that I had a new boyfriend when we were checking in.

I lay thinking about Magnus. I had enjoyed our first few dates together. We had agreed to meet at his hotel rather than in the Oran Mor as we both thought its Friday night buzz had made it difficult to talk. He had been a perfect gentleman, hadn't even suggested that I go up to his room for a nightcap, and his goodnight kisses had been short but sweet. I was beginning to like him even more than I thought I would and was debating with myself whether it was time to invite him home for a meal.

After breakfast of porridge and toast, I showered and put my cycling gear on. Just as I was leaving, my phone rang. It was a number I didn't recognise but I pressed the button automatically.

'Is that Jessica Aitken?' a woman's voice asked.

'Yes, it is,' I replied, putting on my author's voice.

'This is Pam Crosby. John's wife.'

For a moment I was perplexed. I had been expecting a phone call about business not about John.

'John?'

'Have you forgotten him already?' the woman said, her voice beginning to rise.

'No, of course, not. You've caught me by surprise. I'm just about to leave for an appointment and my mind was on that. Is there something I can help you with?'

I decided to be reasonable.

'Help me with. It would have been helpful if you had never had an affair with my husband. You've broken up our home and my children are distraught. I don't know how you could do that.'

I could hear the woman sobbing down the phone and actually felt sorry for her.

'Look I'm sorry that you feel I was to blame but it takes two to tango as they say. I didn't know he was married at first and I never thought he would leave you for me. It was me who finished with him and told him he should go back to you and his family.'

'You told him,' the woman screeched. 'Well he did try and wheedle his way back in but there's no way I'm going to take him back now. He told me he had finished with you.'

The woman was becoming hysterical and I decided I better end the conversation.

'Look I need to go, or I'll be late for my appointment. I'm sorry things have worked out the way they have.'

'Sorry, you will be sorry by the time I've finished with you.'

The woman's voice was low and menacing.

I hung up the phone feeling unsettled. I won't think about this now I told myself, feeling like Scarlett in *Gone with the Wind.*

5

Jessica

I liked the feel of the cold air whistling through my helmet as I made my way onto Hyndland Road and down past Cottiers to my meeting. I did wish Glasgow had more cycle lanes though as it was a precarious business trying to avoid potholes as well as buses and cars. It took me only five minutes to reach the community hall where the circle meetings were held but I was late, of course, so everyone was sitting waiting for me. Saying sorry wasn't my style so I just sat down and waited for things to start. My stomach was still churning from the conversation with John Crosby's wife, but I decided I was going to tell the group about Magnus anyway.

'Who would like to check-in first this week?' Barbara said, looking pointedly at Evie. She obviously wanted to make it easier for her, but I decided I would go first.

'Good morning everyone. My feelings are mixed-up today. I received an upsetting phone call just before I left and it's made me jangly but on the positive side I'm happy to tell you that I've met someone new and we are getting on well together,' I said, beaming my smile perhaps less brightly than normal at them.

'Did you not fall out with your boyfriend not that long ago Jessica?' asked Evie.

'Yes I did.'

'How did you meet your new boyfriend so quick?'

'He's a fan if you must know. We've been chatting online for quite a while now and we've had three dates so far.'

'I thought I saw you with someone in the *Oran Mor* a few weeks ago. Was that him?' asked Greer.

I could feel my beam dimming and wished I hadn't said anything. Maybe it was too soon to start a relationship with someone else but what right did she have to stick her nose into my business.

'What is this? You're only supposed to be here to support *her*,' I said, pointing at Evie, 'not to stick your tuppence worth in.'

'Okay thanks Jessica. Who wants to go next?' interrupted Barbara. 'What about you Evie? How are you feeling today?'

'I'm feeling great Barbara. I've been offered a house by the housing association and they've given me a moving-in date which means I'll have my own place by the time this little girl is born,' said Evie, rubbing her swollen stomach proprietorially. 'Greer's applying for grants for me and she's going to come with me and help me pick furniture and stuff.'

Oh, good for Greer I sneered inwardly. Miss goodie two shoes.

'Is it a little girl you're having then?' asked Lottie, smiling at Evie.

'Aye. I'm so excited.'

I could feel my blood pressure rising as I watched the two younger women gushing on about Evie's baby. Could they not see that all she was doing was bringing another girl into the world to be abused; to repeat the cycle that they had been through. There was no way I was ever going to have a baby.

'Can we stop talking about babies and get on with what we're here for,' I said, with a frown.

'I've not checked in yet,' said Lottie, frowning back at me

'Sorree! How are you this week?' I said, smiling tightly at her, forgetting to be nice.

'Well I wasn't feeling great when I came in this morning but hearing Evie's good news has just cheered me up.'

'Would you like to share with us what was upsetting you Lottie?' asked Barbara.

'Maybe later.'

We all got our knitting out and there was some chatter as Greer showed Evie again how to knit. I decided to concentrate on my knitting and let them get on with it. I wanted to make some progress with it so that I could have it ready for Mum's birthday. It was only a month away now. I wished Mum and I could get on better. When Dad died, I had hoped that our relationship would improve but if anything, it had got worse. Mum was even more crabbit now that she didn't have the booze to self-soothe. I often wondered what my life would have been like if my twin brother had survived our birth. According to Cathy, his death had completely changed my mum and dad. I could understand them being upset at the loss of my brother as I constantly felt that a part of me was missing, but I often wondered why I hadn't been enough to help them get over his loss. Perhaps I had wanted too much. According to my mum I was a needy child who always wanted attention.

I was awoken from my reverie by a change of atmosphere in the room. The chatter had died down and Lottie was speaking.

'Today is the fifth anniversary of when I killed my baby,' she said, two large tears spilling over.

I couldn't help staring at her, fascinated by the way one of the tears ran through the piercing on her nose. No-one said anything as we waited for her to continue.

'I got pregnant when I was sixteen and my mum and dad made me leave home. The doctor recommended a termination and I agreed, thinking that Mum and Dad would let me move back in. But they didn't. My little girl would have been nearly five by now if I had let her live.'

Evie got up and went to give her a hug, tears streaming down her face now too.

'Sorry Evie,' said Barbara. 'Touching isn't allowed at our meetings. Ground rules you know.'

Evie hesitated in mid hug and glared at Barbara.

'Well I think that's a daft ground rule,' she said, with a swing of her ponytail as she sat back down.

Greer patted Evie on the hand.

'That applies to you too Greer,' I couldn't help saying, while throwing her a bright smile.

'Barbara's right Evie. I don't like being touched. It creeps me out,' said Lottie, smiling apologetically at Evie. 'I became a prostitute you see when I was homeless, and I just hate anyone touching me now. But thanks for caring.'

'We all care about you Lottie, don't we girls?' said Evie, looking round everyone for affirmation of their feelings for Lottie. Everyone nodded, including me but I was losing interest and picked up my knitting again.

'I know that I am forgiven because Jesus has forgiven all my sins, but I can't help feeling sad,' continued Lottie.

So she was a born again. I sometimes wished that I could be

born again, have all my past mistakes wiped out and be made new and clean.

'She'll be well safe with Jesus Lottie. You don't need to worry about her,' said Evie.

She hesitated a moment and it was clear she was thinking intently about something.

'Would you like to be my wee one's Godmother?' she said, offering a woman she hardly knew the welfare of her child.

Lottie looked at Evie with a huge delighted smile. 'I would be honoured Evie,' she said. 'Thank you.'

I wriggled in my chair, feeling unsettled by all this kindness. The blind leading the blind, I thought. I was glad when Barbara wound up the meeting and I was free to go.

6

Greer

It was Friday again, but she wasn't going out with Marie so had decided she would send for a curry. She already had a bottle of wine chilling in the fridge. As things turned out it was just as well she wasn't going out as one of her other clients had taken an overdose and was in the Queen Elizabeth Hospital. Her manager had asked if she would mind going over to see how he was doing. The young man had no-one else to support him and Greer was more than happy to visit. It meant, however, that it was well after her finishing time when she returned to the office to hand the pool car back. As she walked home down Queen Margaret Drive and onto Byres Road she thought about the last circle meeting. Evie had been in a reflective mood.

'What did you think of the meeting?' she'd said, smiling over at Greer but continuing on without waiting for her to answer. 'I feel sorry for Jessica and Lottie. I think Jessica's only grumpy because she's unhappy and I thought Lottie was very brave today telling us about having the abortion. I feel so sorry for her having to get rid of her baby. Do you think I did the right thing asking her to be Godmother?'

Greer smiled inwardly as she remembered their conversation. Evie was such a kind wee soul but definitely too trusting. Imagine her feeling sorry for Jessica Aitken.

'I'm not sure, Evie. You've only known her a few weeks.'

'I know, but I feel as if it will make her feel better.'

'I can understand that, but will it make you feel better. You know sometimes you've got to think about yourself and what's best for you.'

'Well I don't have anyone else Greer,' Evie had said, tears starting to form in her eyes.

Greer knew this to be true and wondered what would become of the girl once she moved out of supported accommodation and into her own house. She wondered if she would be able to cope. Having a baby and looking after it on your own wasn't easy for anyone but for a vulnerable young girl like

Evie, it would be extra difficult. She was glad that she would be working with her for a few months after she moved in.

Her thoughts were interrupted by her mobile ringing and she smiled when she looked at the screen.

'Hello Sean.'

'Hi Mum. Are you able to talk?'

'I'm just walking up the road.'

'It's about Sophie.'

'Sophie?'

'Well not Sophie but Sophie's daughter.'

Greer sat down on the seat in the bus shelter that she had just reached, her hand with the phone dropping from her ear to her knee. Sophie had a daughter. She couldn't take it in. How could her daughter have her own daughter and she not know about it. She became aware of Sean's voice in the distance.

'Mum, Mum, are you still there?'

She raised the phone to her ear again.

'Yes, I'm here Son.'

'I know it's a shock Mum and I'm sorry to spring it on you like this, but she's coming to Glasgow tomorrow and I needed to give you some notice before she turned up on your doorstep.'

'Look Sean my signal's going, and I can't hear you very well. I'll phone you when I get home.'

This was a lie, but she needed time to think. She tried to stand up, but her legs felt wobbly and she sat back down again. She didn't know how to react and didn't know how Sean wanted her to react. He hadn't seen Sophie change the way that she had. He had decided to stay in Manchester and left her and Sophie to face the fall-out from what his father had done. She thought about Sophie and wondered what she was like now. The last time she had seen her she had been a sixteen-year-old teenage rebel, today she would be a forty year old woman. A woman with a daughter of her own.

'You can't tell me what to do Mum. I'm going, and you can't stop me,' she had screamed at Greer the morning she had left. Greer put her hand up to her cheek as she remembered the sting from the slap Sophie had given her when she had grabbed her arm in desperation and tried to reason with her. But there had been no reasoning with Sophie. She had gone completely off the rails and nothing Greer said made any difference. She had stood and watched with tears coursing down her cheeks as her daughter picked up her bags and slammed the door behind her, rejecting her mother and her life in Scotland. She had phoned Sean and told him, but he had been totally disinterested. It was like he had put them all in a box and didn't want to have to take them out again.

Her thoughts returned to where she had left them that morning as she lay in bed waiting for her alarm to ring. When Paul's sobs had subsided a little, he looked up at her.

'It's Debbie, you know the girl I was telling you about that I've been helping with her English.'

'Yes. The one you gave Sophie's wee earrings to at Christmas. What about her Paul?'

'She ... the headmaster called me up this afternoon and told me that she has accused me of ... kissing her and trying to have sex with her.'

Greer felt her stomach lurch and her head begin to pulse.

'You tried to have sex with her?' she whispered.

'No. I didn't.' Paul stood up glaring at her. 'That's what she's accused me of. I would never have sex with a pupil. What do you take me for?'

'Then why has she made this allegation? I don't understand.'

'Neither do I but I've been suspended pending further investigation.'

'Investigation? Are the police involved then?'

'Not yet. There's to be an internal investigation first.'

'So, they'll prove she's lying, won't they?'

'Oh Greer,' he had said, coming over and putting his arms around her. 'I hope to God they do.'

When Greer got home, she phoned Sean. She felt calmer now and was ready to hear what he had to say.

'Hi Sean, it's Mum. That's me home. So, tell me again.'

'Sophie's daughter is coming to Glasgow. She found me on *Facebook* and sent me a private message.'

'I can't believe Sophie has a daughter and I don't know

about it.'

'I know Mum. I was shocked too when I got her message.'

'When did she get in touch?'

'Just yesterday. I wasn't sure how to tell you. I know that Sophie left under a cloud and for her not to tell you she had a daughter is unforgivable. I wasn't sure how you would feel.'

'She's my granddaughter, Sean. Naturally, I would want to see her. Is she coming to Glasgow to live do you know?'

'I'm not sure about that but she wants to come and stay with you and asked me to let you know. She didn't want to just turn up on your doorstep. She can come and stay with you, can't she?'

'Yes, of course,' Greer said automatically, but wondered if she really meant it. She couldn't stop the sinking feeling that was beginning to take hold and make her long for a glass of the pinot lying in the fridge.

'When is she planning to come?'

'Tomorrow, I told you Mum.'

'Right, well I better go and get things ready for her then. I'll give you a ring when she arrives.'

Greer hung up the phone, went to the fridge and poured herself a large glass of wine. She gulped it down and poured another one feeling relieved when it began to help her relax a little. She thought about Sophie again and what her granddaughter might be like. She realised she didn't even know her granddaughter's name. What if she was another version of that unhappy girl who had left twenty something years ago? Greer didn't think she could cope if she was. She didn't bother ordering a curry. She much preferred the numbing effect of the wine.

Jessica

As I got ready for my date with Magnus, I thought about the last circle meeting. What was that girl Evie thinking about allowing Lottie to be her child's Godmother? What a joke? Although as a Christian maybe she was the only one who would be suitable for the job. I smiled as I thought of Magnus and wondered if he would invite me up to his room tonight. I called a taxi and was soon on my way down to the Grosvenor.

When I jumped out of the taxi at the entrance to the hotel, I spotted Greer at the bus stop with a phone to her ear. I felt myself become instantly annoyed at the sight of her. I wasn't sure why I disliked the woman so much; she seemed a reasonable person and she was a fan but for some reason every time I saw her I had a negative reaction. I knew I had let my mask slip in the circle meeting; for some reason it was starting to bring out the worst in me. Then I noticed that something was going on. Greer looked as if she was getting some bad news from the way she sat down on the seat in the bus shelter and stared into space with her phone lying in her hand. I wondered what it might be and hoped she would tell us about it at our next meeting. Perhaps it would give me an idea for a story.

Magnus was waiting in the bar of the hotel when I arrived. He was reading the paper and looking comfortable as he supped his pint. I stood for a moment looking at him and wondered where this relationship would lead if anywhere. Just enjoy the moment I told myself. The hotel bar was sophisticated but also cosy, all dark wood and beige carpets. A coal fire was twinkling in the corner. I felt cosy too as I sat down beside Magnus making him look up from his paper.

'Jessica!' he said, giving me an enthusiastic hug. 'It's lovely to see you. What can I get you?'

'Fresh orange and soda for me please Magnus.'

'So, how's your week been?' he asked, as he sat my drink down on the table in front of me.

'Yes, it's been good. I've been making progress with my latest book which means I can get my publisher off my back. She wants me to have it ready in time for the summer holiday trade. That's always a lucrative time for me. People like nothing better than a good murder mystery to read while they lie frying at the pool.'

'Yes, some people go over the top with the sunbathing don't they. I prefer an active holiday myself. What about you?'

'Oh yes, I much prefer walking or sightseeing to sunbathing. My skin burns easily so it's not comfortable for me. How's your week been?' I remembered to ask Magnus.

'Well, I've just finished a short story and wondered if I could bring it next time for you to look over. It's a bit on the rough side yet.'

'Of course, what's it about?'

'Well, it's aimed at young adults. A kind of morality tale with zombies in it.'

'Not quite my thing but I'll have a look anyway.'

I felt disappointed. For some reason I had hoped to mentor Magnus. Helping someone always made me feel a little superior inside but I knew nothing about young adult novels or zombies for that matter, so I didn't think I would be of much help.

After dinner, we went back through to the bar again which by this time was busy with couples out for Valentine's. I had completely forgotten it was the fourteenth of February the day before.

'Why don't we go up to my room? It'll be quieter than this bar and we can talk.'

I was delighted at Magnus's suggestion. This was our fourth date and I was hoping that we could take things on to the next stage. When we got up to the room, he took off his shoes and smiled as he rubbed his feet.

'Sorry my feet are killing me. I've been on them all day. Would you like a drink?' he said, opening the mini bar.

'No thanks I've had my quota for tonight'

'Your quota?'

'Yes. Remember I told you. I only ever have half a bottle of wine. My parents were alcoholics you know so I don't want to end up like them.'

'That must have been difficult for you.'

'Yes, it was. But I don't talk about it. My therapist tells me to live in the moment and not to worry about the past so that's what I try to do. What about you? What are your parents like? Are they still alive?'

'Oh yes, they're still alive. They were okay as parents go. He was a social worker and she was a teacher. Both retired now of course. Typical middle-class family. Never any domestic dramas. I think they would like to see me settled of course and give them a grandchild.'

'Do you have any brothers or sisters?'

'No. What about you?'

'No. I did have a twin brother, Darren, but he died at birth.'

Magnus seemed to be stuck for words.

'It's okay. I feel that a part of him is still with me. When I was young, he used to talk to me or at least I thought he was talking to me. It was my way of feeling less lonely without him I suppose.'

'Why don't you have a drink? One won't hurt you.'

'It might, so I won't bother thanks.'

'Do you play scrabble?' he asked, putting back the little bottle he had taken out for himself.

I felt something akin to gratitude at his thoughtfulness although it didn't bother me when other people had a drink. I never felt the urge to have any more than my quota which I found strange given the genes I came from.

'Yes, I do as a matter of fact. I have an app on my phone.'

'So do I,' he smiled. 'Let's have a game then.'

I smiled and played, but my thoughts were elsewhere. What was up with the man? He seemed to prefer playing scrabble to becoming more intimate. It wasn't until the night was coming to an end that I realised I had enjoyed it. No fumbling and worrying about whether or not this was the right time to have sex. I had enjoyed the companionship of the game and the easy chat.

Magnus walked me down to get my taxi. It was bitterly cold, and the pavement was glistening menacingly with frost. The taxi was already waiting and before I got in he put a red envelope into my hand and looked into my eyes. He then lightly touched my cheek and pushed my hair behind my ear before kissing me lingeringly on the lips. I was surprised at how sweet it felt and something in me softened.

'I hope you don't think I'm being presumptuous getting you a Valentine card. I know it's a bit juvenile, but I really like you Jessica.'

'I really like you too Magnus. Thanks for this.'

I'd never had a Valentine card before and looked down shyly at the envelope, feeling like a teenager again.

'Thanks for a lovely evening,' I said, meaning it. 'See you next Friday.'

'Can't wait.'

As I was getting into the cab I turned back towards him. I had decided it was time.

'Why don't you come to mine for dinner next week. I cook a mean chicken curry.'

He hesitated for just a second and I thought he was going to say no. I felt a stab of disappointment so was delighted when he went on to say, 'Okay. Text me your address.'

As I lay in bed thinking of Magnus, I decided he was a bit of sweetie for getting me a Valentine card. There wasn't much written in it, just the usual slushy message asking me to be his Valentine with his name written in bold black ink at the bottom with two kisses. I sighed as I snuggled into the luxurious mattress and pulled the duck filled duvet over me. My shutters were slightly open as normal, and I lay for a while watching the sleet drift past in little flurries at the mercy of the wind. I hoped it wouldn't turn to snow as I had an important meeting with my publisher tomorrow. I might drop something into the conversation about Magnus and his zombie story to see whether young adult literature was a genre Dorothy might be interested in publishing.

Barbara

At last they were alone. Ella had gone to the party and Ben was at his friend's house playing games. It had been agreed that she would pick them both up at 10pm that night so no wine for her. She didn't really mind as she wasn't a big drinker, but she felt something to relax her might have been good given that she and Rory were going to discuss what was going on with him and why he was so moody. She found herself biting her lip, a sure sign that she was nervous. As a counsellor, she was always checking in with herself and how she was feeling. She wondered how Rory was feeling. Was he nervous too? Did he have something to tell her that would change everything? She realised that she was catastrophising and should just get the conversation underway rather than sit in this nervous silence putting off the moment of truth. Rory had already downed a half bottle of wine with dinner, but she asked him if he would like another.

'Yes, thanks. It might make it easier for me to explain what's been going on.'

She poured the Merlot into his empty glass and then sat down opposite him. She felt herself going into counsellor mode; she would be non-judgemental and would really listen to what he had to say. He took a deep breath in, had a gulp of his wine, then got up and started pacing. This made her even more uneasy. Why didn't he just get on with it.

'So about three months ago I got an email at work from a woman called Mia Cooper. She said she was my daughter.'

'Your daughter?' she couldn't help her cry of surprise. So much for listening and not saying anything.

'Yes. She told me that I had slept with her mum when she was fifteen and that she had been the result.'

Barbara was shocked. What age had he been? What age was the daughter? Had Rory been with this girl's mum at the same time as he had been with her? Did his daughter want to come back into his life? What would that do to their family? She bit her lip again and waited for him to continue. Questions could come later.

'She was contacting me not because she wanted to let me

know that I was her father but because she had read in the paper that I was up for Chair of the Law Society and she didn't think it was right that someone who had sex with a underage girl should be in a position of power like that.'

She found herself agreeing with Rory's daughter but kept quiet while he continued.

'But, and here's what she was really after, she said that she would remain quiet about it all, but it would cost me.'

'Cost you. She wants money?'

Ignoring her question, he continued.

'I'm sorry Babs that I didn't share it with you, but I was so shocked. I didn't know how you would react. I've been doing some digging and hired a private detective to try and find out who she is and who her mum is.'

He sat down beside her and took her hands in his.

'Ask me anything you like. It's such a relief to have told you. I know I've been a right arse for the last few months. Please forgive me.'

So, it was life-changing. She hadn't been catastrophising, she had been seeing the future.

'Rory', she said, pulling her hands free. 'I don't know what to say. I have so many questions whizzing around my head. I was worried that you were having an affair or something, but this is huge. It changes everything.'

'What do you mean?'

'I don't know if I can continue to live with a man who has taken advantage of an underage girl.'

'But I didn't Babs. Please listen to me.'

'And what about the effect on Ben and Ella if this Mia wants to come into your life,' Barbara continued, ignoring him. 'And the blackmail. What if she goes to the papers? It means not only the post with the Law Society is out of the question, but your job could be in jeopardy. You could be struck off or banned from practising. My God what a disaster.'

'Babs, please listen to me. I've found out that Mia's mother is Sophie Fraser. I was at school with her. Her dad killed himself after a girl had accused him of grooming her for sex. I recognise now that Sophie must have been in turmoil as she started drinking, taking drugs and was having sex with anyone and everyone. She was only fifteen at the time, but I was only seventeen. It's not as if I was an adult who exploited her. I was just a daft teenager whose hormones where raging and was delighted when sex was handed to me on a plate. She was my first time, but it was a horrendous experience. She was sick all over the bed afterwards.'

She imagined the scene and felt sick herself at the thought of it. How could her Rory have taken advantage of someone like that. He'd never mentioned it when she had talked to him about her past. Did being so young excuse him? She felt herself growing cold and moved away from him. He was continuing to talk but his words were distant as her mind went back to that unbearable night on holiday when she had been raped. She remembered the pain, the shame and the vomit spread in stinking clumps over the bed and it was all replaying in her head like a scene from a horror movie. All the negative thoughts about herself came crowding back. Had her attacker been like Rory, a young man with hormones raging and had she somehow encouraged him because she was drunk? Had she offered herself on a plate? With her heart racing she could only stare in horror at her husband.

'Barbara, Babs.' Rory was squeezing her hands gently trying to get her attention. 'Talk to me darling.'

She looked at him like he was a stranger and for the first time in their relationship she didn't want to be with him.

'I can't do this just now Rory. I need to get out. I can't be in the same room as you.'

The look of hurt on his face made her want to howl but she couldn't ignore what he had done to that girl and what he had brought into their lives.

7

Jessica

I hummed to myself as I got ready for the circle meeting wondering what would happen today. I remembered seeing Greer at the bus stop on my way to meet Magnus last week and hoped she would say something about what her phone call had been about. Perhaps I would ask her if she didn't volunteer anything. Greer was good at sticking her nose into other people's business, so it was only fair she should share her stuff too. I checked my phone and there were lots of emails as usual when I clicked on the little envelope icon but one stuck out. It was from someone called Avenging Angel with the heading Homewrecker. I clicked on it wondering who it was from. *You bitch. You home wrecker. Everyone is going to know about this. Don't think you're going to get away with it.*

I didn't recognise the name of course. Avenging Angel. Who could it be from? I thought it must be someone related to John and I supposed I was a home wrecker if truth be told. Perhaps it was his wife as she had already been on the phone giving me an ear bashing, but it had the tone of a younger person and the name was like something from those games that young people play. What did they mean everyone is going to know. I felt scared that they might go to the papers. This was a disaster.

I phoned Dorothy and asked her what I should do.

'It's up to you lovey but my motto is that no publicity is bad publicity. Let them do their worst.'

'But I've only started going out with a new guy and don't want to put him off with a lot of bad publicity about my ex.'

'Yes I can see that that wouldn't be good. Why don't you wait and see what happens. If it is one of John's kids then they won't go to the papers. They'll just be wanting to troll you.'

'What about Pam though. She sounded so menacing when she phoned me.'

'I don't think you need to worry about her coming round and sticking a knife into you, but I do expect you might be cited in her divorce petition, so you better be prepared for that.'

'Okay Dorothy. Thanks. See you soon.'

Cathy came in and I realised I was late again for the meeting. She looked freezing and I felt bad that I hadn't made our usual pot of tea.

'Sorry Cathy, I'm going to have to go. Please make yourself whatever you want. Put the fire on in the lounge if you want and get heated up before you start.'

Greer

Greer picked Evie up as usual for the knitting circle. She was now in her own house and they had spent some time last week getting it kitted out. It was still in Maryhill, not that far from her supported accommodation, so it meant Evie was familiar with the area and felt comfortable. She had been fortunate getting a house rather than a flat as most of the housing association's stock was tenemental but as Evie was classed as vulnerable she had priority in terms of the association's allocation's policy. A house had become vacant just at the right time.

'I'm so lucky Greer to have a house with a back and front door. It's something I've always dreamed of and it means my little one will have a garden to play in,' she said, as she locked her front door and waddled down towards the car.

Evie's movements reminded her of when she was expecting Sophie and her thoughts went back to last week when she was waiting for her granddaughter to arrive. When the door entry finally buzzed, and she let her granddaughter into the close, she was unable to keep the look of surprise off her face when she opened the door. Standing on the threshold was a woman who could have been her daughter but clearly wasn't as she was twenty odd years younger than Sophie would be now.

'Hello, my name's Mia. I'm your granddaughter.'

Greer stood staring at Mia unable to speak.

'So, are you not going to invite me in Nana?'

Greer's heart melted when she heard the word 'Nana'.

'Yes, of course. Sorry. This is such a surprise.'

She took the girl's suitcase and ushered her inside.

'Let me look at you. You're so like your mum.'

Greer also noted that she had Paul's eyes, dark blue with little flecks of grey. She smiled at the young woman who smiled back confidently. Something about her made Greer's stomach turn over. She looked so much like Sophie had done when she was young, and Greer wondered if she also held some of that anger that her mother had carried away with her. Greer was disappointed that Sophie hadn't come with

Mia. She would have liked to see her again and if possible, heal the breach between them. But maybe she would be able to do that through her granddaughter. She knew her life was going to be turned upside down, but she relished the prospect. She had been living a half-life for far too long

Greer and Evie arrived at the Circle and took their seats in their usual place. Barbara smiled her welcome at them but didn't speak. Greer poured them all a glass of water and was about to take a sip of hers when Jessica arrived late. She didn't say anything, no apologies, just sat down and waited.

'Are you alright Jessica?' asked Evie. 'You're awful quiet.'

'Yes. You?'

'Yes thanks.'

'What about you Greer?' Jessica said, turning the attention to Greer. 'I saw you at the bus stop last week and you looked as if you'd had a shock. Hope it wasn't bad news.'

'Remember Greer isn't a part of the group Jessica,' said Barbara.

Greer was taken by surprise at Jessica's comment. She had been totally unaware that Jessica had seen her when she got Sean's phone call and wondered if she was just being nosy or if she really cared whether she had received bad news or not. Today Greer wished she were a real part of the group and could share the news about her granddaughter, but she decided it wouldn't be appropriate.

'Actually it was really good news, thank you for asking Jessica. It was kind of you to be worried for me.'

Lottie went next and told them that she was feeling better than she had the last time and thanked everyone for listening to her talk about her grief for her lost baby.

Evie went next.

'Good morning everyone,' she said, smiling round the small group.

Greer was delighted to see that her confidence had grown so quickly in the group. It must be working for her.

'I'm feeling cheerful today. I moved into my new house last week. It has a back and front door and a garden,' she beamed a smile that wouldn't have looked amiss on Jessica's face.

'But as well as that, for the first time I feel that I have made a true friend.'

She smiled over at Lottie as she said this, and Lottie looked down shyly.

'Lottie and I have been in touch via text and we are now friends on Facebook.'

'That's nice for you,' said Jessica. 'Shall I check in now?'

'Yes, of course,' said Barbara.

'I'm doing okay. My publisher had a look at the first draft of my novel which is due out this summer and has given me the thumbs up. Also, I've invited Magnus up to my house for dinner the next time he's in Glasgow and he's going to bring a short story that he's written for me to read. I don't think I've got much more to say today so hope you don't mind if I just get on with my knitting. It won't be long till my mum's birthday and I want to have it finished for her.'

'Does anyone have anything they want to share this week, or shall we just get on with our knitting?' asked Barbara.

'Can I go?' said Evie, putting her hand up like a child in a classroom.

'Yes of course,' said Barbara.

'Well I'm feeling quite good. Tom phoned me to ask how things were going. He seemed really interested in what was going to happen to the baby. I think he might be building up to ask if he can come and stay with me. I would really like it if he could. It would be like a fairy tale come true. Tom and me together with our little girl.'

Evie's face was bright with happiness as she envisioned their future together.

'His wife can't have children you see,' she continued, 'so this would be like a dream come true for him too.'

'What if he wants the baby but doesn't want you?' asked Jessica

'What do you mean?' asked Evie, becoming alarmed

'Well just saying Evie. If he and his wife can't have children, perhaps they would want your baby. You need to be less trusting of that man.'

'But he couldn't get my baby could he Greer?' Evie said, turning toward Greer who took her hand.

'I think Jessica is just being mischievous Evie. I don't think

Tom would be able to take your baby anyway. He has been discredited because of what he did with you so wouldn't be considered a fit father.'

Evie looked at Jessica.

'I don't understand why you're so cruel Jessica.'

'I'm only being realistic Evie. Life isn't a fairy tale; you're not a princess and Tom certainly isn't a prince.'

Greer wished Jessica had just stuck to her knitting. She was a real bitch when she wanted to be but there was a ring of truth in what she was saying. Perhaps Mr and Mrs Bannerman had planned this all along and had used Evie for their own ends.

Barbara

Barbara sat in the lounge with a small glass of Sauvignon Blanc. Only she and Ella were at home and Ella was in her room sulking as she was still grounded. When Barbara had picked her up from June's party last week, it was clear she had been drinking and this was a strict no, no for Barbara and Rory. Too many things could go wrong when young girls were out of control and vulnerable. Look at what had happened to her.

Her thoughts went back to last week and Rory's confession of what had been bothering him. She had hardly spoken to him since then and had moved into the guest bedroom. She had told the kids she was having trouble sleeping, which was true, and that she didn't want to disturb their dad. She needed time to think so that she could make a rational decision about what to do. She had talked to her supervisor about Rory and that had helped her to see that her experience wasn't necessarily the same as what had happened to the girl Rory had had sex with. He was only seventeen, not much older than Ben was now. The man who had raped her had been in his twenties. But it didn't change the fact that he had taken advantage of a young girl. She hoped that Ben had more compassion.

But the whole thing just seemed so fantastical. Why would Rory's daughter only be contacting him now? Why hadn't her mother been in touch? She realised that she was resistant to the thought that she was his daughter. She thought that the girl must be making it up for her own ends. But what were her ends? What did she want? Rory had decided that it would be best to get a DNA test done. That was the only way that they would be able to settle the question of whether or not she was his daughter. She wanted to support Rory, of course she did, but the thought of him having sex with an underaged girl and also having a child with someone other than herself was disturbing. But she had to put her own feelings aside for the sake of her children. They were her priority now. She had to do what was best for them and their long term future no matter what the cost to herself.

She decided to go up and see how Ella was getting on. She didn't want to leave her sulking too long. It was important to try and keep the conversation going and not let even more resentment build up. She knocked softly and then went into her daughter's room. Her daughter immediately closed her laptop and looked up with guilt written all over her face. Not wanting to cause more trouble, Barbara decided to ignore it and sat down on the bed beside Ella.

'How are you darling? I know you're unhappy that you're grounded, but you know that your dad and I will not tolerate you taking alcohol at your age. Alcohol is a dangerous drug. It affects your brain and makes you lose your inhibitions. But inhibitions are there for a reason. They keep you safe.'

'I know Mum, we've had all this in school,' Ella said, raising her eyes to the ceiling. 'I'm not a kid you know.'

'I know. You are a very clever and kind young woman,' said Barbara, giving her daughter a hug.

'Don't think you can get around me that way,' said her daughter, shrugging off her mother's embrace. But Barbara noticed she had a little smile playing about her lips.

'I just came up to see if you wanted to watch a movie with me. I'm feeling lonely downstairs all on my own.'

'I'm in the middle of something just now Mum so can you give me ten minutes maybe,' she said, giving her mother a look that said she was willing to be friends again.

'I'll open some popcorn. See you in ten.'

Barbara felt relieved that her daughter was thawing a little, but she wondered what she was up to on that computer. She would try and get into it when she was at school next week to see what she could find.

8

Jessica

I was surprised to find that I had butterflies while waiting for Magnus and realised I was nervous about him coming to my home for the first time. When he arrived a little later than expected, he handed me a shopping bag all apologies for being late.

'Sorry Jessica, sorry. I had difficulty getting a taxi.'

'You're here now Magnus, that's what matters. Let me take your jacket.'

I could feel the cold that had seeped into his heavy leather jacket as I hung it up on the coat stand. It smelled of him, and I became excited at what I hoped was going to happen.

'Wine and something for the house,' he said, pointing at the shopping bag. 'I hope you like them.'

I put the wine in the fridge and then opened the package which was wrapped in pretty pink paper. I was pleased that I was good at disguising my feelings. Inside were two paper tissue boxes which I thought looked rather cheap and nasty. They were covered in black lacquer and had cherry blossoms painted on the sides.

'Oh, they're beautiful Magnus,' I lied.

'I'm glad you like them. Now let me see your home Jessica. Show me where you write. I've fantasised about if for a long time now.'

I laughed, thinking how different our fantasies had been. I led him through to my writing room. I loved this room and hoped he would too. It was painted in sunshine yellow and had white wooden shutters on the windows which were closed over on the night. A restored rosewood antique writing desk that I had bought on-line from a dealer sat in the bay window facing out onto the garden. The desk had been an extravagance, but it made me feel I was a real writer like Jane Austin or Charlotte Bronte.

I loved watching the changing seasons from my desk and spotting the birds and other wildlife that frequented my garden. Tucked under the desk and looking quite incongruent against the beautiful wood of the table, was an ultramodern ergonomic chair covered in yellow leather that had also cost a fortune, but I had decided that my back was worth it. On the desk was a laptop in pearly white with my notebook at its side opened to reveal my squiggly written thoughts on my latest story.

On a shelf above my desk were a set of twenty crime novels all written by me. I kept them there in case I hit a block. They were a reminder that I had done it before and could do it again. My little misery lit memoir wasn't among them. It was set aside in the bookcase on the far side of the room where I kept novels, reference books, biographies and so on. It was out of print now and although it had helped to set me on the road to becoming a successful novelist, I wished that I had never written it. Luckily very few of my fans seemed to have connected me with the memoir so I supposed I had better tell Magnus about it but not tonight.

'Your home is beautiful, just like you,' he said, after I had shown him around the rest of the apartment. 'So how are you?'

'Not too bad thanks. My publisher was pleased with my first draft so that's good news. Did you bring your story for me to have a look at? Dorothy has contacts who are into young adult stories, so she might be able to point you in the right direction if your story is good enough.'

'That's fantastic Jessica. I wasn't sure you would remember. But yes, I've brought my story along,' he said, taking an A4 brown envelope out of his briefcase. 'What's for dinner, I'm starving?'

My apricot chicken curry was well received and afterwards we sat on the settee together in front of the fire. It was gas but looked authentic with its black coals set inside the Victorian fireplace that had been part of the original house. It wasn't long before he took me in his arms. His kisses were soft but sensual and I found it extremely erotic when despite his obvious arousal he withdrew from our embrace, rose from the settee, and pulled me up. He fastened the top buttons on my blouse which had come loose during our snog, his long fingers brushing against my throat while gazing into my eyes.

'I think we should stop now before we go too far Jessica.'

As far as I was concerned we hadn't gone far enough. I wanted to take him through to my bed and rip his clothes off, but I liked that he was showing me some respect. To help calm our arousal, I decided to offer him a nightcap and found myself drinking down one of John's Macallans and water without regard to my quota. We had a game of scrabble and as he got up to leave he suggested we should have a game online during the week. I was pleased that he wanted to spend more time with me even if it was just online.

When he left, I took out his story. "The Liar" I read. Although excited at the thought of reading it, I knew I was too tired to do it justice so decided to leave it until the next day. Perhaps he would have some talent and maybe I would learn something about zombies and YA fiction. It might even inspire me to write something in that genre myself.

I lay in bed thinking of the evening and felt pleased that Magnus and I seemed to be making progress. He had talked quite a lot about the stuff in the papers about Harvey Weinstein and the success of the The *Me Too* Movement. I was pleased that he didn't seem to be one of those men who thought that women only had themselves to blame for what happened to them.

'It's such a difficult matter though isn't it. Two people telling different stories about what took place between them. In any sexual encounter there are generally no witnesses to confirm or deny what truly happened.'

This had made me think of my own situation with Mr Fraser. The only reason that my allegation seemed to stick was that a couple of witnesses had corroborated parts of my story. If they hadn't been willing to come forward to say what they had seen, it would have been my word against his and I had no doubt who would have been believed.

'What about you Jessica? Any *#MeToo* incidents in your life?'

I wasn't ready to give him chapter and verse on my experiences of sexually inappropriate behaviour so said what I believed to be true.

'Well I'm a woman Magnus and I think most women have

experienced some kind of *#MeToo* incident in their lives. It goes with the territory of being female. That's why I'm always careful.'

'Yet you're here with me alone in your home. How do you know I'm not a serial rapist?' he'd smiled.

'I don't but I generally get a vibe if someone's dodgy and I'm not getting it from you,' I'd said, foolishly believing my infallibility at sniffing out predators.

9

Barbara

The first person to arrive was Jessica but she wasn't in her cycling gear.

'Not on your bike today Jessica?'

'No, I had a late-night so just took a taxi.'

'Was it good?

'Was what good?

'Your late night. Were you at a club or a party?'

'No. I don't do clubs or parties. I just couldn't sleep.'

'Oh, I'm sorry to hear that. Is there something bothering you?'

Jessica looked at Barbara obviously weighing up the pros and cons of confiding in her. Barbara wondered why this was a dilemma for her. She had been counselling her for a few years now and Jessica had confided a lot of personal information to her.

'If you must know, Barbara, my mum's fallen out with me and I've been getting upsetting emails.'

'Upsetting?'

'Yes. They're saying horrible things about me and I'm worried that they're going to put things on Facebook. It could be a disaster for me.'

Barbara refused to use Facebook and other social media platforms. She felt they were intrusive and potentially dangerous. She felt vindicated in her views as she listened to Jessica.

'They are accusing me of being a home-wrecker, but I didn't know that John was married when we first got together. It was only later and by then I had fallen for him and things had moved on.'

'I see. So, what are you going to do? Are you replying to these messages?'

'No. I wouldn't give them the time of day. Obviously if they went public, I would need to say something.'

'Do you know who they are from?'

'No. They're using pseudo names; Avenging Angel and

Mockingbird. That would imply that they are young people as I think they are the names of superheroes in those Marvel films or computer games. The thing is they are becoming more and more threatening and I can't sleep because of them.'

Before Barbara had time to reply, Evie and Greer came into room, but she made a mental note to check her daughter's laptop. Those names sounded familiar and she remembered that guilty look on her daughter's face when she had gone into Ella's room to speak to her. She hoped to God she wasn't involved in sending these messages to Jessica. It would only add to the stress they were already under because of this woman who was claiming to be Rory's daughter. At least they would know the truth soon.

Jessica

After speaking to Barbara I took my phone out of my bag again, but I was scared to look at it. There were now two people sending me messages: Avenging Angel and Mockingbird. Their messages were becoming more threatening and I was worried that they might go further than nasty emails. What if they knew where I lived? They still hadn't gone public, but I was sure it was only a matter of time. I didn't know what to do. Dorothy had told me that a little notoriety wouldn't do my reputation any harm, but I didn't want to spoil things with Magnus. Also I didn't want Mum to know that I'd been with a married man.

'Morning Jessica. It's a miserable day isn't it?'

I looked up at Greer but didn't respond before returning to stare at my phone. I realised I must be giving myself away as Greer continued

'Is everything okay Jessica? You look upset.'

'I'm fine. Just let me be.'

Evie, who had just come into the meeting from the toilet, stuck up for Greer, of course.

'She's only trying to be nice to you Jessica, but you don't know the meaning of the word.'

I looked at Evie and realised I probably didn't. Hardly anyone had ever been nice to me and I thought back to my mum's birthday last week. I had arranged to visit her in the afternoon and take along the cardigan I had knitted at the circle meetings which, if I say so myself, had turned out rather well. I was sure Mum would like it. On my way I had bought a huge cake and a card which implied that Mum was the best in the world, even although she was far from it. Nevertheless, I found myself longing for some words of appreciation from her. When I arrived, the house was like an oven and was filled with cigarette smoke. I opened a window much to her annoyance.

'Happy Birthday Mum,' I said, kissing her wrinkled cheek. My stomach turned as the stench of nicotine reached my nostrils. 'I've brought you a present. I hope you like it. Why don't you open it while I put the kettle on?'

'Just leave it there. I'm watching *Murder She Wrote*. Wait till it finishes.'

I had felt the familiar feeling of disappointment and sat down on the settee while Mum finished watching her programme. As I watched Jessica Fletcher solving yet another crime, I wondered why it was still so popular. Hadn't it been out in the eighties and nineties. It was hard to believe that the series was being re-run yet again. I had actually taken my pen name from the character in Mum's favourite television programme even although she was an old woman, but I had hoped it might please my mother. Some hope!

As I looked round the room I noticed as if for the first time that there were no photographs of me. There was only one of Mum and Dad on their wedding day. Mum looked radiant as a bride should and I felt sad that life had changed her from that lovely young woman to what she had become. I did take comfort though from the fact that my brother and I were wanted and had been made through love. That at least was something. A lot of other children came into the world unwanted and unloved. Look at Evie. I didn't blame Mum for how she had treated me, and I still hoped that somehow we could become close.

Eventually the programme finished.

'You can get that tea now. Remember don't make it like dish water. I like it strong.'

When I came through I could see that Mum had opened my present, but the cardigan was lying on the floor at the foot of her chair with the wrapping paper carefully folded on the table.

'Don't you like your present Mum?'

'Yes, it's nice but I would never wear anything like that. You know I only like dark colours.'

'I know but I thought with spring just around the corner you might like something colourful for a change.'

I smiled my bright smile at Mum but as usual it didn't work.

'It's your brother's anniversary next month so I would like to go up to the cemetery. Can you arrange to get me a taxi?'

'Oh, you don't need a taxi Mum. I can take you and as it's my birthday we could go out afterwards for a lunch to that nice place at the church that's just opened.'

Mum looked at me as if I was a freak.

'I prefer to go on my own and I don't think it's appropriate to celebrate anything on the day that your brother died. Just order me a taxi if you don't mind.'

I don't really remember all that clearly what happened next just that a red mist took over my brain and I hurled the tea things and cake at the wall and found myself screaming at Mum.

'I'm alive, why can't you celebrate that? My brother's dead. It wasn't my fault that he died. It was probably yours. I bet you were drinking even back then, and it affected him. I hate you. You've never loved me, and you've always been nasty to me. Even when I told you about Mr Fraser you didn't believe me.'

'How dare you say that I caused your brother's death. I was so looking forward to having the two of you.'

As the mist lifted and I managed to bring myself under control again, I was horrified to see tears pouring down Mum's cheeks.

'I've never been able to get over losing Darren because of you talking to him and about him constantly. I never had time to grieve. You were a constant reminder of what I'd lost.'

'Oh Mum, I'm so sorry. I didn't mean what I said.'

But Mum carried on speaking ignoring me.

'I know I wasn't the best mum when you were growing up, but I don't understand why you've turned out the way you have.'

'But I've done well Mum. I'm a successful author and have a nice home. Why can't you be proud of me?'

I knew my voice was whining now and that this would only annoy her even more.

'Proud of you,' Mum scoffed. 'I could never be proud of a snivelling slut like you. You're so needy and always have been.'

Suddenly she grabbed my arm. I was surprised by the strength of her grip as she pulled me towards the living room door.

'It's a pity you've not become a nice person to go with your nice home.'

Before I knew what was happening she had pushed me into the hall and was screaming at me.

'Get out of my house now and don't come back. I've had enough of your tantrums. You're not a little girl anymore. Grow up.'

Barbara's voice broke into my troubled thoughts and when she asked if anyone would like to share I found myself telling my Mr Fraser story to the group.

Greer

When Greer arrived with Evie at the meeting room, Evie had to go to the toilet. While she was waiting for her, she noticed Jessica looking at her phone. She seemed upset so Greer decided to ask her if everything was alright but, Jessica was rude and cut her off. Evie heard her and stuck up for her, but it made no difference to Jessica. Greer wondered what was bothering her as she had seemed nice when the circle meetings first started but had been quite bitchy recently. After everyone had checked in, Barbara asked if anyone had anything to share and Jessica asked if it she could do it. Greer was a little surprised at Jessica's subservient attitude. However, she realised that something had upset Jessica, so she supposed she was entitled to use the group in a therapeutic way as much as the others even if she was a bitch.

'I don't know if you know, but when I was at school, my English teacher groomed me and tried to sexually assault me,' she began.

Evie let out a loud oh sound but didn't say anything. She just stared at Jessica with tears in her eyes. As Jessica continued, her voice became soft, and Greer thought she sounded just like a young girl. She felt moth wings flutter in her stomach at the subject matter.

'It was really hard for me back then. My mum and dad were alcoholics and I didn't have much support at home so when Mr Fraser showed an interest in me and took me under his wing, I was suspicious. I was rude and obnoxious to him sometimes, but secretly I was flattered that someone seemed to like me. He used to give me extra tuition and I did well. He said he was hopeful that I would get the grades I needed to go to university. It was like a fairy tale.'

By this time Greer's stomach was filled with a kaleidoscope of moths. Mr Fraser. It couldn't be the same Mr Fraser could it? But by the time Jessica had finished her story, Greer knew it was.

She could hear Paul's voice all those Christmases ago telling her he had driven one of his pupils home after the school dance and that he had given her the little package he had bought for Sophie because he felt sorry for her. She had no inkling that the girl was Jessica. Hadn't the girl's name been Debbie something? Greer's insides had turned to liquid and her stomach began to cramp. She needed to get out before the others noticed that something was wrong.

'I need to go the toilet. Sorry. Excuse me,' she said, getting up quickly. She ran into the toilet and vomited violently.

10

Greer

She was dreading going to the circle meeting after Jessica's revelations last time. She had no idea how she should behave towards her now or even whether she should still attend the meetings. Surely it was a breach of confidentiality or something. Perhaps she should speak to Barbara about it. But what about Evie? Would she be brave enough to go to the meetings without her? She had certainly grown in confidence since they had begun attending the circle so perhaps she would be okay without her being there.

For once her granddaughter wasn't in the bathroom holding her back.

'Mia,' she called through to her granddaughter. 'That's me off to work now.'

The bedroom door opened and out walked a sleepy looking Mia.

'Nana could I borrow some money please. I'm a bit short until I get my benefits.'

'How's the job hunting going?' she asked, trying not to sigh as she looked in her purse for some notes.

She loved that her granddaughter had chosen to come and stay with her, but she was on a limited income and found it hard enough to manage without having another mouth to feed.'

'I'm meeting someone today and it might mean that things will change for me.'

'Oh that's good. Am I allowed to know any more?'

'Not yet Nana. I'd rather wait until I know for sure.'

'Okay. See you later darling,' she said, handing over a £20 note.

Barbara

She sat in the meeting room waiting for the others to arrive. She wasn't in the mood today, but had to keep going, maintain some semblance of normality. Today she was going to meet her husband's daughter at the DNA Testing Clinic. Rory had asked her to go along as he didn't feel comfortable meeting the girl on his own. They hadn't said anything yet to the kids. They would wait until the test had been done and then decide how they would go about introducing this new sister to the Ben and Ella. She was dreading it.

She was so pre-occupied she didn't hear Jessica coming in.

'Morning Babs you're not looking so hot this morning. Something up?'

She must be in a mood as she was calling her Babs. She only called her that when she wanted to annoy her but today she couldn't annoy her with that. She had much larger fish to bother her than Jessica Aitken.

'Good morning Jessica. I'm okay. It's kind of you to ask. I had a restless night. How about you? You're looking better than you did last time.'

'I feel a little embarrassed about telling my story at the last meeting. I was upset about falling out with my mum and about those trolls.'

'You know you don't have to be embarrassed Jessica. Everyone here is a friend and everything you share is confidential. Please don't worry about it. Help yourself to water. I think I hear the others coming.'

If truth be told Barbara was concerned about Jessica's revelation to the group regarding her experience. Although Jessica's story wasn't new to her, she wondered what had caused her to bring it up in the circle. Unusually for Jessica, she had seemed so vulnerable which surprised Barbara as she very rarely presented herself in that way. Barbara hoped that Jessica wasn't heading for another breakdown. She had been a wreck when she had first come to her for counselling and it had taken a couple of years to get her back on track. Everyone in the meeting had been supportive although poor Greer had needed to use the toilet suddenly. She hoped she was okay.

At the end of the session Barbara breathed a huge sigh of relief. Everyone seemed on edge today but then again, she was on edge so maybe she was projecting that onto her clients. She decided to do a simple meditation just to calm herself before walking along to Kelvingrove Art Gallery and Museum where she had arranged to meet Rory. She wondered how he was feeling. They had discussed whether he should withdraw his nomination for the Law Society but in the end, they agreed that it would be better to wait and hear what the girl had to say and whether there was substance to her claim that she was his daughter.

As she walked along Dumbarton Road, her thoughts became preoccupied again with the problems facing her family and she arrived at the Art Gallery on autopilot all her mindfulness training going out the window. Rory was waiting for her at the corner of Kelvin Way and Dumbarton Road and it took them about five minutes to reach the clinic. She loved this area. The blonde sandstone buildings were so beautiful, and it was good to see that more were being reconverted back into housing rather than being used as offices or clinics

They sat down together nervously. Normally she would have held his hand, but she was still angry at him, so they sat in silence not touching. The clinic was busy, and she wondered if everyone was here for a DNA test or were there other reasons that people came to a clinic like this. A woman in a white coat came out of a door on the far corner of the room and called 'Rory King and Mia Cooper.' Barbara's heart missed a beat as a young woman on the opposite side of the room stood up at the same time as Rory. She was petite with long straight brown hair and wore leopard skin leggings with a black puffer jacket. She was glad to see that she looked nothing like Rory or her children.

Jessica

Barbara didn't look up when I came into the room and I began to feel anxious. Had telling my story at the circle meeting annoyed her. I decided not to let the therapist see my anxiety and called her Babs. I knew that always annoyed her but today it didn't seem to have any effect on her. She had replied absently and had gone out to look for the others as if she didn't want to continue our one to one conversation. This of course fed my insecurities where Barbara was concerned, and I became sure that I must have said something to make her annoyed with me.

Just then Evie, Greer and Lottie arrived and for the first time I was pleased to see them.

'Hello you three. How are things?'

I was surprised when Greer put her head down and didn't say anything as normally she was chatty. Evie responded but as usual everything came back to talking about Tom, her hero.

'Hi Jessica,' said Evie. 'You look great in that cycling gear. I wish I could go a bike. I'm rubbish at keeping my balance. I remember going on a trip with Mr and Mrs Bannerman to Millport. Mrs Bannerman was really pissed off with me because I kept falling over and holding them back. Only Tom was kind to me and whispered nice things when he came over to pick me up.'

'Come on Evie don't get all sentimental over that man. He's not worth it.'

'Well I still think he'll come and stay with me and the baby when she comes.'

Evie sat with her arms folded glaring at me.

Barbara came in and sat down. I thought she looked worried about something and realised that maybe it had nothing to do with me after all.

'Anyone want to share this week?' asked Barbara

'I would like to if you don't mind,' said Lottie.

'Yes of course.'

'Well my head is all over the place. I got a phone call from my dad to say that my mum is in St Margaret's Hospice and was asking for me. You can imagine what a shock that was. I haven't heard anything from them for so long. I wish it had been in different circumstances though. My mum looked very pale and thin when I went along to see her, but she smiled when she saw me and took my hand. My dad was there but he didn't say anything to me, so I think he must just have contacted me because Mum had asked him.'

'Is she very ill Lottie?' asked Evie.

'Well she wouldn't be in a hospice if she weren't,' I said, not meaning to be as mean as I must have sounded.

'I would give you a hug Lottie, but we're not allowed,' said Evie, looking pointedly at Barbara.

'Thanks Evie, you're a real friend.'

I looked at the two girls and couldn't help wishing that I had a friend. I had never found it easy to make friends and most of the people in my life were acquaintances or professional people like Dorothy, my publisher. Magnus was a friend, but I was hoping that he would become more. I had read his story and although it wasn't very well-written, it had unsettled me. It was set in zombie land, but it could almost have been my Mr Fraser story but with a different ending.

I had been a bit off with Magnus when I had last spoken to him. He had taken to face-timing me a couple of times a week and kept asking if I had read his story. He had looked disappointed when I said I'd had a quick read but would need to spend more time on it. I wanted to digest the implications of what he had written and what I would say to him about it. I would need to tell him his writing was shite, but I wanted to say it in such a way that he wasn't devastated. Everyone had to learn. I was disappointed though. For some reason I had thought he would have potential and that I could take him under my wing, but it wasn't looking that way.

And we still hadn't made love despite our foreplay and Magnus's suggestion that we should try cyber-sex seeing as we couldn't see each other very often. I wasn't sure about it. I would feel a bit strange masturbating in front of my phone. But sex was something I understood, and I wanted him more than I had ever wanted anyone before. I also wanted the power that I believed sex could give me over him. It had always given me the upper hand in my previous relationships but now it felt that all the power was with Magnus.

11

Greer

She decided it was time to tell Marie the truth about her past. How was she going to explain who Mia was unless she did. Also hearing Jessica telling her story and realising who she was had upset her and brought the past into the present with a huge bang. She had suggested to Marie that they go for a meal rather than to a busy pub for a drink as she wanted a quiet spot to tell her. She was nervous in case her friend felt hurt that she hadn't confided in her from the start. What if it changed their relationship? She needed to take that chance.

'I've got something to tell you,' she launched in, as soon as they sat down.

'Okay. Let's order a drink first and then you can tell me over dinner. What're you having? I fancy the steak.'

'I'll have the fish.'

Marie signalled to the waiter and as usual did her best to flirt but the young man wasn't interested in someone old enough to be his granny.

'So, Greer what is it you want to tell me?'

'Well it's a bit of a story Marie and I'm not sure how you'll take it. I'm sorry I didn't tell you before, but I was trying to make a new life and put the past behind me when we met. I was in desperate need of a friend and I didn't want to put you off.'

'Put me off. Why would I have been put off?'

She took a deep breath and said the words that she had been dreading saying to her friend.

'My husband was accused of grooming a young girl and trying to molest her.'

Just as the words were out the waiter came over with their drinks and Greer could tell that he had heard by the way his hand shook as he put their drinks on the table. He didn't look at her or say a word, only made a quick getaway back to the bar. She bet he couldn't wait to tell his colleagues. Shit she hoped no-one she knew worked here. She looked at Marie who for once was speechless.

'Say something Marie.'
'What a bastard. I hate flaming paedophiles.'
'He said he was innocent.'
'Well he would, wouldn't he?'
'I believed him.'

Marie took a gulp of her wine and pushed her chair back.

'I need to go to the loo.' she said. 'I think I need to throw up.'

Greer's throat went hard as she tried to swallow down her disappointment. I'm going to lose my friend after all she thought.

Jessica

One of the things that I had always been able to do was sleep and I was finding it difficult lying awake till all hours of the morning thinking about who was trolling me and what I should do about it. Inevitably I also had flashbacks to things that had happened in the past which added to my distress. I was also worried about my relationship with Mum. I hadn't seen her since her birthday and she still wasn't picking up her phone. I had been surprised at just how angry I had felt that day. Normally I was able to keep my feelings under control where Mum was concerned, but something had become unleashed and I wasn't sure she would ever forgive me.

As well as all these worries, I was also troubled that my relationship with Magnus still hadn't been consummated. Although he came up to my house for our Friday date nights now, he still insisted on going back to his hotel at the end of the evening. So despite our heavy petting we still hadn't had full blown sex. This was leaving me so jangly and restless, I was even considering his suggestion that we have cyber-sex. He'd brought me a sex toy the last time I'd seen him, and had suggested that instead of playing scrabble on our FaceTime date nights that we play with that instead. I was still resisting and had begun to wonder if Magnus really did like me or whether he was just with me as he thought I would be able to help him with his writing career.

That made me think back to when I had told him that his short story still needed a lot of work before it would be ready to send to a publisher for consideration. I had been anxious about telling him, but he hadn't appeared to be too bothered.

'Thanks for taking the time to read it Jessica. I know I have a long way to go but I wondered what you thought of the moral of the story.'

'To be honest I found it quite upsetting that someone would go to those lengths to discredit another person that they had loved. You would need to be really screwed up to do something like that.'

'You seem a bit rattled Jessica. Did the story upset you?'

'No don't be daft. It's just that I've been anxious about

speaking to you about your writing in case you would be annoyed.'

'Come here silly,' he'd said, taking me in his arms and kissing away all my worries.

I felt restless and couldn't decide whether to go for a run or go to the gym so checked my phone. I had a couple of hours to kill before Magnus would be face timing me. I had a bottle of wine chilling in the fridge as he had suggested that we have a drink together as it would make it more like a date and would help us relax. When I opened my email I saw immediately that there was another message from the trolls. Attached to their email was a link and without thinking I clicked on it. I was horrified to see that it was a suicide site. It was only then that I noticed the words on the email. *Just thinking! You'll get lots of ideas here Jessica. Make us happy.*

For some reason I thought about Mr Fraser and wondered whether he had got hate mail after what happened with me. I began reading through the posts on the site and was amazed by the content. A chat room dedicated to talking about how to kill yourself. It was gross. There was no way I would ever do that. I had too much to live for, but I was rattled and poured myself a glass of wine not bothering to wait for Magnus. I still hadn't told Magnus about the trolls in case it would make him finish with me, but this was getting serious. I might need to contact the police as Dorothy had suggested.

12

Greer

She could hardly believe it was time for circle meeting again, such a lot had happened. Firstly, telling Marie about Paul. At the point when Marie had got up to go to the toilet, Greer had been sure that their friendship was over and had almost left the restaurant. However, their meals were served as she was about to go and luckily Marie came back just at the right time.

'Are you okay Marie? Were you sick?'

'No don't be daft. I just needed a little bit of time to think about what you told me. Right tell me everything.'

It had taken about two hours to tell her the whole story as Marie kept interjecting and asking questions. The upshot was she was still Greer's friend, but her view was that her husband 'had done the deed otherwise why would he have killed himself.' That was the question that she had asked herself thousands of times. If he didn't do it, why did he decide to jump from that bridge? She remembered what it had been like. The week before he had been calm and quiet. She realised now that it was because he had come to a decision about what he was going to do. Prior to that he had literally been tearing his hair out.

If only she had recognised it, perhaps she could have stopped him. If only she had told him how much she loved him and believed him, if only she had gone to see the girl who had accused him and got her to see sense, if only she could have given him a reason to live. That was all she could think of after he died. If only. But he was obviously devastated by the allegations and the thought of the inevitable court case that would follow after the investigation was complete must have sent him over the edge. Although confident on the surface, Paul had suffered from bouts of depression throughout their married life. He had put this down to being given up by his birth mother for adoption and although Mr and Mrs Fraser were the kindest of parents he had still been left with the feeling that he wasn't good enough. She knew that shame could make people act in all kinds of self-destructive ways and could only imagine the negative voices going around and around in Paul's head. He hadn't had enough resilience to fight. Nor had she.

Jessica

I didn't sleep again and decided to drive to the circle meeting. When I arrived, I checked my phone scanning to see if there were any emails from Mockingbird or Avenging Angel but there were none. They seemed to have given up as I hadn't heard anything from them in over a week and all without me having to go to the police. I wondered why but not enough to try and investigate. I was just grateful that it appeared to be over. However, there was an email from someone called *Iam-Mia* and the heading this time was Liar, Liar. I was about to open it when I was interrupted.

'Morning Jessica. Are you not on your bike today?' said Evie.

I smiled tightly.

'Morning pumpkin. No not today. You just keep on growing don't you?'

'I know. It's lovely isn't it?' said Evie, rubbing her tummy and not getting the underlying barb in my words. She was a bit thick.

I noticed that Greer wasn't looking at me again and wondered what was wrong with her. She hadn't been the same since that meeting when I had told my Mr Fraser story and I wondered why. As Barbara was still faffing about getting water, I decided to open the email. It was all I could do not to cry out when I saw what it said.

I know that you lied about your teacher and I'm going to make sure you pay for it. Keep an eye on your post.

Before I could take in what it meant, my thoughts were interrupted by Barbara's voice.

'Lottie won't be coming this week. Her mother died at the week-end and the funeral is today.'

'She didn't tell me that her mum had died. I thought she would have let me know. I'm supposed to be her friend,' said Evie in a whining voice.

'I'm sure she will tell you Evie, but it must have been a big thing for her. The pastor from her church talked her dad into letting her go along to the funeral so I expect a lot has been happening for her just now and the last thing she would be thinking of would be contacting her friends,' said Barbara.

'Yes, just because you're letting her be Godmother to your baby doesn't mean you have to know everything about her,' I added.

I found it easier sometimes to be bitchy especially when I was scared or anxious. Hearing that Lottie's mum had died made me think about my own mum. What if my mum died without forgiving me? When Mum had given up alcohol, as part of her programme of recovery, she had to apologise to people she had hurt. I had been more than willing to forgive her when she said sorry but somehow it hadn't changed things between us. Perhaps I had forgiven her too readily and hadn't explained enough what it had been like for me as a child.

But it was more than that. There was something spiteful about Mum. Poor Dad had been on the receiving end of her malevolence for years and as for me no matter what I did to try and earn her love, nothing was ever good enough. The cardigan I had knitted for her birthday was just one example. Sometimes she threw me the odd crumb of love, but it was always quickly overshadowed by her next criticism of something I had done. She clearly still resented me being alive instead of my brother and didn't feel that my birth was worth celebrating.

I hadn't started another knitting project yet so just sat pretending to listen to the sporadic chat while the knitting needles click-clacked in the background. Normally I found the sound of the needles soothing but today my stomach was churning thinking about this latest email. Sometimes life was just crap.

13

Jessica

When Magnus arrived on Friday night he was laden with a huge bouquet of roses and a bottle of champagne.

'What's this?' I cried in delight, taking them from him. I loved getting presents.

'Since I can't be here on Sunday for your birthday, I thought we should celebrate tonight. I hope that's okay.'

It was more than okay in my eyes. I had decided that tonight was the night and two bottles of champagne should do the trick. I laughed and led him to the kitchen where I opened a bottle of champagne that I already had chilling in the fridge. He smiled as I poured the fizz into two glass flutes.

'Happy Birthday when it comes Jessica. You look lovely tonight. Have you done something with your hair?'

'I was at the hairdresser today, so she managed to tame these curls,' I said, twisting one in what I hoped was a provocative way.

We drank the champagne before having dinner, so we were both a little tipsy and when he took me in his arms, I knew it was going to happen. I loved the feel of his muscular arms holding me and the smell of his body, a mix of citrus and musk. I took his hands and pulled him gently towards my bedroom. I kissed him tenderly at first and then more urgently pulling him down onto the bed and unbuttoning his shirt. His body was smooth, not rugged and hairy like John's. I pushed John from my mind and concentrated on Magnus.

'Magnus, this is what you want isn't it. I'm not coming on too strong.'

'No Jessica. I want us to be closer but I ...

'What is it Magnus?'

'I don't want you to think that I'm taking advantage. We've only known each other a few months.'

'I know that Magnus, but this just feels right for me. I hope it feels right for you too.'

He didn't answer but his kisses told me that he felt the same. As our lovemaking progressed, I felt something change in me. I realised I had never made love before only had sex. I was blown away by Magnus's passion, creativity, and tenderness to such an extent that I screamed with joy and by the end was crying like a baby.

'Oh Magnus,' I breathed. 'I've never felt like this before. I love you so much.'

'I love you too Jessica,' he said, wiping away my tears with his fingers. 'I didn't hurt you did I?'

'No, no I'm just feeling a bit overwhelmed. You've given me something that's been missing my whole life.'

I was in a golden bubble of happiness. When I made up my mind that tonight was the night I thought it would be the usual sex romp which I enjoyed, but this was different. I was in love and apparently so was Magnus.

'Will you marry me Jessica? I'm still married but when I get divorced would you do me the honour of becoming my wife.'

I couldn't believe what Magnus was saying. No-one had ever asked me to marry them before and I had never contemplated it as something that would happen to me. The only experience I had of married life was of my parents and that was something I had hoped to avoid. But Magnus was different. We would be different. My heart swelled with hope.

'I can't believe you've asked me,' I said, the tears spilling out again. 'I was hoping we could move in together if all went well tonight. But this is even better. My answer is Yes! Yes! Yes!'

Giggling and holding hands, we made our way back to the kitchen and chatted over dinner about when we could get married, where it would be and where we would go on honeymoon. Afterwards we sat in the glow of the fire burning warmly in the hearth and held each other. I had never experienced such happiness, apart from that time when Mr Fraser had given me the little silver earrings at Christmas. When I thought of Mr Fraser my mood dipped and I shivered.

'What's wrong my darling. Are you cold? Shall I get you a warmer jumper.'

'No, I'm nice and cosy Magnus. It was just an old ghost walking over my grave as they say.'

I knew I would have to tell Magnus about what had happened with Mr Fraser but not tonight. I didn't want anything to spoil tonight.

14

Jessica

When I woke up in the morning, I felt a bit woozy. I had drunk too much, but hey I had something to celebrate. I could hear Magnus moving about in the kitchen and curled up again under the duvet hoping he might come back to bed even although we had made love most of the night. I couldn't get enough of him. It was strange being on the other side of the fence. In the relationships I'd had before, it was the men who couldn't get enough of me and I had loved the power it had given me. But this was different. I was no longer thinking of power and control. All I wanted was to be with Magnus. It was then that I noticed one of the tissue boxes he had given me sitting on my bedside table.

'Ugly little thing,' I said, taking a tissue, 'but I love you.'

The next thing the door opened and in walked Magnus with a tray. I hoped he hadn't heard my criticism of his gift.

'Breakfast in bed for you my girl,' he said, kissing me on the lips. I felt self-conscious knowing I had morning breath as I hadn't yet brushed my teeth, but he didn't seem to mind as his tongue searched greedily for mine and we again made love.

He had made me porridge with fruit and honey and a very welcome cup of tea which I drank thirstily even although it was cooler now. After I had eaten, we settled down and started to chat. He didn't need to leave until midday, so we had a few more hours together. I hoped that we would continue where we had left off earlier, but Magnus seemed set on talking.

'Tell me more about yourself Jessica. If we are going to be married, I want to know absolutely everything about you.'

'What do you mean *if* we are going to be married?' I laughed, digging him in the ribs. 'You go first. I want to know all about you too.'

While he talked about his past life, I thought about John and how Magnus might react. He sounded very conventional and might think having an affair was wrong. I began to feel nervous at the thought of telling him what had happened. Would he dump me? I couldn't take the risk. I loved him and wanted to hold on to him forever. But when he had finished and said it was my turn to talk, I found the words popping out of my mouth unbidden.

'I'm worried that you might not want to marry me when you hear about my life. You might hate me.'

He sat back his eyes quizzing me.

'I could never hate you,' he said hesitantly. 'What could you have done that's so bad that I could hate you?'

'I had an affair with a married man and I'm now getting frightening emails from trolls. I'm worried that they'll try to hurt me or expose me to the papers,' I blurted out.

'Do you know who's threatening you Jessica? You must go to the cops. This isn't right.'

'I know but I don't want my mum to know that I went with a married man. She already hates me and if she knew that she would just throw it back at me as evidence that I'm a bad person.'

'You're not a bad person Jessica. You're lovely.'

He put his arms around me and held me close.

'I'm not squeaky clean you know so you don't need to worry that I'll think less of you because you had an affair.'

'Does that mean you had an affair when you were married Magnus?'

'No, not that but I wasn't very considerate, I was always working away from home and not giving time to my marriage.'

I thought he looked sad and for a moment I felt a little jealous. Did he love me as much as he had loved his wife? But he brightened up quickly and continued with our conversation.

'So, what else is there to know about you? What other secrets are you hiding from me?'

I felt myself grow cold. Although he was saying it in a jokey manner, I wondered if he had found out about my memoir. I thought I had managed to separate that first story from my crime novels by using the pen name of Jessica Aitken. But I supposed it wouldn't have been that difficult to make the connection. I decided now was the time to come clean.

'When you asked me before whether I had any *#MeToo* incidents in my past I told you I didn't, but I wasn't telling the truth.'

I got up and went through to my writing room and came back with my memoir.

'This is a memoir I wrote when I was at university. I wrote it as part of my degree course, and it helped me get the First I told you about. Afterwards, my tutor passed it on to an agent friend of his and he found a publisher for me.'

I thought about my tutor. It had almost been a replay of what had happened with Mr Fraser only Patrick hadn't killed himself. He had been twenty years my senior and I had been bedazzled by his intellect, charisma and of course his interest in me. He had been my first sexual encounter and I had thought I was in love but that had changed as I grew in confidence, excelled in my subject, and found out he was married with two children. It was easy to coax him into getting his agent friend to send my memoir to a publisher when I slipped into the conversation that we would have to be careful to make sure that his wife and kids didn't find out what we had been up to. He had got the message without me having to use a direct threat and he enjoyed our little affair too much to give it up. He was still on my Christmas card list and sometimes I invited him to my book launches and sometimes he invited me to 'lunch', so it hadn't ended too badly for either of us.

'I think you should read it Magnus, and then see how you feel about me.'

'I know how I feel about you Jessica. I love you. I want you to marry me. Nothing will change that. But if it makes you happy I'll take your book with me and I can read it when I'm whiling away the lonely hours without you.'

I smiled at his hyperbole but hoped he would be lonely without me. I was missing him already.

When he had gone, I checked my phone and clicked on the icon from *IamMia.* I wondered how I was going to break this news to Magnus. How was I going to explain that I was being accused of lying in my memoir.

15

Jessica

It was my birthday. I had tried to phone Mum, ostensibly to see if she wanted a lift to the cemetery to visit Darren, but I really wanted to tell her about Magnus and his proposal. However, as usual there had been no answer. I decided to go along to Dalnottar Cemetery myself to lay some flowers and perhaps if she were there she would speak to me. She was there but she didn't speak to me. Just looked me up and down and then got into the taxi that was waiting for her without saying a word. I laid my flowers on Darren's grave and noticed the little stone that we had erected for my dad after he died. His ashes were buried beside Darren. It made me wonder where my ashes would be laid. If Mum had anything to do with it, it wouldn't be here. I began to cry and started talking to Darren.

'Hello Darren. I miss you so much. If you have any influence over the living can you try and get Mum to forgive me. I feel so alone. Sometimes I wish I were dead.'

I was taken aback by this. Hadn't I said only recently when I clicked on that suicide site that I had too much to live for to think about killing myself. Now I had even more to live for. I shuddered. What was happening to me?

When I got home my phone was ringing. My heart swelled with hope. Mum must have had second thoughts.

'Hello Mum?' I said breathlessly.

'Jessica Aitken?'

It was a woman's voice but not my mum's.

'Yes.'

'I'm from True-Life Magazine. We've been approached by a source who says that you lied about what you said happened to you in your memoir. We're giving you an opportunity to respond before we print the story. Have you anything you would like to say?'

I was stunned and it was a moment before I found my voice.

'Who is this?'

'Nancy Gardener. I'm the Features Editor of the magazine.'

'Who told you this? Whose your source?'

'I'm sorry I can't tell you my source just now but if you were to agree to an interview, perhaps it would become clearer who is making the accusation.'

My mind was racing. I didn't know what to say so I stalled for time.

'I'll need to think about it. Can you give me your number and I'll get back to you?'

'I prefer to phone you,' the voice said. 'I'll give you a week.'

Then she hung up before I had a chance to say anything else.

Magnus was going to FaceTime me later for my birthday and I had bought a bottle of prosecco. Without thinking I took it from the fridge, opened it and poured a glass. It took me all my time not to spill it as my hand was shaking so much.

I had a good chat with Magnus and the couple of glasses of Prosecco I had drunk before he facetimed me had loosened my tongue and I found myself telling him about going up to see Darren and how Mum had been. He was lovely and so supportive that I found myself engaging enthusiastically in cyber sex when he suggested it. It seemed okay to me now that we were having a proper relationship. By the time he hung up I felt much better. I hadn't told him about the phone call as he hadn't mentioned my memoir but if these allegations were going to come out into the open he would know soon enough as would all my fans.

I was just settling down to go to sleep when I heard a voice.

'Happy Birthday Jessica.'

I sat up in bed and switched on the bedside lamp.

'Whose there?'

I wondered briefly if it was Magnus. But he was miles away so it couldn't be him.

'It's me. It's Darren. Thanks for coming up to see me today. You have a good sleep now. Night, night.'

I was sitting bolt upright by this time. What had just happened? I must have fallen asleep and been dreaming. It was the only explanation. Dead people didn't talk.

16

Greer

On her way to pick up Evie, she thought about Lottie. She wondered how she was doing and whether she would be at the meeting this week. The poor girl had only had a couple of weeks with her mum before she died. All those years wasted. This made her think about Sophie. Her daughter had wasted even more years being angry with her and she wondered if they would ever be able to make up for them.

She thought back to the time when everything had gone wrong. At first, Paul had only been suspended from his work but then Social Work had been called in and Sophie had been put on the At-risk Register as she was only 15. Sean was at university and had been classed as an adult, so it didn't affect him. Greer could still remember the feeling of shame when she went into work and the Senior called her in to reassure her that her job was safe and that they would support her in whatever way they could. But she knew that word would get around the team and it was only the way of things that there would be gossip.

It had been a nightmare time. She had struggled. She didn't know what to believe. Her training told her always to believe the victim, but she thought she knew her husband inside out. They had known each other since they were teenagers and he had always been kind and thoughtful. Why would he want to groom a young girl not much younger than his daughter and try to assault her. When they decided they wanted to get married he had been gentle and understanding when they had first made love together so the idea that he could force a young girl to do something against her will was just unbelievable. But she knew from her work with young folk, that the people they thought they could trust most were the very ones to abuse them. Evie was a prime example of someone who had been duped by an adult who was supposed to take care of her.

Sophie had no doubts about Paul's innocence. It was only later, after his suicide, that she appeared to have doubts. She had gone into a self-destructive spiral that had led to her leaving home and having this daughter who had now turned up on Greer's doorstep all these years later. She had lost count of the number of times she had watched in horror as Sophie arrived home late at night full of drink and probably drugs, her clothes dirty and dishevelled, her make-up smudged and her hair like a bird's nest. Nothing she did could stop her girl from doing what she had made up her mind to do. Grief could be such a destructive force.

Paul's mum had asked her to take out a civil action against the girl as the case would of course not to go court as Paul could no longer be charged. But Greer didn't have the strength at that time. She couldn't face it and what if the judge found in favour of the girl. Although she knew that girls could make things up to get attention, she also knew that they could be very convincing. How many times had she been duped and manipulated by young girls and boys that she was trying to help? It was sometimes the only way they could function in what to them was a hostile world.

When she arrived to pick Evie up, she was still going on about Lottie not telling her about her mum dying.

'But she would have been all tied up with the funeral and getting back into the good books of her family. She wouldn't have had time to think about phoning you.'

'I don't care. I feel let down by her and after me telling her she could be my baby's Godmother. Well that won't be happening now I can tell you.'

'Well you must do what you think is right for you.'

Perhaps it was for the best anyway. Evie hardly knew Lottie.

Jessica

I didn't feel like going to the circle meeting. I wasn't in a good place. I had that dehydrated feeling from drinking too much and I'd hardly slept a wink after hearing Darren's voice. I thought back to when I was little. I used to talk to him all the time although Mum's slaps had put a stop to that. I wondered what was happening to me. When Dad died a couple of years ago, I had really lost the plot. I was in tears all the time, dreamed of him constantly and began to hear his voice. My doctor had suggested I see a psychiatrist as the anti-depressants he was giving me weren't working.

Dr Kumar was nice enough and we spent several sessions together, me talking and him doing all sorts of tests. By the end of it he said I had a borderline personality disorder. I refused to believe him. This type of diagnosis was a get out of jail card for psychiatrists as far as I was concerned when they couldn't pigeonhole you into a recognised mental illness. When I rejected his proposed treatment, he suggested that I might benefit from some talking therapy and that was how I met Barbara. Thinking of Barbara made me decide to go to the circle. I wanted to tell her I was getting married and about the email from *IamMia*.

I phoned a taxi and saw the driver looking at me strangely as I got in. It wasn't till I got to the centre and saw my hair and clothes in the bathroom mirror that I realised how dishevelled I looked. I hadn't showered or changed my clothes from yesterday and my curls had grown wild again. I felt embarrassed when Barbara came into the toilet behind me.

'Good morning, Jessica. Are you okay?'

I could see the concern on her face as she took in my appearance.

'I don't know Barbara. On the one hand I'm so happy as Magnus has asked me to marry him but I think I'm getting sick again.'

'Why? What's happened?'

'I thought I heard a voice last night but also those trolls are really doing my head in.'

Her face became bright red and she looked really angry.

'Are you still getting emails from Mockingbird and Avenging Angel?'

'No, they seem to have stopped but now I've started getting emails from someone called *IamMia*.'

Her face went back to its normal colour but now she looked puzzled.

'*IamMia*? What does she want?'

'She's accusing me of lying in my memoir. I'm at my wits' end Barbara and I don't know what to do.'

'Perhaps you should make an appointment to see Rory, my husband. He deals with cyber bullying and could maybe help you put a stop to them. I'll text you his details. You go through to the meeting now and try not to worry. I'll be through shortly.'

'Morning Jessica. Are you okay. If you don't mind me saying you're not looking too good,' said Evie.

'Lack of sleep,' I said. 'Nothing to worry about.'

Just then Lottie arrived, and I was surprised to see that Evie went into the room without acknowledging her.

'Morning Evie,' said Lottie, as she sat down. 'Did you hear about my mum?'

'Yes,' said Evie. 'But I thought you would have told me yourself Lottie instead of leaving it to Barbara to let me know.'

'I can't believe you're annoyed at me when such a devastating thing has happened to me. My mum just died and you're complaining about me not telling you. You might not have had a mum that cared about you, but I did.'

'Well she didn't care about you that much did she when she threw you out when you got pregnant.'

'Take that back Evie. My mum had her reasons.'

Lottie stood up and approached Evie. I felt a tingle of anticipation when I saw her raising her hand as if she were going to hit her. But Greer was up on her feet as quick as a flash and stood between the two girls and to my delight it was Greer who received the blow intended for Evie.

'What on earth is going on in here?'

It was Barbara coming back from the toilet.

'It was her,' said Lottie, pointing at Evie. 'She made me do it. She said my mum didn't care about me. But she did, she did,' she sobbed, before lying on the floor and curling up into a ball.

'Are you alright Greer?' said Barbara, noticing the bright pink mark on her face.

I thought Greer was lucky it wasn't worse. Lottie was a big girl and looked like she could do a lot of damage with those hands of hers.

'Yes, I'll be fine. I think we need to get someone to come and take care of Lottie.'

'What about me?' screamed Evie, who by this time was weeping loudly. 'She said my mum didn't care about me.'

'Well she didn't,' I said, deciding to throw some fuel on the fire. 'You told us that yourself.'

'If I wasn't pregnant, I would punch your lights out, you cheeky cow.'

'Calm down, calm down everyone.' said Barbara, raising her voice to be heard above the din. 'What's wrong with you all today?'

'Greer would you mind pouring a drink of water for Lottie.'

'And me,' said Evie, not wanting to be left out.

'Come on Lottie. Come and sit up here and I'll phone your pastor. It's been much too soon for you to come along. You're probably still in terrible shock from your mother's death.'

'Can you phone my dad,' Lottie hiccupped, as she pushed herself up from the floor.

'Of course. Does that mean you've made up?' she said, dialling the number that Lottie gave her. 'Hello Mr MacGregor. It's Barbara King here from the knitting circle Lottie attends. I'm afraid Lottie is terribly upset, and it would be helpful if you could come and pick her up. I don't think she's stable enough to travel home alone.'

There was a silence and then Barbara continued.

'Yes, I understand. Okay.'

I couldn't help a secret smirk as Lottie looked up at Barbara with puppy-dog eyes, but I knew from the way Barbara had ended the call that Daddy wouldn't be coming to pick up his little girl.

'I'm sorry Lottie. Your dad can't come. I'll phone your pastor to come instead shall I?'

Lottie began to scream. 'I want my daddy! I want my daddy!'

I had to cover my ears at Lottie's loud piercing screams and shouted over the din at Barbara.

'For goodness sake Babs do something about that noise. I can't stand it. This place is a real nuthouse today. I think I'll go home now.'

But I didn't go anywhere. I sat in my chair surveying the scene, feeling reluctant to leave them. I knew that when my dad died I had felt like screaming my head off and I could sense that perhaps I might be heading to that dark place again.

'Here Lottie have a little drink. It will help to calm you down,' said Greer, giving her a drink. 'Come on now you're okay, you're okay,' she soothed, patting her on the back.

'Thanks Greer,' Barbara mouthed at her, and went over to Evie who had calmed down now. After taking a sip of water Evie rose and went over to Lottie who was still sitting beside Greer.

'I'm sorry Lottie,' she whispered. 'I didn't mean to upset you. Please forgive me.'

Lottie looked up. 'Thanks Evie. Can we be friends again? I didn't mean what I said.'

'Yes of course we can.'

I couldn't believe that they were making up again after all that hullabaloo but noticed a pang of jealousy. If they could make up why couldn't my mum and me do the same.

Barbara

It was mayhem when she came back from the loo. Everyone seemed to be shouting and it looked as if Greer had received a slap as her cheek was bright pink. Just what I need. As if I don't have enough on my plate she thought remembering the emails she had found on her daughter's computer last week. There were lots of emails between Ella and June discussing how they could make Jessica Aitken's life a misery which were then followed up by emails from Avenging Angel and Mockingbird threatening to expose Jessica on social media.

She was shocked and disappointed in her daughter. She thought she and Rory had brought her up to be better than that but obviously they hadn't done as good a job as they thought. She had put an immediate stop to it and ignored her daughter's protestations that she was invading her privacy by going into her emails.

'Your privacy. What about that woman? What about her privacy? I know you think she's responsible for breaking up June's family, but her dad had a part to play too remember. And your language. It was cruel and degrading. I am thoroughly ashamed of you.'

At that Ella had broken down.

'I'm sorry Mum I just wanted to support June. I promise I will never ever do it again.'

'You're damn right you won't,' Rory had shouted. 'You are banned from using any computer, phone or whatever for the foreseeable future. Didn't you realise that what you were doing was illegal? If Jessica Aitken had gone to the police you could have been charged with cyber bullying.'

When she and Rory had talked about it later, they agreed that their anger had been fuelled by their fears about Rory's illegitimate daughter and the effect on their lives that she was likely to have. If Ella was misbehaving now when she had no reason to, what would she be like when she found out she had an older sibling.

'What a complete fucking mess,' he had said, pulling his hair roughly back from his face.

All these thoughts were coursing through her head at the

same time as she was trying to handle Lottie's breakdown. When she spoke to Lottie's father, he told her that he blamed Lottie for his wife's death. There was no way that he was going to have anything to do with her, so she had better find someone else to take her home. In the end it was Lottie's pastor who picked Lottie up. She breathed a deep sigh of relief when everyone had gone.

17

Jessica

I walked back from Partick hoping that it would help me shake off the trauma of the meeting. All that screaming and crying had done nothing for my own peace of mind. In fact it had made me want to scream and cry too. The walk didn't help. The weather was cold and damp. The daffodils were starting to wilt and despite the budding blossoms on the trees, there was no hint of Spring warmth yet. As I unlocked my front door I felt a reluctance to go inside. My stomach was full of tension. What if Darren spoke to me again.

I had no sooner closed the door, than my bell tinkled and I opened it again.

'Special delivery Ms Aitken,' said a man with a courier badge hanging from his neck. He handed me a large brown envelope. 'Can you sign here please.'

I signed the machine with my finger and wondered how they would verify a signature if there was ever any dispute about a delivery. I took the envelope with me into the kitchen, pulled a bottle of wine from the fridge and poured myself a glass. I realised how agitated I was as this was something I rarely did no matter how stressed I was. I wondered if the envelope was from Dorothy with fan mail. Yes some people still wrote letters. Snail mail wasn't dead yet. I was grateful to my readers for their loyalty so answered all fan mail personally. I opened the envelope, as reading the positive messages from my fans always cheered me up. It opened easily but when I lifted the flap I could see photographs inside rather than letters. Intrigued I pulled them out and spread them on the worktop. It took me a while to realise what I was looking at. They were of a naked couple having sex their bodies entangled and contorted into the most unlikely positions and I'm ashamed to admit that I felt slightly aroused at the sight of them.

I turned the envelope upside down to see if there was anything that would tell me what the photographs were and why they had been sent to me and out popped a typed note.

On it were the words *You would make a good porn star Jessica. What would your public think? Check your email. Signed IamMia.* I grabbed up one of the photographs and peered at the couple. The man's face was unidentifiable, but the woman's face was mine. But how? How had someone been able to photograph me like this, in the most intimate of situations. I remembered the email from IamMia who had told me to look out for the post. This must have been what the email was referring to. But how was this connected with saying that I had lied about Mr Fraser. I didn't get it. What the fuck was happening.

I didn't know what to do, who to turn to for advice. I didn't want to tell Magnus that I was in porn photographs. He would think I was a slut. My heart was thumping. Why was this happening to me? Was it John? Was he trying to get revenge? I looked at the photographs again. The photos definitely weren't of me and John. The man's body was smooth and hair free unlike John's. It must be Magnus. I dreaded to think what Magnus would think when he saw them.

The note had told me to check my emails and sure enough there was one from *IamMia*. My hand was shaking as I picked up my glass of wine, downed the contents and poured another one before clicking on the little icon. *Unless you state publicly that you lied about Paul Fraser or pay me £50,000, the photographs that I sent you will be posted on your Facebook page,* the email read. The pictures would ruin me if they were posted online but so would me admitting that I had lied about Mr Fraser. I would have to pay the £50,000. But I couldn't give in to blackmail. How would I know that they wouldn't keep coming back for more?

18

Jessica

Time was moving on and I didn't know what to do about paying out the money. Magnus wasn't coming tonight and I was gutted. I had got so used to seeing him every Friday but apparently his mum was ill. I couldn't help feeling a bit peeved that she had become ill now as I had planned to tell him about the photographs and the email but it would need to wait until I saw him. It wasn't something you did on FaceTime.

I was becoming paranoid. I kept checking my phone for emails. I was also drinking a lot more than usual. Trying to distract myself, I poured myself a glass of wine and turned on the television. There was a report on the news that Harvey Weinstein was trying to do a deal with the women who had accused him of sexual misconduct. He had the money to pay them off but what kind of message would that send out to all the women who had signed up to Me Too. I felt sorry for them sticking their necks out like that. He had the look of a powerful man who thought he could do what he liked and get away with it. I hoped by some miracle that he wouldn't.

My phone pinged and I almost jumped out of my skin. I was terrified to look and was so relieved when I saw it was from Barbara giving me the contact details for her husband. It had been nearly a week since she told me she would text me the details and I thought she must have forgotten. I decided to phone there and then and got an appointment to go in and see him the following day. Feeling somewhat relieved I poured another glass of wine.

My phone began to ring but I didn't jump. The wine was having a nice numbing effect. It was Dorothy.

'Hello Jessica. How are you?'

'I'm tickety boo. How about you?' I giggled. 'Did you see what I did there?'

'Have you been drinking Jessica?'

'Just a little.'

'What's going on? You don't normally drink very much.'

'Have you ever heard of a Nancy Gardener. She phoned me,

I can't remember when now so much has been happening, to tell me that a source has told her that I lied in my memoir and would I like to comment.'

'Yes I know Nancy, but I only saw her today and she never mentioned you.'

'She didn't? Does she know you're my publisher?

'Yes I think so. Look I'll phone her and try to find out who her source is and what's going on. And you my girl, you put that wine away and get something to eat.'

I liked when Dorothy called me her girl. I wished sometimes that she was my mum.

19

Barbara

She sat and thought about how her life had changed. They had received the lab report and it had confirmed that Mia Cooper was indeed Rory's daughter.

'I'm so sorry Babs to bring this on our family. What are we going to do? Will we have to tell the kids? Do you think if she gets what she wants she'll keep quiet?'

'Don't be crazy Rory. Once someone has you in their power, they will never stop blackmailing you. We will have to tell the kids. There's nothing else for it. She is their half-sister after all. And what about you? Don't you want to get to know your daughter?'

'As far as I'm concerned, I don't have a daughter. She was conceived in a drunken moment and she's only my biological daughter not my real daughter. I wish I knew what she wanted.'

Despite her antipathy towards Mia, she felt her husband was being harsh. It wasn't his daughter's fault that she had been conceived in a drunken moment. She felt her anger at Rory rising again and decided to tell him about the email that Jessica had received and that she had suggested that he act for her.

'What? Mia's trying to blackmail Jessica too. But why on earth have you said that I would act for her? I could be even more compromised than I currently am.'

'Don't you see that if you act for her rather than another solicitor you can control the situation. We don't want Ella getting into trouble with the police do we?'

'No, you're right. Good idea,' he smiled wanly.

'And also, you are going to have to talk to Mia to find out what she wants now that she has confirmation that you're her father. At the same time, you can explain to her that what she's doing to Jessica could get her into serious trouble. Threaten her with going to the police. That would give you some bargaining power against her.'

Before he could respond, his phone rang.

'It's Mia,' he mouthed.

'Hello Mia. Yes, we've received the lab report. Yes, I think an early meeting would be best. Shall we say Monday morning at nine in Cafe Nero. It's generally quiet in there at that time and we can talk about what you want.'

She could hear the girl's voice on the other end of the phone but couldn't hear what she was saying. Despite her anger at him, Barbara realised that she didn't care what Rory had done as a young man, everyone had things from their past although not everyone had a child to show for it. What she cared about were her own children and how they would react to this news. They still didn't know what the girl wanted but it would become clear when they met her.

'What did she say?'

'Just that she wanted to meet me and not to worry. She wasn't intending to tell my children or anything like that. She just wanted me to do something for her.'

'Do something for her. I wonder what she wants you to do.'

Jessica

I had taken Dorothy's advice; put the wine away and had something to eat so was feeling much better than I had yesterday. Rory King's office was in one of those old sandstone buildings in Bath Street in Glasgow city centre, but it had been tastefully modernised inside. The walls were light grey, and the floor was covered in laminate a slightly darker shade of grey than the walls. There was a pleasant waiting room with soft blue seats and a water cooler which I was pleased to see. I took a cup of the cold water and reflected that it tasted much nicer than the wine that I was beginning to drink too much of.

When Rory King came out to take me through to his room, he looked slightly harassed.

'Good afternoon Miss Aitken,' he began, after we were both seated. 'How can I help you?'

'Well I've been receiving emails over the last few months that I've found upsetting. First of all there were these ones from Mockingbird and Avenging Angel.'

I passed over photocopies of the emails I had received including the one with the link to the suicide site. He picked them up and I could see a look of shock on his face. Wait until he saw the next lot.

'Luckily, those ones seem to have stopped but I have now received these emails plus compromising photographs, and I don't know what to do.'

I laid out copies of the emails I had received from *IamMia*, some of the less explicit photos that had been sent to me together with the covering note that had come with them. He studied them and then looked at me. I felt myself blush.

'Do you know who this Mia person is?'

'No.'

'Do you know why anyone would make these accusations? I take it they're not true.'

'Of course not.'

'Have you gone to the police?'

'No. I don't want the publicity. That's why I've come to you. Barbara said you dealt with cyber bullying.'

He ran his fingers through his hair, as if this would help him to figure out how he could help me.

'Can you leave this with me, and I'll see what I can find out. I might be able to trace who this IamMia is and put a stop to her plans.'

'Yes okay. But I hope you can do something. I don't think I can take much more of this.'

20

Jessica

When I woke up that morning, I had a little frisson of happiness for a moment as I remembered it was Friday and that Magnus would be coming to stay with me later, but it was quickly replaced by a quiver of fear when I remembered all that had been happening recently. I hoped that Rory King would come back with something soon. I realised I hadn't heard anything from Dorothy and wondered if she had been able to talk to Nancy Gardener about me yet. Thinking of Dorothy made me decide to do some writing. If everything went pear-shaped I didn't want it to be because I hadn't been doing my job.

I went for a run after I had finished and came back feeling energised and ready for my lunch. Cathy had left me a sandwich of tuna and avocado salad on wholemeal bread, my favourite and I made a cup of tea to drink with it. I sat for a while thinking about what I was going to tell Magnus. He should have read my memoir by now so it would be easier for me to tell him about the emails and the photographs. But I dreaded to think how he would react, especially to the photographs.

Magnus arrived at his usual time and we had dinner and a couple of glasses of wine. I hardly spoke the whole time I was so wound up.

'Is something wrong Jessica? You're very quiet tonight? You're not annoyed that I didn't come last week surely?'

'No, I mean yes, there is something wrong Magnus but I'm dreading telling you.'

'Come on. We're going to be married. You can tell me anything.'

'Did you read my memoir?'

'Yes. Is that what you're worried about?'

'A little. I didn't know how you would feel about being involved with someone with a past like mine.'

'I can't tell you how much I admire you Jessica. To have got over everything that you've been through and make a success of your life the way you have. It's bloody amazing.'

He was looking at me with so much tenderness that I started to cry again.

'Come on Jessica. It can't be that bad. Tell me what's bothering you.'

'I've been getting emails from someone called Mia who is accusing me of lying in my memoir.'

'Lying?'

'Yes and she says that if I don't pay her £50,000 she will go to the papers. I've already had True-Life Magazine calling me.'

'Shit, that's not so good. But it would be her word against yours wouldn't it?'

'Yes, but that's not all.'

I went through to my bedroom and brought the envelope with the photographs inside and passed them over to him. He looked at me curiously.

'What's this?'

'They are compromising photographs of us having sex and the sender is threatening to make them public if I don't say that I lied in my memoir or pay £50,000.'

He poured the pictures onto the table and I could see a look of disgust on his face as he went through them one by one.

'My God Jessica. What the fuck have you been doing? Have you been secretly filming us, and someone's got a hold of the film?'

I was stunned. Magnus had never sworn at me before.

'I'm in the middle of a messy divorce and if my ex gets a hold of these I'm done for.'

'It's alright Magnus. No-one would know it was you. Your face isn't recognisable.'

'Don't be so naïve. It wouldn't take a genius to work out it was me. I don't know what to say Jessica. Do you have the money? Can you pay this Mia person?'

'Yes, I have the money, but I would need to give notice to the bank to get it.'

'Well I think you should get on to the bank right away.'

'But I'm hoping I won't need to. I've been in touch with a solicitor who specialises in cyber bullying and he's going to try and find out who's been trolling me.'

'Why did you go to a solicitor? Why didn't you talk to me first?'

'I'm sorry Magnus. I had planned to tell you last Friday but your mum got ill so I didn't have the chance. I can see now that I should have told you on the phone.'

I took his hand hoping he would stop being annoyed with me and continued to explain.

'When Barbara suggested that her husband might be able to help, I jumped at the chance. I didn't know what else to do.'

He withdrew his hand from mine and pushed his hands through his hair.

'And if he finds out who this person is, what then? Will you go the police?'

'I don't know Magnus. What do you think I should do?'

'If you want to prevent these from going public and giving my ex the evidence she needs to fleece me, you need to pay the money Jessica.'

21

Greer

She could hear her granddaughter in the shower singing some modern pop song loudly – something about DDD N A. She had been unusually upbeat this week and had been extra helpful about the house. Greer was relieved that she had gone into the shower earlier than usual which meant she would be able to get into the bathroom and get ready for work on time which had been something of a trial since Mia had arrived.

'I'm heading out Nana.'

'You're an early bird this morning. Have you got an interview or something?'

'Something,' said Mia, tapping the side of her nose with her finger.

'Aren't you going to tell me what you're up to? You've been the like a cat with the cream this week.'

'I'll tell you when I get home,' she said, kissing her on the cheek.

'Bye. Have a good day.'

Greer got ready for work and put her granddaughter to the back of her mind. She was more worried about going to the circle meeting and seeing Jessica again. The last meeting had been a disaster, but she hadn't needed to interact with Jessica much because of the upset between Evie and Lottie but things might be different this week. When Jessica had told her story, she had seemed genuine and for the first time Greer had seen how vulnerable Jessica was. Greer didn't like Jessica much as she had been bitchy in the circle meetings to all of them at one time or another but she had never walked in her shoes so who was she to judge her. She wondered whether she should tell her granddaughter about Jessica being in the group.

She went to pick Evie up and was surprised when the girl didn't answer her door. She decided to check with her neighbour to see if she knew anything and she told her that Evie had been taken into the Queen Elizabeth Maternity Unit in the early hours of the morning. Apparently, her waters had broken, and she had knocked on her neighbour's door in a panic. Her neighbour had phoned for an ambulance. Greer felt relieved that she wouldn't have to go to the circle meeting after all and drove instead to the hospital wondering whether she would be in time to take the role of birthing partner as had been agreed. She didn't want Evie to be on her own. She was little more than a child herself and didn't have anyone who could be there for her at a time when she needed such a lot of support. To her surprise, when she arrived and checked whether she was still in time to be Evie's birthing partner, she was told that the baby's father was in with Evie and her services wouldn't be needed.

Barbara

She kissed Rory lightly on the cheek as they left for their meeting with Mia. She had decided to try and heal the crack that had begun to fracture their relationship, and this was the first step. They were still sleeping separately but all going well they would be back together soon. Her insides were churning but she suspected his were too and it was important that he felt supported. Things like this could split families and she was determined that her family wasn't going to be split. Look at Ella's friend June. Her family had been irreparably damaged by what her dad had done, and she didn't want that for her kids. She wanted to give them a stable loving home as she knew children weren't always as resilient as adults liked to think.

When they reached the coffee shop, Mia was sitting waiting for them looking calm and collected and she couldn't help but admire her. Mia must only be in her early twenties yet here she was about to take on one of Glasgow's top lawyers and get him to do something for her. Perhaps she had inherited his genes as he was very single-minded when he needed to be.

'Good morning,' Mia said with a smile, as she waited for them to sit. 'I fancy a couple of their breakfast rolls.'

Barbara felt her stomach turn over. The thought of eating made her queasy and Rory looked the same.

'Have what you want Mia,' he said. 'Barbara and I will just have a pot of tea.'

Mia went up to the counter and ordered after Rory gave her the money to pay, almost like she was in charge of the meeting.

'So, Mia, can we get straight to the point,' said Rory. 'What is it you're looking for?'

She and Rory had decided that Rory would do all the talking so she decided to sit back and observe her husband and his daughter. She was good at reading body language and thought she might find a chink in the armour of this confident young woman.

'I would like if possible to get to know you and my little

brother and sister.'

Her heart contracted and she noticed that Rory's face had gone pale.

'I know this must be a huge shock for you both and I'll understand if you don't want to have anything to do with me. I knew that would be a possibility if you did turn out to be my dad.'

The food and drinks arrived and nothing more was said until Mia had finished her breakfast. Barbara never ate fry ups and the smell of the breakfast rolls was making her feel nauseous again. The girl was playing with them, and they were letting her. Sitting there pretending to be reasonable but she knew Mia wanted something from them. What had happened to the shit hot lawyer and his top of her game counsellor wife? They were like rabbits caught in the headlights.

'Well that was lovely,' said Mia, wiping her mouth with her napkin. 'Thank you.'

'We are naturally concerned about introducing you to our children,' said Barbara. 'We know very little about you. How come you've only contacted Rory now? You must be in your twenties.'

'It's a bit of a story so here goes. A long time ago, about twenty-five years in fact, my Grandad was accused of grooming and sexually assaulting a fourteen year-old schoolgirl. The effect on him was devastating and he killed himself. My mum went off the rails. You, Rory, met her when you and she were at a drunken party and had sex.'

Barbara noticed the girl's eyes becoming moist as she thought about her mum and what it must have been like for her. Barbara felt close to tears herself.

'I didn't know if you were my father or not. My mum told me that she had slept with several boys in the months after her dad died but she said you were the only one who ever contacted her afterwards to ask if she was okay.'

So Rory's act of kindness had led to this.

'Then you agreed to do the DNA test and it turned out that you were my dad.'

'What do you want Mia?' said Rory, looking defeated.

'Well I think you only took the DNA test because you had so

much to lose if I decided to spill the beans and even if what I said wasn't true your reputation would still be damaged. You also have your children to consider and what about your nomination for Chair of the Law Society. I don't think they would want to appoint someone who may have been responsible for having sex with an underage teenager even if he was only seventeen. You know what the media is like. They can twist anything to make it into a good story.'

She paused to take a sip of the coffee she had ordered.

'As I said before, I would like to be involved in your life, but I get the feeling that this isn't what your wife or you want. So I am looking for some kind of payment. My mum had to bring me up on her own and I think it's only fair that she gets compensated for that. Being a lawyer you must know what kind of child support payments would have been due to my mum had she known that you were my father.'

Barbara found herself relaxing. It was just money she wanted. She didn't want to push to be part of their family. They had money. She was sure they would be able to meet whatever demand she made.

'I'm looking for £250,000.'

'That's a lot of money Mia,' said Rory. 'We're quite well off sure, but we have a mortgage, two cars, two children...'

'I don't want to hear what expenses you've got,' interrupted Mia. 'I just want what my mum is due.'

'This is blackmail Rory. I think we should go to the police.'

'You do that Barbara and let's see what the papers have to say about it.'

'We know you're trying to blackmail Jessica Aitken too. You'll end up going to prison.'

'What are you talking about?'

'Don't pretend you don't know. She's the girl who accused your grandad of grooming her and you've been sending her emails threatening to go to the papers saying that she lied about it.'

Mia stared at them as if they were mad.

'The girl who accused my granddad was called Debbie Halligan not Jessica Aitken. Why would I want to blackmail her? She didn't do anything wrong did she?'

'Well it's a bit of coincidence that you show up in Glasgow now and she receives an email threatening her at the same time. You don't seem averse to blackmailing us so why not her too?' said Rory.

'Fuck you dad,' Mia shouted at him, then got up and barged out of the café without a backward glance.

'What am I going to do?' Rory asked Barbara.

'What am *I* going to do?' answered Barbara. 'Jessica Aitken is my client. This is a disaster. Things could get very messy indeed.'

'But at least Mia seems happy not to meet the kids Barbara if we pay her compensation, so that's something isn't it?'

'Yes, but I don't trust her. Even if we could pay what she's asking I think she would mess things up for us just for the sake of it don't you?'

Jessica

I woke up feeling crap on Monday morning. I wanted to roll over and go back to sleep but Cathy knocked gently on my door with tea and toast on a tray.

'You're late this morning Jessica. Isn't it today you go to your knitting group?'

'Yes it is, but I'm not feeling well.'

'Have you had one too many pet? I couldn't help noticing the bottles in the recycling.'

'Yes I have Cathy. I can't help it. I just feel so bad. Magnus walked out on me at the week-end and I don't know if he's coming back.'

She gave me a hug and wiped away my tears with a tissue from the box on the bedside table.

'You have your tea and toast and then go and have a shower. You'll feel better after that and I'll give you a run down to your meeting. Okay?'

'Thanks Cathy. What would I do without you?'

When I had woken up on Saturday morning, Magnus had gone. He had left me a note saying he needed time to think about things. He wasn't sure that he could continue with our relationship. I was devastated. Even with my track record I had dared to hope that things would last longer than a couple of weeks.

When I arrived at the circle meeting, Barbara was setting up the room.

'Hello Jessica,' she said, 'how are you today?'

'Hello Barbara. I'm okay thanks. Has Mr King been able to find out anything for me about who the trolls are yet?'

'I'm sorry Jessica. I don't know. He doesn't discuss his clients with me.'

'I just thought that since you had suggested that I speak to him he might have told you but that's okay, I'll get in touch with him after the meeting.'

Barbara didn't say anything. She looks as if she has a lot on her mind I thought, for once being empathic. I decided I was going to do my best to be nice today and not wind anyone up.

'It will only be the three of us today,' said Barbara. 'Evie has gone into labour. She's in hospital, so Greer doesn't need to come in today either.'

'Do you know what ward she's in Barbara?' Lottie asked. 'I would like to go up and see her. I've started knitting this shawl for her so hopefully I'll have it finished by next week.'

'I can't really give out any information on any of the members of the circle Lottie but if you phone the hospital, they'll be able to tell you which ward she's in. So, who would like to check in?' Barbara asked, looking at Jessica, but Lottie went in first,

'I'd like to go first if you don't mind. I want to apologise for how I was the last time I saw you. It just became too much for me what with my mum dying and all that. But the good news is that your phone call to my dad was followed up by a visit from my pastor and my dad has agreed that I can move back home. He said it's what Mum would have wanted. He says he hasn't totally forgiven me yet, but everybody needs a second chance and he can see that I've been working hard at changing things. So basically, what I'm saying is that I'm moving back home tomorrow.'

I looked enviously at Lottie. How lucky for her that her dad was letting her move back home. Nothing like that for me. I had gone around to Mum's house to try again but when she opened the door and saw me she immediately closed it again. I was gutted. I had come to expect very little from her but at least I had got to see her every week. Now nothing, nada. I wasn't sure I even had Magnus. He wasn't picking up his phone either.

'How are you Jessica?' Lottie asked, breaking into my thoughts.

'Okay thanks Lottie. I'm really pleased for you. It's not often we get a second chance is it? I hope you and your dad find a way of getting on and making up for the past. Oh, and that's a beautiful piece of knitting you're doing there by the way. I'm sure that Evie will love it.'

'Thanks Jessica.'

After a moment Lottie continued.

'Are you sure you're alright? You seem different.'

'Not as unpleasant as usual do you mean?'

'Well maybe,' Lottie agreed smiling. 'And you haven't come on your bike the way you normally do.'

'No, my housekeeper drove me down today. I wasn't feeling too good, but I didn't want to miss the meeting.'

'Do you want to talk about it Jessica. We're here to listen,' said Lottie, looking over at Barbara.

'Not really Lottie. All I'll say is I was ecstatically happy because Magnus had asked me to marry him on the weekend of my birthday but since then I've been receiving hate mail and it's had an effect on my relationship with Magnus.'

I could feel the tears starting and quickly blew my nose.

'That's terrible Jessica. Have you been to the police? I hear they can trace these kinds of emails.'

'No, I don't want it to get into the papers and I'm sure it would if I went to the police.'

'I'm so sorry this is happening to you. You don't deserve it.'

'Don't I? There's a voice inside my head that says I do.'

As I said this I thought about the voice I thought I'd heard last week.

'Sometimes I hear a voice inside my head but to me it's God talking to me. He's a good friend to me Jessica. Maybe it would help you to come along to my chuch.'

I looked at her and wondered. That church had clearly helped Lottie but I wasn't sure that even God would be able to forgive me.

'No thanks Lottie. All that God stuff's not for me. No offence.'

We sat companionably knitting for a while chatting about this and that, but I noticed that Barbara was unsettled. Normally she had a calm aura about her but today she seemed on edge. Her knitting was sporadic, and she didn't make any interventions in the conversation between Lottie and me which was unusual too. As we were leaving, she suggested that we meet next week rather than wait a fortnight for our final meeting of the circle.

'Now that Evie's had her baby, Lottie's back with her dad and you're getting married Jessica, we might as well wind the meetings up.'

I felt uneasy. Things might be hunky-dory for Evie and Lottie but not for me. I would talk to her next week to see if we could do any more one to one work. I couldn't lose Barbara as well.

22

Greer

When Greer got home from the hospital, Mia had returned from her '*something*' and was sitting playing a game on her tablet.

'Hello Nana, you're home early.'

'Yes, my client went into labour last night and is in the maternity hospital, so I didn't need to go the circle. Also, I didn't need to be her birthing partner as the father of her baby was in with her. I didn't even get to see her.'

'You sound a bit pissed about that Nana. Isn't it better that the father was in with her rather than you?'

'You don't understand Mia. He abused his position and got her pregnant. He had no right being with her but because she's over eighteen, there's nothing we can do about it. Anyway, enough about me. How did your '*something*' go?'

'Very well,' said Mia, smiling. 'I met my Dad today.'

'Your Dad? Isn't he in Belfast with your Mum?'

'No. Kevin isn't my Dad.'

'He's not?'

'No. My mum was already pregnant when she left Scotland with Kevin.'

'Already pregnant. But she never told me.'

'She didn't know. She was quite young you know and didn't recognise the signs. She thought not having a period was because of the stress she was under. It wasn't until she got to Belfast that she realised and unfortunately for her Kevin stuck by her thinking I was his.'

Her stomach clenched as she thought of her daughter all alone and pregnant in a strange city with some random bloke she had just met. Had he been bad to her?

'What do you mean unfortunately?'

'Kevin's a real control freak and he keeps the thumbs on mum, that's all I mean.'

'He doesn't hit her or anything?'

'Don't you want to know who my real dad is then?'

She didn't know if Mia was avoiding her question or just

excited about finding out who her real dad was. She decided to play along and get back to finding out more about this Kevin later.

'So, who is your Dad then?'

'Rory King.'

'Who is he?'

'Rory King, the lawyer. You know. He's been nominated for the Law Society Chairmanship this year.'

'Sorry I don't know anything about the law or the Law Society.'

'Oh Nana. You're so out of touch.'

'Sorry.'

'I wasn't sure if he was my dad or not, but I took a gamble and contacted him to say that I was his daughter and of course he insisted on a DNA test. That's where I was going when I borrowed the £20 from you that day.'

'And the test was positive?'

'Yes, it was. I went to meet him and his wife Barbara today to discuss how he could help me.'

'Barbara?'

'Yes. She's Barbara King the psychotherapist who has been involved in giving evidence in some high-profile murder cases.'

She could feel the blood draining from her face as she took in this information.

'What's wrong Nana, you look like you've seen a ghost.'

'But it's Barbara King who runs the knitting circle that I go to and I suppose I should tell you that the woman who accused your grandad all those years ago also goes to the meetings.'

'Is her name Jessica Aitken?'

'Yes. Why do you ask?'

'When I met Rory and Barbara they accused me of trying to blackmail them and accused me of trying to blackmail this Jessica Aitken too.'

'What do you mean they accused you of trying to blackmail them? Have you asked them for money?'

'Only what Mum's due Nana. He's a wealthy man and he can afford it. I don't think £250,000 is too much to ask for twenty four years backdated child support.'

She could only stare at her granddaughter. Mia had rendered her speechless.

23

Greer

Evie was getting out of hospital and she was going to collect her so that she could help her settle in. Normally, she would have been happy at the thought of helping someone make a fresh start, but today she made her way up to the hospital to collect Evie with a heavy heart. She was worried about Mia and the repercussions of her actions. When she arrived, Evie was waiting for her bright eyed and happy.

'Hello Greer, we're ready and waiting for you, aren't we Charlotte?' she said, nuzzling her little girl's cheek.

After they had completed the paperwork, they made their way to the lift, Evie carrying Charlotte and Greer carrying Evie's bag.

'I can't wait to get home with Charlotte. For the first time I have my own family. I just love her to bits.'

She could see Evie's eyes glistening as she looked at little Charlotte and she hoped with all her heart that things would work out for her. She wondered what had happened with Tom Bannerman. Evie hadn't mentioned him, so she hoped he was off the scene. Just as the thought left her mind, the lift opened, and a couple stepped out. She moved forward to go past them but sensed that Evie had stopped and turned to see what was delaying her. The girl was looking confused as she stared at the couple.

'Hello Evie,' the woman said.

'Hello Mrs Bannerman.'

Oh no. Little Charlotte's dad and his wife. She hoped they weren't going to cause any trouble.

'Is this our Charlotte?' the woman said, peering over Evie's arms to get a look at the baby.

'What are you doing here?' asked Evie, pulling Charlotte close into her chest.

'I wanted to see Tom's little daughter. You don't mind, do you?'

'But I thought you and Tom had split up.'

'Why did you think that?' she said, turning to Tom and

taking his hand. 'We are closer than ever now that we have a new baby in our lives.'

By this time tears were streaming from Evie's eyes.

'What's going on Tom? You told me that you would move in with me and that we would take care of Charlotte together.'

Tom had nothing to say and looked down at his shoes, so his wife responded.

'Stupid girl. He only told you that so that you would let him register Charlotte.'

'But he loves me.'

'No, he loves your baby. We've wanted a family for so long.'

Greer wondered if Jessica was right. Had the Bannermans planned this together so that they could get a child. Surely, they couldn't have been so devious. Just then baby Charlotte began to cry, and Greer decided it was time to get Evie out of there. With her heart beating fast, she approached Evie and gently put her arm around her.

'Come one Evie, time to go. The baby will need fed and changed shortly,' she said, directing her towards the lift which luckily was still waiting. As they got inside, she turned back to the couple and said in a voice that sounded more forceful than she felt.

'If you want access to the baby, I think you'd better get a solicitor Mr Bannerman.'

24

Barbara

She felt sad that it was the last meeting of the circle, but it was mixed with relief that she had an excuse to finish working with Jessica. Things were so complicated first because of Ella's behaviour and now it looked like Mia was blackmailing Jessica. That was just too much of a conflict of interest for her to continue working with her. Lottie had given her a lovely bouquet of flowers as a thank you for all her help over the past few months and Barbara was surprised that Jessica didn't have anything for her.

Expecting her to leave with Lottie, she was surprised when she stayed behind and asked if she could have a word.

'Barbara I was wondering what with the meetings finishing whether it would be possible for us to go back to our one to one sessions?'

She continued to put her knitting into her bag without looking up, stalling for time. What was she going to say to Jessica? She hadn't rehearsed anything as she had assumed it would just end naturally.

'I'm sorry Jessica. That won't be possible.'

'Why not Barbara?'

She could see the anguish and puzzlement on Jessica's face and wanted to comfort her, but she resisted.

'I'm afraid that my husband has discovered some information from his investigations into who has been trolling you that makes it impossible for me to work with you any longer.'

'But he hasn't told me the outcome of his investigation. How come you know? You said he didn't discuss clients with you.'

'I know I did Jessica, but it turns out that there is a personal connection between our family and the people who have been trolling you. Rory will be in touch with you soon to explain the situation. It would be a conflict of interest for me to continue to work with you.'

'A conflict of interest? What's going on Barbara? Who is this person and what have they got to do with you and your husband?'

'I'm sorry Jessica I can't tell you. It would be a breach of confidentiality.'

'Please Barbara,' Jessica begged, between huge gulping sobs. 'Please don't abandon me. I need you. I don't have anyone else.'

She came over to Barbara and tried to grab her hands, but Barbara pulled her hands away.

'Please don't do this Jessica. Please don't make this harder for me than it needs to be.'

'Harder for you. What about me?' Jessica shouted, turning her back on Barbara.

'I'm sorry Jessica. I must put my family first.'

Jessica slowly turned around and faced Barbara. She seemed calmer and Barbara hoped that they might be able to make the break amicably, but she knew that wasn't to be when Jessica leaned down towards her putting her face as close to Barbara's as she could without touching her. Barbara could smell a slight hint of alcohol on her breath and could see the spittle forming on her lips as she growled at her.

'You're no better than a prostitute Barbara. I'm only someone you give love to for money.'

Then she pulled her head back and spat in her face.

Barbara was rooted to her chair and could only stare at Jessica as she grabbed her coat and bag, pushed through the double doors of the exit and left them swinging angrily back and forth, back and forth till eventually they came to a standstill. Barbara sat in the ensuing stillness, but the silence screamed in her ears like white noise. Her hands were shaking and when she tried to stand up her legs refused to hold her. The doors were pushed open again and Barbara cowered back slightly in her chair fearing that Jessica had returned.

'What's happened Barbara. Are you okay? You're shaking like a leaf.'

It was Lottie.

'I forgot the shawl for Evie,' she said, retrieving it from the under the chair she had been sitting on. She had brought it in to show them the finished article as she was going up to visit Evie after the meeting.

'There's something on your face Barbara,' she said, pulling

a tissue from her bag and handing it to Barbara.

As Barbara wiped her face with her shaking hand, she could feel her body reaction changing. She had been in a state of fear but was now burning with rage. She felt contaminated. How dare Jessica do that to her. It was assault.

'I'm alright Lottie. Thanks for the tissue. You get off now and take care. Good luck with your dad.'

'If you're sure Barbara. I could call someone for you if you wish.'

'No. Thanks Lottie.'

Unlike Jessica, Lottie went carefully through the exit doors making sure they closed gently, as if in sympathy with Barbara's vulnerable state.

Jessica

I was still in shock from Barbara's announcement that she could no longer work with me and from my own reaction to it. Firstly, I had lost the plot with Mum and now with Barbara. Barbara had been my rock for the last three years. She had provided a stable steady support for me that I had never received before and I had come to regard her as a kind aunt even although there was little difference in our ages. Losing Barbara felt almost as devastating as my mum's rejection. I had pleaded and begged, but Barbara had been adamant that she couldn't continue to work with me. I would never forget the look of shock on her face when I spat at her and called her a prostitute. I closed my eyes trying to blank out the scene. Now that I'd calmed down, I realised that it was assault and hoped that Barbara wouldn't call in the police. That was the last thing I needed.

I couldn't be bothered doing any exercise so decided to have my lunch instead. Cathy had made lentil soup, so I ladled out a plateful and took some bread and cheese. As I was sitting eating, staring into space, I heard Darren's voice again.

'Hello Jessica. It's your brother.'

I couldn't believe it. I hadn't been sleeping and I was perfectly sober. Perhaps I really was going mad.

'What do you want Darren?'

'I've come to ask you to tell the truth.'

'The truth about what?'

'About Mr Fraser. Why don't you just admit that you told a lie. No-one will know. Only me.'

'But I'm not lying Darren. I know what happened. I was there.'

'Come on Debbie you can tell me. I'm your twin. I know everything about you remember.'

'How do you know everything? You haven't spoken to me since I was five. You left me with Mum and Dad all on my own.'

A sense of abandonment and loneliness closed in on me and I began blubbing like a baby. I grabbed a tissue from the box on the table and blew my nose trying to get myself back under control.

'Well I'm back now sis. Why don't you have a drink, it will settle you down.'

It was only lunchtime but having a drink seemed like a good idea, so I poured a glass of prosecco from a bottle in the fridge. I had bought a few bottles to share with Magnus but of course he hadn't been here to share them with me. It tasted lovely and I felt myself relaxing. For the first time I realised why my parents had used it to self-soothe. I knew I was drinking more often but I wasn't worried. I had been over my quota a couple of times since meeting Magnus, but the world hadn't ended, and I hadn't become a raging alcoholic. Two hours later I had finished the bottle and was contemplating opening another one.

25

Barbara

She was vigorously chopping and slicing veggies for the stew she was making for dinner while discussing with Rory what had happened with Jessica.

'Barbara you need to make up your mind whether to do something about this or let it go. You're doing my head in. You've talked about nothing else since you got home.'

'It's alright for you Rory. You weren't the one that Jessica assaulted.'

'No. If I was, she would have been arrested and charged by now. You're too wishy washy. That woman may be damaged and behaving like an abandoned child, but it doesn't make it okay for her to spit in other people's faces.'

There was silence except for the sound of Barbara's chopping until at last she put her knife down.

'What are we going to do Rory?' she asked, her voice quieter now. 'We can't go to the police about Jessica. We might end up getting Ella into trouble. And what about Mia. If she's blackmailing Jessica as well as us, she could get into trouble too.'

'What if Jessica goes after Mia and hurts her?' Rory said. 'What then?'

Barbara felt a ping of jealousy that Rory seemed to be concerned for Mia's wellbeing and found herself almost wishing that Jessica would do something to her. She had brought such a lot of trouble to their door. It was partly her fault that she had had to finish working with Jessica. None of this would have happened if it wasn't for the scheming little bitch. She was shocked at her thoughts. What was happening to her? If Jessica did hurt Mia, she would be to blame. She would need to sort this out one way or another but not tonight. She had talked about it enough.

'Have you got back to Jessica yet about the trolls?'

'Yes I posted a letter out to her on Friday saying that I had contacted the people who had been sending the emails and that they would stop now; that she didn't need to go to the police or pay out any money.'

'What if your letter doesn't work and Mia goes to one of those true life magazines. Even if she can't prove that Jessica was lying, she can tell them what the fall-out from the allegation was on her family.'

'Yes, I suppose it would still sell because of Jessica's status.'

Rory ran his fingers through his hair as he always did when he was anxious.

'But it also means that it would come out about me being her father. When are we going to talk to the kids Barbara? I can't take the chance that they would read about it in a trashy magazine.'

'I don't think they read that kind of magazine,' she said with a smile, trying to lighten the mood, but Rory looked at her incredulously.

'I can't believe you're making fucking jokes about this Barbara.'

'I'm sorry,' she said, feeling a knot tightening in her stomach at the ferocity of his words. 'I know we need to tell them, but I can't face it just now. This thing with Jessica has really upset me and I need a bit of time to pull myself together before facing another crisis.'

His face softened and he came towards her.

'I'm sorry darling. I've been an arse over this Jessica thing. Come here and give me a hug.'

'We need to stick together Rory. I don't want anything or anyone ruining things for our family.'

Greer

She wondered how Evie was getting on and decided to go and visit her later. It had taken her longer than she had anticipated to settle Evie and baby Charlotte into their house last week because of the unwelcome meeting with Mr and Mrs Bannerman. Evie was upset, of course, as her dream had been shattered. She now knew that there would be no Tom moving in with her, playing happy families. It also looked like she would have a battle on her hands over access to baby Charlotte. Poor Evie. As if life wasn't hard enough for her. She knew Lottie was planning to go over and see her today, but she wanted to just make sure she was okay.

When she went into the kitchen to make something to eat, Mia was looking at her phone with a puzzled expression.

'Anything wrong pet?' she asked.

'It's a text from Rory King. He says he needs to speak to me about Jessica Aitken, but I can't get a hold of him. His phone seems to be switched off.'

'Soup and sandwich for tea today. Is that okay? Perhaps we can have a chat about all this while we're eating.

'Okay Nana.'

When the food was ready they sat down together at the table. Greer appreciated having someone to share her meals with, but she wasn't looking forward to this conversation. Her mouth was dry as she thought about what kind of life Sophie might have had. From what Mia had said before, it didn't sound as if it had been good.

'I wonder why Rory wants to speak to me about Jessica Aitken. If it's so desperate he should have his phone switched on. So what do you want to know Nana?'

'I suppose what kind of life your mum's had and what your plans are in relation to this new dad that you've found. Are you planning to stay in Glasgow, or will you head back to Belfast once he gives you the money you've asked for? And what are you going to do with all that money?'

'Okay here goes. When I was growing up, I didn't know anything about what happened to Grandad. Mum never talked about the past and neither did Kevin. When she realised she was pregnant, she assumed it was Kevin's and felt relieved when he asked her to marry him. So far as I knew I was Mia Cooper, the daughter of Kevin Cooper. It was only when I heard Mum and Dad arguing one night that I realised he might not be my father. I decided to get a DNA test done and took his toothbrush to a testing centre. It turned out that he was not my father after all. I was relieved as he's not a nice man.'

Greer wanted to ask her what she meant but Mia continued on with her story.

'I didn't tell Kevin what I had discovered as I wasn't sure how he would react. He can be quite volatile, but I told Mum and I was shocked when she told me she didn't know who my dad was if it wasn't Kevin.'

'What made you think that Rory King was your dad then?'

'When at last Mum opened up to me about what had happened with Grandad and how she had gone off the rails, she told me the only person she could remember sleeping with other than Kevin was Rory King as he had phoned her afterwards to see if she was okay. It was then I decided to contact him.'

'What about your Mum? What does she think of all this?'

Mia's face clouded over.

'I haven't told Mum in case she tells Kevin. He's a control freak and she's really under his thumb. I want to get some money so that I can help Mum get away from him.'

'Are things that bad between them?'

'Yes, although if you asked Mum she would say things were fine. It's like she's blinded to Kevin's faults and blames herself for things that go wrong between them.'

She was upset at this description of Sophie. She had been such a hothead when she was young, it was hard to think of her becoming a victim.

'Would you mind if I phoned your Mum? Do you think she would talk to me?'

Mia looked horrified.

'Oh God no Nana. You can't phone her. Kevin doesn't know I'm in Scotland.'

'Why are you so scared of this Kevin? Why do you want to

get your mum away from him?'

'I told you. He's a control freak. Just butt out Nana,' she shouted.

To her surprise Mia jumped up from the table, her chair crashing to the floor, and slammed out of the room leaving Greer looking after her in dismay. A few moments later she heard the front door slamming shut and wondered where on earth Mia was going. So far as she knew she didn't know anyone in Glasgow yet apart from Rory King.

26

Jessica

The drink made me bold and I decided to phone Magnus. He hadn't been in touch since he had left last week, and I was bereft. I needed him more than anything now that Barbara had finished with me. His number just kept ringing out, then eventually went to voicemail.

'Magnus, Magnus where are you sweetheart? I need you. The most terrible things are happening. I'll do anything you want. I'll pay the money. Just come back to me please, please.'

I looked at the letter from Rory King that had been waiting for me when I got back from the meeting today. Basically it looked like he had managed to identify the trolls and was confident that they would now stop harassing me. He was also saying not to pay over any money but that was the opposite of what Magnus wanted me to do. I would need to show Magnus the letter and see what he thought. Magnus was my priority. I didn't want to lose him and if he wanted me to pay over the money then I would.

Seeing Rory King's name at the bottom of the letter, made me think of Barbara and I felt sick at the thought of what I had done and hoped that things wouldn't be made worse by Barbara going to the police. I wouldn't blame her. What I had done was disgusting. I found myself in floods of tears again as I thought about Barbara. I loved her and was so sorry for what I had done. I decided to phone her and ask her to forgive me.

Barbara

She was in the middle of sorting out the washing getting it ready for going into the machine when the front doorbell rang.

'Can someone get the door,' she shouted, but no-one responded, and she was forced to go herself as the bell continued to ring insistently. Feeling peeved at being interrupted in her task, she opened the door with a frown.

'Hello,' said Mia.

Barbara didn't respond for a moment and then looked behind her quickly calculating where the children were and whether they would be able to see or hear who was at the door. She stepped down quickly onto the pathway, closing the door over behind her.

'What are you doing here?'

'I'm here because I've got nowhere else to go. I've had a fight with my Nana.'

'But you can't come here. The children still don't know about you.'

'Well perhaps now's a good time to tell them.'

'I don't think so. Look there's a café on the corner why don't you go down there, and I'll get Rory to come and talk to you in ten minutes.'

'No. I don't want to and if you don't let me in, I'll just keep ringing the doorbell until you do.'

Barbara began to boil with rage. How dare Mia come to her home like this and threaten her into telling the children about her. Barbara pulled herself up to her full 5ft 8in height and glared down at the girl.

'You will go to that café and I will send Rory along to see you in ten minutes. If you don't do what I say I'll phone the police, and have you arrested for harassment.'

Mia hesitated for a moment, then smiled.

'Your too easy to wind up Barbara. Your husband's been trying to get me on my mobile, but he didn't respond when I phoned him back. I thought it might be urgent that's why I came over. But I'll do as you say. I'll wait for him in the café. Sorry if I've upset you. I really don't want to cause any trouble for your family.'

She looked the picture of innocence, but Barbara knew what she had been doing to Jessica. She was a cold calculating blackmailer. Barbara went back inside and stood with her back against the closed door her heart racing.

'You okay Mum. Who was at the door?'

'Oh, just someone selling something I didn't want Ella. Where's you Dad darling?'

'He's playing a game with Ben.'

'Will you ask him to come through to the kitchen while I finish sorting the washing please. Tell him I need to speak to him.'

'Are you sure you're okay Mum? You look a bit flushed.'

'I'm fine but I need to speak to Dad now.'

♦ ♦ ♦

Rory had a smile on his face as he came out of the study and she could hear Ben telling him to hurry back as he wanted to thrash him at whatever game they were playing, but it quickly faded when he saw Barbara's face.

'What is it Barbara?'

She was aware that Ella was still standing in the hallway.

'I've got something confidential to talk to your Dad about Ella so I'm going to close the door. It's to do with a client. You go and continue the game with Ben.'

She waited until Ella languidly made her way through to the study to make sure she couldn't hear what they were saying.

'What's going on Babs?'

By this time, she could see Rory was becoming frustrated at all the cloak and dagger.

'It's Mia. She's just been at the door. She says she's been trying to phone you in response to the text you sent her about Jessica.'

He checked his phone and showed her that it was out of power.

'Shit. What did you do?'

'I threatened her with the police if she didn't go and wait

for you in the café. You'll need to go and talk to her Rory.'

The door burst open and in walked Ben and Ella who had obviously left their game to listen to what this confidential issue was their parents were talking about.

'Go and talk to who?' said Ben.

Her heart sank as the two teenagers looked at her and Rory expectantly. It was clear they thought they were talking about some kind of surprise for them and weren't worried so when she told them to come and sit down, she could see they were unprepared for the shock of finding out they had an older sister.

'A sister! But how can that be? You and Mum have been together forever. It's not possible,' said Ella, tears streaming down her face. 'I don't want a sister.'

She knew how much Ella liked being the apple of her Dad's eye and that she wouldn't want anyone else coming in and taking her place. Ben on the other hand became quiet, taking in the implications. He continued to sit on the kitchen stool, but his leg jiggled up and down, up and down and he began to bite his nails. Barbara could imagine the thoughts running through his head. Had his dad been leading a double life? Was he a bigamist or was it just a sordid affair he had had? Or worse maybe it was she who had a daughter. Perhaps she had got pregnant before she met his father and the baby had been put up for adoption.

'I can't believe it,' Ben exploded. 'You two are part of the establishment. I can't believe that you would do anything like this. What hypocrites you are. Look how you went on at Ella when you found her trolling someone and when she had had a bit too much to drink one night.'

'It's our job as parents to keep you and Ella on the straight and narrow,' began Barbara, but he cut through her words.

'So, which one of you is the parent?'

'I am,' said Rory. 'But it happened when I was just a lad not much older than you are now Ben and I didn't know anything about her until a couple of months ago.'

'A couple of months ago. And you didn't tell us. Were you hoping we wouldn't find out? Were you going to keep her a secret? You are disgusting Dad.'

'This is a big shock for us all,' said Barbara, going over to her son and putting a hand on his arm, which he quickly shrugged off.

'I don't want a hug Mum. You can't kiss this better. I'm going up to my room. I need space to think.'

The door slammed shut behind him and the silence that followed was heavy with implications. Ella stopped sobbing and went to her Mum.

'I wouldn't mind a cuddle Mum.'

Barbara let out a sigh of relief and took her daughter in her arms and held her tightly.

'Look I need to go,' said Rory, looking meekly at Ella. 'When I come back, I'll tell you everything. Okay darling?'

'Okay Dad.'

She ran into her father's arms and held him like there was no tomorrow. Barbara looked on feeling hopeless, wondering what this would do her family. As Rory gently removed Ella's arms to go and meet Mia, Barbara's phone rang. Her heart sank as she saw Jessica's name. She hesitated, then pressed the red phone icon. She couldn't be doing with Jessica as well as Mia today.

27

Greer

She wasn't too worried yet about her granddaughter. She thought she would come back with her tail between her legs when it was time for dinner, so she decided to go and visit Evie as planned. While she was there Lottie arrived and handed Evie a parcel with a baby balloon attached.

'Lottie,' Evie beamed, delighted to see her friend. 'Come and meet Charlotte. I've named her after you as you are going to be her Godmother.'

'Oh, that's so kind of you Evie. I am indeed honoured. Can I hold her?'

'Of course. Here you are Lottie.'

Tears began to form in Lottie's eyes as she looked down at the little bundle of love that had been passed to her, but she smiled widely.

'She's beautiful Evie, just like her mum.'

Suddenly Evie began to cry.

'I think she's like her dad Lottie. I was so hopeful that Tom and I were going to be together. He was wonderful on the night that Charlotte was born. My waters broke during the night and I was frightened, so I phoned him after going through to my neighbour. He came to the hospital right away and was waiting for me when I arrived. When they asked if he was the father, they just assumed that we were together and let him come into the delivery suite with me. I even let him register Charlotte.'

'Why are you so upset Evie?'

'Because when I was leaving hospital he came up with his wife and it was clear that it was Charlotte he was interested in, not me and Charlotte.'

'Did he put his name on the birth certificate when he was registering Charlotte?'

'Yes. I mean I was happy that he had as he was acknowledging that Charlotte was his daughter. I wanted him to have rights. I wanted my little Charlotte to have a dad and have a better start in life than me.'

'But think about what Jessica said. What if he tries to get custody of Charlotte?'

Greer could see that Evie was getting upset and decided to try and change the subject.

'Well he'll have a fight on his hands, won't he Evie. So how was the last day of the circle with just you and Jessica?'

'Well the meeting was fine. Jessica was much nicer than usual, but I think something happened between her and Barbara after I left. I had to go back to pick up something that I had made for you Evie and Jessica nearly knocked me down as she came out. When I went into the room, Barbara was sitting shaking like a leaf in her chair and she had a big glob of spit on her face.'

'Wow that doesn't sound cool,' said Evie. 'Spitting is a terrible thing to do. I wonder what could have happened.'

Greer felt herself going cold. Was this all connected somehow with what Mia was doing. She felt powerless as if a tsunami were about to devastate the quiet existence she had been living up until now. How many lives were going to be affected by the decisions her granddaughter had taken. She took her leave of the girls who were still speculating a bit too gleefully about what had happened between Barbara and Jessica.

Jessica

I stared at my phone wondering what to do. Barbara hadn't answered my call and although I wasn't surprised, I sat in hope that she might give me a ring back. As I stared at the phone, I got notification of an email delivery. The thought of who it might be from made me shiver. But then I reasoned that it couldn't be from *IamMia* as Rory King had dealt with her and the other trolls. So to say I was disappointed when I saw it was from her is an under exaggeration. I could also see a little paper clip which meant there was an attachment. I poured another drink and drank it down before pressing the email open.

Here's a little video of you. Have a look. I don't think you would want anyone to see this. Here are the account details to put the money into. You have until the end of the week and then this goes viral.

I clicked on the video expecting it to be of me and Magnus in bed together, so it took me a minute to realise what I was looking at. It was me sitting in my lounge on the sofa making full use of my sex toy and whispering provocatively into my phone. I was mortified and felt totally disgusted with myself. I couldn't bear for anyone to see this. Why on earth had I agreed to have cyber-sex with Magnus? I was going to have to pay the money over despite what Rory King had said.

Seeing as Barbara wasn't answering my calls, I decided to text her. Not only would I apologise for spitting at her, but I would also tell her about IamMia so that she could let Rory know that whatever he thought he had done hadn't worked and I was going to have to pay out the money. As a writer I could express my emotions very eloquently, so the text was a long one and by the end of it I was smiling. I thought I had done a good job of telling Barbara how I felt and was convinced that she would get back to me. While I was waiting, the phone rang but it wasn't Barbara.

'Hello Jessica, it's Dorothy here.'

'Hi Dorothy. How did you get on? Did you manage to speak to Nancy Gardener?'

'Yes I managed to get a hold of her, and she told me that

she hadn't phoned you and that no-one had been in touch with her making any allegations. It looks like whoever is trolling you made that phone call to put more pressure on you to pay. I think you should go to the police Jessica.'

'I can't Dorothy, I've been sent the most horrendous video of me in a compromising situation and I've decided to pay what she is asking. I would die if anyone saw it. She's sent me the details of how to pay the money so I'm going to sort it out this week.'

'If you think that's best. There's something else I need to tell you Jessica.'

'What is it now. I don't think I can cope with any more problems Dorothy, I'm at the end of my rope.'

'Nancy was intrigued by my questions and thought it might make the basis of a good story for the magazine. She wants to interview you and find out the detail of what's been going on. I've put her off, but I think now she has a nose for a story she might contact you for real this time. Just be careful is all I'm saying.'

'Okay Dorothy. You're the boss.'

I gulped down my prosecco.'

'Are you drinking again Jessica?'

'It's only prosecco.'

'It's only Monday evening Jessica. Look I think we need to have a meeting. When would suit you? I can fly up to Glasgow any time you want.'

'Thanks Dorothy but I can't think straight just now. I'll phone you back when I'm feeling better.'

I pressed the red button to end the call. It must have been Mia phoning me pretending to be Nancy Gardener. It would tie in with the threats. I checked my texts to see if there was any response from Barbara. Seeing there was none I began to sob again and pulled a tissue from the box.

28

Greer

She had half expected her granddaughter to be waiting for her when she got back from Evie's, but the house was empty. She decided to go out and look for her in the hope that she might find her in one of the local coffee shops that she liked but no luck. It was growing dark by the time she made her way home and she hoped a light would be on in her flat, telling her that Mia was home. But when she turned the corner and looked over eagerly at her window, it was dark and her blinds were still open.

She decided to phone Marie and tell her about Mia. It was a relief to have Marie to talk to now about Mia and Paul and everything that had gone on in the past. She realised how isolating it had been holding that secret to herself for all those years. She recognised now that was the reason she hadn't made many friends. She hadn't liked getting too close to people in case they asked her a lot of questions about her past as she found it hard to lie. She had kept herself to herself just in case anyone ever got wind of it. And yet it wasn't her shame. It was Paul's.

After her chat with Marie, who did her best to cheer her up as usual, Greer tried Mia's phone, but it again went to voicemail. She was at a loss as to what to do. She paced up and down the living room waiting and hoping that her granddaughter would come home. She felt that history was repeating itself; her on her own waiting for Sophie to come home praying that she was safe. She found herself wishing her granddaughter had never come to Glasgow but then felt guilty. She loved her and was glad that she had come and that she had the chance of getting to know her, but all this upset was so unwelcome.

She needed to do something to find Mia. But where to start. Who did she know in Glasgow? The only person, so far as Greer knew, was Rory King her new-found father. But she didn't know where he lived. She looked him up on Google and there were several listings for him. He was obviously quite an expert in his field. As she read his profile, which included a photograph of him with his wife Barbara, she thought of her connection to Barbara through the circle. Hadn't Barbara given her a card with her number on it. She had used it only the other day to tell Barbara about Evie going into labour. She rummaged through her bag looking for the card and found it tucked in the front pocket.

She gazed at the card and saw that Barbara had lots of letters after her name, was a member of the British Association of Counsellors and Psychotherapists and offered one to one support plus group work. There was no address on the card, but her phone number and email address were there. Deciding not to procrastinate, she thumbed in the numbers on her mobile and listened while the ringing tone sounded in her ear.

'Pick up, pick up please,' she said in a kind of silent prayer. But her prayer wasn't answered as there was a click and the connection was lost. She decided to send a text. Perhaps if Barbara saw that it was Greer who had been trying to contact her, she would phone her back.

Barbara

Her phone pinged. It was Jessica sending a rambling text telling her how sorry she was. She almost didn't bother reading till the end as some words were unintelligible so when she saw what was at the end she was glad she had continued reading. Jessica was telling her that she had received another email from *IamMia* who had sent a compromising video of her and had also sent details of where to pay the money. Jessica needed to speak to Rory right away and would Barbara get him to phone her back as he wasn't answering his phone.

She knew that girl was up to no good. She would get Rory to phone Jessica when he returned from his talk with Mia. She wondered how he was getting on with her. Ella was quieter now and was sitting watching a game show on the television. Ben was still in his room refusing to come out and talk to her. She knew now that whatever happened with Mia, her family was changed forever.

She looked out the window and saw Rory walking up towards the front door. She was relieved to see he was on his own. He had been away for quite a while so hopefully he had put Mia in her place and convinced her to go home to her Nana. She felt sorry for the granny whoever she was. She went out to greet Rory when she heard his key in the door and Ella followed at her back.

'What's happened? You've been away a long time.'

As Rory was about to answer her phone began to ring. She glanced at it expecting it to be Jessica again, but it was an unknown number. She quickly pressed the cancel button.

'We had a long chat. I said that I would give her some money but that she must stop sending these emails and photographs to Jessica. I gave her a copy of the letter I had written to Jessica, but she said she didn't know anything about Jessica until we told her and flatly denied trying to blackmail her.'

'Did you believe her?'

'Yes, I did, funnily enough.'

'It's just that I've received a text from Jessica saying that Mia has sent her a video and is threatening to post it on Facebook unless she pays up. She wants you to phone her back.'

'I'll do it later. I think we need to speak to the kids before I do anything else. She was genuinely sorry that she had upset you tonight by coming to the door and she didn't want to cause any more trouble. She was going to head back to her gran's when I left her. She did say that she would like to meet her brother and sister though if they wanted to meet her.'

Her heart sank at this prospect and then her phone pinged again. This time it was a text from the unknown number. Curious she clicked on it thinking it might be Jessica using a different number.

'What's wrong Barbara, you've gone white?'

'I don't think she's gone home to her Nana. Look at this text.'

'Who's Greer. How has she got your number?'

'She's a support worker for one of my clients and she attends the circle meetings that I run, the one that Jessica Aitken attends.'

'And she's Mia's grandmother?'

'It looks like it. She talked at one of the meetings about getting good news, but she never mentioned a granddaughter coming to stay with her. She is such a nice woman and has been a help to me in that group. I can't believe she's related to Mia.'

'Dad.' It was Ella. 'You said you would tell me everything when you came back so can you do that please.'

Rory pushed his hands through his hair.

'Of course, darling but I think it would be better if Ben was here. I don't want to go through it all twice. Will you try and persuade your brother to come down please.'

Ella left the room and they could hear her slow steps going upstairs. She obviously wasn't in a hurry to get to her brother and ask him to come down.

29

Jessica

When my tears dried up I was surprised to see that my bottle of wine was empty so I decided to open another. Before I could go through to the kitchen, the doorbell rang, and I went into the hall to see who was there. A young woman with long brown hair wearing a black puffer jacket and leggings was standing. She had a backpack slung over her shoulder. I opened the door.

'Hello,' I asked. 'Who are you?'

'I'm Mia.'

'What do you want?'

'I want to talk to you. Rory King said that you had received blackmail threats and photographs and that you think I sent them.'

'Come on in,' I said, opening my front door. 'Would you like a drink? I'm just about to have a Prosecco'

'I don't drink, but you have one if you like.'

'Don't mind if I do,' I said, disappearing through to the kitchen and coming back with the bottle of prosecco.

'What can I do for you then?' I said, opening the bottle with a pop. 'I don't normally drink much you know but things have been bad lately because of you. What do you want from me Mia?'

'I don't want anything from you. I only came to tell you that I haven't been sending you emails or anything. I don't want to get into trouble with the police.'

I looked at her, then without saying anything I put a copy of her emails and the photographs on the coffee table.

'That is your email address isn't it?'

She looked through the emails and the photographs.

'I swear to you, it wasn't me who sent you these. That is not my email address. How would I even have got these photographs?'

'So why has Rory King written to me saying that I won't be receiving any more emails and yet I got a horrible one again today. He must think it's you and that he can stop you for some reason.'

'Rory is my dad. He thought it was me who had been trying to blackmail you because of the name on the emails. He also thought that because he was going to give me some money, I wouldn't need to blackmail you anymore.'

'But if it's not you, who is it?'

I began to sob at the thought of all the hateful messages and that porn video I had received. I shrivelled inside at the thought of it going viral. I just knew it would finish me. To my surprise Mia got up and gave me a handful of tissues from the ugly tissue holder. She even looked sorry for me. Perhaps she wasn't a bad person after all.

'I don't know Jessica,' she said, sitting back down again, 'but if you did lie about my grandad, then you deserve all you get. What you did had a terrible effect on everyone involved. My Gran had to give up her home and her job, my mum took to alcohol and drugs and got pregnant with me and my uncle Sean never came home from Manchester.'

I looked at her and was stunned that my actions had had such terrible repercussions? I had felt guilty about Mr Fraser killing himself, but I had never thought about his family and the effect on them. I began to cry again.

'I'm so sorry. I really loved your Grandad you know he was the only person who ever showed me any kindness back then.'

'If he was so kind, then why did he try to abuse you. That wasn't a kind thing to do.'

'No it wasn't but if I had known what would happen, I would never have reported it.'

'My gran says you go to the knitting circle that she's been going to. She didn't know who you were to begin with, or she wouldn't have continued to go along.'

'Your Gran? Don't tell me that Greer Gibson is your Gran,' I sneered, my unreasonable dislike of the woman surfacing again. 'I knew there was something about her. I bet she's been stalking me all along. Weirdo.'

'Don't call my nan a weirdo.'

Mia was up on her feet and I could see her little cheeks turning pink.

'Sit down. Have a drink. Don't be so touchy.'

Mia sat back down again, and I patted her on the hand. I was surprised at how mellow I was feeling.

'Look Mia I'm prepared to give you something if you stop sending these horrible photographs and videos.'

'But I told you I haven't sent any photographs or videos.'

'But you'll need to sign paperwork and give me back the original photographs and video. I'm not planning on being fleeced for the rest of my life.'

'You're drunk. Didn't you hear me? I didn't send any emails or photographs. I'm out of here.'

As she moved towards the door she knocked against the coffee table causing the bottle of prosecco and the tissue box to fall to the floor. The prosecco poured out of the bottle with an effervescent splosh but worse than that, the tissue box broke open. Magnus's present was broken. How was I going to tell him?

'Look what you've done. You've broken it,' I wailed at Mia's receding figure.

She didn't reply, just banged out of the door. When she had gone, I went over and picked up the tissue holder wondering if I could fix it but when I examined it more closely I could see that in fact it wasn't broken. There was an opening in the box which housed a little pen drive and it was this that had fallen open. I knew immediately what it was; a hidden camera and the pen drive gave the owner the facility to download what was captured onto their computer. I remembered using something like this in one of my books. I was stunned. Those photos and the creepy video of me must have been taken on it but who would do this to me? Who could it be?

While to anyone else it might have seemed obvious, I was rather befuddled with alcohol, so my mind whirled back in time thinking who had been in my house but really there were few people. Only Cathy, John and Magnus. All of them had a key but I immediately discounted Magnus. He loved me. He wouldn't do anything to harm me and what possible motive would Cathy have. I had known her most of my life. The only person it could be was John. He had been hurt and angry when I finished with him and quite violent, so it was possible. Although he had returned his key he could have had another one cut. So, was John wreaking revenge on me for finishing with him or perhaps it was Pam his wife. She had more or less threatened me when she phoned that time and it was probably her who had sent those horrible messages that I had got at first. It was the only explanation that made sense.

But then I remembered that it was Magnus who had given me the tissue holders. But why would Magnus want to harm me? He loved me. My stomach turned to mush, and I ran to the toilet vomiting up my stomach contents. I had just come back through to the living room and sat down when I heard the door opening. I still felt a bit shaky from being sick, but my heart soared at the thought of Magnus coming back to me, despite what I had just discovered.

'Hello darling,' he said, but stopped dead when he saw the bottle of prosecco with its contents spilled on the floor and the pen drive sticking out of the tissue holder.

'Magnus, Magnus you've come back to me,' I cried, jumping up from the couch and going towards him.

'What's going on here? You haven't been drinking all day surely and what's happened to the tissue box?'

I could see he wasn't happy with me and I went over to him grasping the lapels of his jacket. I was desperate. I wanted him back in my life and to know that we still had a future, but I needed to know what the camera meant.

'I'm sorry Magnus. I was really upset. I heard Darren again even although I was stone cold sober, and I had a visit from *IamMia,* but she said it wasn't her whose been trying to blackmail me.'

He removed my hands from his lapels and pushed me lightly away from him while I continued my sob story.

'She knocked over the prosecco and the box. I thought it was broken but it wasn't. It had fallen open and inside was that.'

I pointed at the pen drive.

'What the f…,' he said, picking it up and staring at it.

'What does it mean Magnus? Did you give me those tissue holders so that you could spy on me?'

'What's wrong with you Jessica. You're talking like a madwoman. Why would I do that?'

He looked at me as if trying to decide whether to tell me something or not.

'If you must know someone gave me those tissue boxes. I didn't say because I gave you them as a present and I didn't want you to think I was a cheapskate.'

'Who was it Magnus? Who gave you them? Did they know you were going to give them to me?'

'It was a doctor client of mine who lives in Manchester. Sean Fraser his name is. I told him I needed to get a present for you but that I didn't have a lot of time as I was driving up to Glasgow that night. He said he had these tissue boxes which I could have if I liked them. He had bought them for a friend, but he could go and buy some more as he wasn't seeing her until the following week.

'Sean Fraser?'

'Yes. Why? Is it important?'

'Paul Fraser's son was called Sean.'

'Well there must be a lot of Sean Frasers in the world. It would be too much of a coincidence if it was him.'

'Not really Magnus. Look what's been happening. Perhaps it's been him whose been sending the emails and the video.'

'Video. What video?'

Shit I hadn't wanted to mention that, so I continued on as if I hadn't heard him.

'Mia said it wasn't her. Maybe it was that Greer woman. It turns out she's Mr Fraser's widow. Maybe she and her son were in it together.'

I was finding it difficult to breath and was gasping for air. If it was them, then Mia was in it too. Magnus grabbed me by the shoulders, a look of disgust on his face no doubt at the smell of stale booze and vomit coming from me.

'Calm down Jessica. You're starting to lose it again. Take deep breaths. In and out, in and out.'

I eventually calmed down. Even although I knew Magnus was annoyed at me, I felt comforted by him speaking to me and holding my hand.

'Tell me about the video you mentioned earlier.'

'It was sent in today together with details of where I should pay the money.'

'Was I on the video?'

'No, only me. It was taken while we were having our date night. I can't bear for anyone to see it Magnus. I've decided I'm going to pay the money.'

'I think that's for the best sweetheart. When will you be able to do it?'

'Tomorrow I think. I'll need to make a special arrangement with the bank.'

'Hopefully, that will put all this to bed, and we can get on with our lives. Look why don't you go to bed and sleep it off and then we'll discuss it when you waken up tomorrow. You get ready for bed and I'll bring you a nice hot drink.'

Feeling relieved that he was being softer with me, I staggered my way up the hall to my bedroom like an obedient puppy, where I discarded my clothes on the floor, did the toilet and brushed my teeth in the ensuite before lying down. The door opened and Magnus came in with a mug of what smelt like hot chocolate.

'Drink this honey. It will help you to sleep.'

'Have you put something in it?'

'No, don't be silly. I don't think mixing booze and pills is a good idea. Do you?'

He sat with me while I supped the drink and I must admit that it felt comforting. When I had finished he took my mug, switched off the bedroom light and closed the door quietly. Before I knew it I was fast asleep.

PART TWO
UNRAVELLING

'The web of our life is of a mingled yarn, good and ill together.'
William Shakespeare

30

Ewan pressed the call end button on his phone and sighed. He had been looking forward to his day off after having worked the week-end. Suzie, his girlfriend, was supposed to be coming around that night so he had planned to do some shopping and cooking following his regular morning swim. But, Detective Sergeant Molly Smith had just phoned to tell him a body had been found in a house in Kirklee and he knew from experience that he would be tied up for most of the day and probably the evening too. He decided not to phone Suzie until he found out the lay of the land.

He had instructed Molly to take on the role of Crime Scene Manager. It would be her job to look at the crime scene and decide what specialisms they would require from the Scene of Crime Officers. It was important to make sure that evidence wasn't contaminated by having too many police officers and others moving around the crime scene. She had obviously acted quickly as when he arrived the forensic team in their white suits were already there as was Molly and Detective Constable Jamie McDougall. Ewen would be the Senior Investigating Officer with back up from Molly and Jamie.

'Morning sir', said Molly. 'The victim is a white male. Looks like he was beaten with a prosecco bottle and then stabbed in the eye with a knitting needle. He was found by Jessica Aitken's cleaner, Cathy Brown. She's over there in the car sir if you want to talk to her.'

'Thanks Sergeant. I'll have a look at the victim first and then have a word with her,' he said, pulling a protective suit over his clothes.

When he got inside the house, there were several people in white protective clothing walking about taking photographs, measuring, and bagging items. Molly led him to where the victim was. He was glad that they hadn't moved him yet as he liked to see the body in situ. He pushed his glasses to the top of his nose and looked down. The victim was lying flat on the floor behind the couch. He had been a tall man, perhaps about six feet, with black hair. He was wearing a blue suit, a blue shirt and a tie in bright primary colours in a jazzy design.

On his feet were a pair of black brogues with blue socks inside. He had a knitting needle sticking out of his right eye. There was an empty prosecco bottle lying not far from the body with blood and hair stuck to it so no doubt his head would be caved in at the back. There was already a biologist taking samples and checking for blood splatters in the area.

'Good morning Detective Inspector.'

Ewan's mood dropped as he recognised Jade Scott's voice coming from behind him. Shit why did it have to be her.

'Hope we've not spoiled your day off?' she said, with a slight sneer.

Jade was one of the pathologists who worked with the police. That was how he had met her. She had assisted on a case involving a refugee who had been found dead in the back of a van when he worked for the human trafficking unit. They had dated for a couple of months, but it hadn't worked out. Mostly because he had been on the rebound after Maggie, his exwife, had left him for her new partner, Fiona. At that time, all Ewan had wanted was to prove he was attractive to women and have sex with whoever was willing. Jade had been willing, but she had expected more and had been disappointed when Ewan made it clear he wasn't looking for a new relationship. He felt bad about how he had treated her and wished that he could explain but what was the point. She thought he was a rat and nothing he could say would change that.

Although it had been over two years since they had been an item, their history made it a little awkward working together because of her hostility but Ewan decided that the only way through it was to be courteous and professional and not rise to any bait that she threw his way.

'Hello Jade. Good to see you,' he lied. 'So, anything you can tell me?'

'Not yet.'

'Looks like cause of death was the knitting needle.'

'Maybe.'

'Any idea of time of death?'

'Difficult to say.'

Just then one of the white coats shouted Molly over and Ewan could see him holding up a tissue box. Molly went over and began chatting to him. Deciding that talking to Jade wasn't going to be fruitful, he went over to see what it was.

'Something important?' he asked, as he approached Molly.

'It might be. It's one of those spy cameras. If it has a video capability we might be able to see what happened to him.'

'Good. Keep me advised will you.'

He returned to Jade who was examining the body more closely. Rather than asking her when the post-mortem would be and risk a 'difficult to say' answer he asked her to let him know the time of the autopsy when she had arranged it.

'Yes sir,' said Jade, making a salute with her right hand.

Ewan decided to go and interview the cleaner. As he approached the patrol car he could see a sixty-something woman with grey bobbed hair sitting with a packet of tissues in her hand. She looked up as he opened the door and sniffed a welcome at him. Her eyes were red from crying.

'Good morning, Ms Brown, I'm Det Inspector Ewan McNeil, I won't keep you long but it's important that you tell me everything you can remember while it's still fresh in your memory.'

'Fresh in my memory! I don't think I'll ever be able to forget it,' she said, her eyes filling with tears again. 'I only came in this morning because I was due to go on holiday at the weekend and I wanted to give the place a last clean before I left. Tenerife I was going to, but I don't think I'm in the mood now. Not after walking in and seeing him like that. It was horrible that knitting needle sticking out of his eye. And the smell. Who would do such a thing?' she sobbed, pulling out several more tissues from the packet she was holding and blowing noisily into them. 'And what about Jessica? What if the murderer has harmed her? You'll need to find her Inspector.'

'We'll do that Ms Brown but I wonder if I could ask you some questions. Who knows, what you have to tell us might help us find Jessica.'

She began sobbing again and he waited until her sobs had subsided before beginning to question her.

'Can you tell me what time you arrived?'

'It's *Mrs* Brown by the way. I arrived just after ten o'clock. That's the time I always come, and Jessica has a cup of tea waiting for me, but Jessica didn't know I was coming. It was supposed to be a surprise. Well it was a surprise for me I can tell you.'

Ewan got in quickly before she started talking again.

'Tell me what you saw and heard when you came into the house.'

'Well I have a key, so I opened the door as usual and called out that it was only me. I was surprised when she didn't reply. I thought that possibly she was having a lie in with that new boyfriend of hers, Magnus, like in that Mastermind programme you know. "I've started so I'll finish," he used to say, but then I remembered that Magnus only came to stay on a Friday.'

'And then what happened?'

'I hung my coat up, went into the kitchen and saw that the light was on. I thought it was strange, but I wasn't particularly worried. There were some dirty dishes lying in the sink, so I put them in the dishwasher then went through to the living room. It was stinking of alcohol and another kind of sickly sweet smell. I wondered if Jessica had had a party or something as she wasn't a big drinker herself, well not until recently. She had started drinking quite a lot in the last couple of months when I think about it. I had to take her to her knitting circle one morning because she couldn't drive herself.'

'And then what happened.'

'The room was dark as the shutters were closed so I couldn't see all that clearly even although the lamp was still on. "Jessica," I called, but she didn't reply of course.'

Cathy gulped two huge breaths then continued.

'I went around the side of the couch and the first thing I saw was an empty bottle of prosecco lying on the floor covered in what I didn't realise was blood and hair. That's when I spotted him. He was lying at the back of the couch with that knitting needle sticking out of his eye. Do you know who he is?'

'I was hoping you could tell me.'

'I've never seen him before in my life,' Cathy began to sob again, and Ewan decided she had had enough for today.

'When are you going on holiday?' he said. 'We will almost certainly want to question you again.'

'I'm going on Saturday.'

'Right that gives us a couple of days. I'll get Constable McDougall to take you home now and he'll arrange to have another chat with you before you go.'

'I don't need a lift thanks. I have my own car.'

'Right, well take your time driving home. You've had a shock.'

'You can say that again,' she said, getting out of the police car.

Ewan returned to talk to Molly and Jamie who were standing looking a bit useless.

'Any sign of Jessica Aitken?'

'No sir, she seems to have disappeared,' said Jamie, 'I wonder if she did it?'

'Best not to make assumptions. Hopefully, we'll get more information from the Pathologist and the SOCO's soon.'

But I won't hold my breath he thought to himself glancing over at Jade.

31

When they got back to the office, Ewan held a meeting to see what they knew already and what immediate action they could take.

'Okay team. Let's write up what we know.'

Molly was first to go.

'Well in terms of the victim, we don't know very much. The cleaner told us that Jessica's boyfriend was called Magnus (no second name), but she never met him so can't identify him as the victim. We can't find any paperwork belonging to him in the house so can't identify him that way.'

'Any clothing or other personal items belonging to him in the house?'

'Some underwear, shirts, a couple of brightly coloured ties, deodorant, aftershave and a toothbrush. Oh and a phone, a car key and one of those remote control things that open a garage were found in his jacket pocket.'

'So it sounds like he drove to Jessica's apartment.'

'The garage is empty sir, but it's not to say he didn't park in the street outside. I'll see if I can find out anything.'

'What about Jessica? What do we know about her?'

'We know that she is an unmarried woman in her late thirties who lives on her own in the flat in Kirklee where the body was found. We know she is a popular and successful crime writer. Her mother is still alive and lives in Knightswood. Her name is Lizzie Halligan. She has no other close relatives.'

'Enemies?'

'Hard to say. As a celebrity she could have attracted a lot of nutters,' said Jamie.

They wrote up what they knew on the board and then decided how they should begin the investigation.

'Jamie, you find out if there were any regular visitors to the house that we can eliminate from our inquiries. Speak to the cleaner first. She was in a state of shock when I spoke to her so she might be calmer now and able to fill in some of the blanks. She's going on holiday on Saturday, so we need to catch her before she goes.'

'Right sir, I'll get on to that straight away.'

'Meanwhile, Molly and I will go and speak to Jessica's mother. See if she knows where Jessica might have gone.'

Ewan and Molly made their way to Jessica's mum's house in Knightswood. It didn't take them long to get from Paisley to the semi-detached inter-war council house where she stayed. She answered their knock straight away and didn't bother to look at their ID.

'I've been expecting you. I heard the report on the news that a body had been found in Jessica's flat. Do you need me to come and identify her?'

She had the face of a heavy smoker; wrinkled and grey. Ewan had no sooner thought this than she lit up a cigarette. He wanted to ask her to put it out as they were at work, but he decided she might be more amenable to talking if she was relaxed rather than tense from nicotine cravings.

'Good morning Mrs Halligan. I'm Detective Inspector Ewan McNeil and this is Detective Sergeant Molly Smith. The body we found wasn't Jessica's. In fact we were hoping you might be able to tell us where she is.'

'No. Come on through. Would you like a cup of tea?'

Ewan was surprised at how matter of fact the woman was considering she had just been given the news that it wasn't her daughter's body that had been found.

'Yes, that would be nice. I'll give you a hand,' said Molly.

When they were settled with their tea, Ewan began to question her.

'So, Mrs Halligan, do you have any idea where Jessica might be?' asked Ewan.

'No, I've no idea.'

'Do you think she's capable of killing someone?'

'She has got a bit of a temper. In fact, on my birthday she had a real go at me and ended up throwing the teapot and the cake she had brought at the wall, but I don't know that she would kill someone. It's more likely that she would be the one to be killed. That's why I wasn't that surprised when I heard a body had been found at her house.'

'What do you mean Mrs Halligan?'

'Well she's in and out of relationships all the time. She

had only finished with her last boyfriend a week before she started going out with this new one. Flighty she is. No loyalty.'

'Do you know the name of her last boyfriend?'

'John something. He was an estate agent. She bought her house in Kirklee through him. But I didn't meet him. She never brought her boyfriends to meet me.'

'So, you didn't meet Magnus her latest boyfriend? We're having difficulty identifying the body found in Jessica's house and were hoping you might be able to identify him if it is her boyfriend.'

'Sorry can't help you.'

'How do you get on with your daughter Mrs Halligan? Are you close?'

'Not particularly. We were on speaking terms until the incident on my birthday, but we haven't spoken since then. She came round to the house one night, but I shut the door on her. I didn't want to see her again after that.'

'So you're not close.'

'She led her life and I led mine. Her twin brother was stillborn you know, and I think it did something to her. She was always saying that I wished that she had died instead of him and God help me sometimes I did wish that. She was such a difficult child; always wanting attention and doing anything to get it.'

'Can you tell us about Jessica's personal life. Any friends that we should speak to, any clubs she was in, that sort of thing.'

'She didn't have any friends. She was a bit of a loner, apart from the boyfriends she picked up and threw away like confetti. She talks a lot about her publisher Dorothy Hamilton, and she was in a knitting group, something that her counsellor ran. Maybe she had some friends in that. She knitted me this cardigan at it.'

She indicated the cardigan she was wearing. It was baby blue and knitted in delicate looking wool. Ewan didn't know much about knitting but it didn't look as if it would have been easy to knit. He wondered briefly whether it was one of the knitting needles Jessica had used to knit this cardigan that had been jabbed through the victim's eye.

'You must be proud of Jessica, Mrs Halligan. She's a fantastic novelist and it looks like she's a fantastic knitter too,' said Molly.

'Yes, Debbie has her talents. I just wish she was a kinder person.'

'You mentioned a counsellor earlier, Mrs Halligan. Had Jessica been suffering from depression? Had something happened to her that made her need to see a counsellor,' asked Ewan.

'It was after her dad died. For some reason she went into meltdown, crying all the time and unable to write. She kept saying she had been traumatised by her upbringing and what that teacher, Mr Fraser, had done to her. The doctor eventually suggested she go see a psychiatrist after the anti-depressants he gave her seemed to make her worse. But she didn't stick with him either and that's when she began seeing her counsellor.'

Ewan could hear the conversation fading. It had suddenly occurred to him who Jessica Aitken was, and he was back in 1995 when he was seventeen. He remembered he had a crush on a girl called Sophie Fraser, but she was only ever interested in being friends. That was until Debbie Halligan made the allegations against Sophie's dad and he jumped from the Erskine Bridge. She was never the same after that. She began hanging around with the wrong crowd and got into alcohol and drugs. He remembered one night at a party she was off her face and had tried to come onto him; offering herself on a plate. He hadn't taken advantage though, but he knew that some of the other boys had. He wondered what had happened to her. The family had left Milngavie after the teacher killed himself and he had never heard anything about Sophie since.

'Sir.'

Ewan was diverted from his reverie by Molly's hand lightly touching his sleeve. I just wondered if you had any more questions for Mrs Halligan.'

'Can you tell us anything about what happened when Debbie accused the teacher Mrs Halligan? It must have been a difficult time for you.'

'What do you want to know?'

'Well how did you find out what was going on? Was there any evidence to suggest that your daughter was being groomed? What effect did it have on your daughter? Was there any contact from the teacher or his family?'

'We didn't know that it was happening. My husband and I had a drink problem at the time and to be honest we hardly knew what time of day it was.'

She averted her eyes and Ewan assumed she was feeling embarrassed at having to admit her past alcohol addiction to strangers.

'Probably just as well. If Debbie's dad had known, he would have murdered the bastard.'

'And once it became known, I assume that social services and the police got involved.'

'Yes, social work got involved. It turned out to be the making of her. After Paul Fraser killed himself she seemed to change. Grow-up. Mature. And she was clever was our Debbie. When she started at secondary she began to handle all the household money and bills, made sure me and her dad had something to eat and gave us just enough booze to keep us going. She also started to experiment with drink and drugs herself and I suppose she could easily have gone off the rails but after Mr Fraser died, she changed. She took up sports like running and cycling, gave up the booze and hash, and began to work really hard at school so that she could get into university.'

Ewan wondered if she was proud of her daughter. She seemed to be ambivalent towards her.

'We didn't notice any change in her behaviour before it happened, but then we weren't in any fit state to notice anything.'

She smiled a self-deprecating smile at them.

'And the teacher. Did you know him? Did any of his family get in touch with you?'

'We didn't know any of Debbie's teachers. We never went to parents' evenings you see. He came here one night I remember even although he wasn't supposed to. He killed himself before there was any police investigation. Didn't want to put his family through the trauma of a court case the papers said, but I reckon it was because he was guilty.'

'You believed your daughter then, Mrs Halligan.'

'Not right away. At first, I thought it was just her way of getting attention. She was well known for it. There always had to be a drama. But that night the teacher came here I could see that she was genuinely upset and that changed my mind. He begged and pleaded with her to withdraw her allegations and in fact her dad had to throw him out of the house she was becoming so distressed. It was after that he jumped.'

'Finally, Mrs Halligan. Can you tell us the name of Jessica, sorry, Debbie's therapist?'

'Yes, her name's Barbara King. Been on the telly and that a few times so you should be able to find her easily.'

Ewan got up from his chair and held out his hand.

'You've been very helpful Mrs Halligan. Thanks for the tea. We'll be in touch when we know anything.'

32

'What happened in there, sir, you seemed to be on another planet,' Molly asked, as they got into the car.

'Yes, I know. I'm sorry Sergeant. Did I miss anything?'

'Just Mrs Halligan going on about her daughter always wanting attention and paying a counsellor to get it.'

'I suppose she could afford it, but it must have been difficult for her being brought up by alcoholic parents and then being abused by her teacher. It's a lot to go through in childhood.'

On the way back to the station, Ewan's phone rang. It was Jade telling him the time of the post-mortem. He decided they would need something to eat as they would definitely get no dinner tonight, so they stopped off at McDonalds. He picked up three meals for Molly, Jamie and himself to keep them going. Not the healthiest choice, but it would have to do. After they had eaten, Ewan called a meeting to discuss what they knew and what they still needed to do. He kicked off the discussion.

'Well Jessica's mum couldn't suggest anywhere that she might be or really tell us all that much about her daughter. She was a loner she said, had no close friends although has had a lot of romantic liaisons. She is a member of a knitting group run by the therapist Barbara King and she is close to her publisher Dorothy Hamilton. She split up from her boyfriend John something, a local Estate Agent, in January so that might be relevant. The biggest thing she told us though was that Jessica had been groomed and sexually molested by her teacher when she was fourteen and that it had resulted in the teacher committing suicide.'

'Could it be that Magnus is in some way connected to the teacher's family and was threatening Jessica?' said Molly.

'But it's so long ago. If Jessica was fourteen when it happened and she's about forty now, then it would be over twenty years ago,' said Jamie, screwing his face up as he made the calculation.

'It's a good point Molly and one we should bear in mind. Jamie could you try and find out what happened to the teacher's family and where they are now. But before you do tell us what the cleaner had to say.'

Jamie read from his notes and Ewan could almost hear the conversation that had taken place.

'Well I don't want to speak ill of Jessica, I am very fond of her, but she was a bit flighty. She seemed to have different boyfriends every few months. Never stuck with them. But this latest one Magnus seemed to be different. She only saw him once a week as he was a travelling salesman for a drug company. Stayed in the Grosvenor Hotel until recently. No, I don't know the name of the company. But she said he was different. He seemed to like her and had asked her to marry him. She was really happy, but she seemed to change in the last few weeks. She was drinking a lot more and seemed on edge a lot of the time. I mean she had only split up with John Crosby for a week when she started going out with Magnus. I only know his second name because he was the estate agent who sold my daughter's house at Anniesland. So far as I could gauge it wasn't a happy ending as there was a whisky stain on the wall and a broken glass lying on the floor one morning when I came in. Jessica just asked me to tidy it up without giving me an explanation. She also asked me to give John his stuff when he called round as she would be out. "Tell him I'm out if he asks," she told me. He didn't ask. He looked a bit pissed off, if you know what I mean, and just took the bags and left without a word.'

'Good work team. I'm going to head over to the Queen Elizabeth mortuary for the post-mortem. We'll reconvene in the morning and decide our next course of action.'

33

Post-mortems were one of the jobs Ewan disliked. Watching a person who had lived a life just like him being cut up like an animal distressed him. He used to wonder how pathologists could do their job but going out with Jade for a while had given him an insight into why she could do the job she did and actually enjoy it. She seemed to be able to get past the physical discomfort that he felt from the smells and the cutting with a mixture of humour and the feeling that she was helping the victim and their family. She never forgot that the body she was working on had been someone's son, daughter, father or mother. He had to admire Jade for that.

After the post-mortem, he headed for home. As he made his way up the stairs to his flat, he took a few sniffs hoping no residue from the mortuary smell was clinging to him. Suzie was sitting reading and was so absorbed she didn't hear him come in. She looked cosy in her pink and blue polka dot pyjamas and was obviously enjoying her book. Sometimes he had to pinch himself at the way things had turned out between them. In 2016 he had been a recently divorced father of one who had suffered a breakdown after his best friend Andy had been killed by a suicide bomber in Syria. He and Suzie, who was Andy's widow, had formed a relationship after he had delivered a case to her in Spain where she had moved after Andy died. Although it had been a struggle for them both, they were now at the stage of talking about moving in together and he harboured hopes of marrying her one day. He bent over and kissed her copper curls and she looked up smiling and pointed to a lump in her cheek. The empty chocolate wrapper told him what the cause was.

'Hi, sorry about tonight. Hope you've had something more than chocolate to eat,' he said, taking off his glasses and rubbing his eyes.

'Yes thanks, although I would have preferred your cooking,' she said, getting up and walking into his arms. Her lips and tongue tasted sweet as they kissed.

'There's some *pasta arriabata* left over if you want to heat it up. I'm reading one of Jessica Aitken's novels. I heard on the news today that a body was found in her house this morning. Is that the case you were called in to work on today?'

Ewan glanced over at his bookcase and could see that one of Jessica Aitken's novels had been removed from the half dozen that had been sitting on the top shelf. Although Suzie thought he was a bit anal, he always kept his books in alphabetical order by author so that he could find what he wanted easily.

'Yes, it was,' he said, going over to the bookshelf and picking up one of her books. He turned it over, looking for her biography. The photograph on the back cover showed a slim woman of about forty with blonde curls smiling out at her public with white even teeth and piercing blue eyes that made you think she was looking only at you. It told Ewan that she had been educated at Knightswood Secondary School in Glasgow and had gone on to University to study English Literature and Creative Writing. Her hobbies included keeping fit, cycling and knitting.

'I see she went to Knightswood Secondary. Did you know her Suzie?'

'I don't think so. I don't remember anyone called Jessica Aitken around that time.'

'That's just her pen name. She was called Debbie Halligan back then.'

'No I don't remember her. Is she the prime suspect then?'

'At the moment, things seem to be pointing that way, but we'll see.'

Ewan knew it was unprofessional to discuss a case with Suzie but since he was only confirming what was in the newspaper he decided it wasn't too much of an offence.

34

Ewan hadn't long joined the Major Investigation Team at Osprey House as he had been part of the human trafficking team before, so he was still finding his feet. Like many of his colleagues, he hadn't been a big supporter of Police Scotland when it was set up in 2013. Change was never easy, he understood that, but it just felt that it was going to be too big. There was also the added problem of the difficulties faced by the last two Chief Constables who had both left under a cloud. However, he knew that having a dedicated team that concentrated on serious crime worked, so he was enthusiastic about his job.

As he made the journey to work through the Clyde Tunnel from Hyndland he thought about Suzie which, as always, put a smile on his face. He had awoken at 7am and as he always did when Suzie was staying with him, he just lay gazing at her sleeping body and marvelled that she was there beside him. She was beginning to stay at his flat more and more which he was delighted about. They had had a rough road getting together but he was hopeful that things would settle now. She looked so peaceful sleeping there that he didn't want to wake her. He could lie and look at her for ever.

'Are you looking at me again,' a sleepy voice said, as Suzie began to stir and stretch.

'Of course. What better way to start the day than to look at the woman I love?'

He kissed her lightly on her hair and she turned languidly into his arms. He felt his body responding to her warmth and began stroking her neck and placing kisses on her hair. She smelled of strawberries from the body butter she moistured with each evening.

'You smell delicious Suzie. I want to eat you all up.'

He pushed her gently on her back and she looked up into his eyes smiling that little smile that said, 'well go on then.' He began caressing her breasts, felt her nipples rise in response and heard her sigh of pleasure. He loved the times when they could spend the morning in bed, making love and chatting. It was a special time that he never stopped being grateful for, especially as the first time they had gone to bed together had been a disaster.

For some reason he hadn't been able to make love to her. He had been angry and upset with himself but had taken it out on her. It was nothing like when he had been with Jade. Having sex with her had never been a problem probably because he wasn't in love with her and if he was being honest was probably only using her. But Suzie was different. Even back then he knew she was much more important to him than Jade had ever been. Although Suzie knew about Jade, he hadn't gone into detail and hoped that their paths would never need to cross.

Suzie had a late start, but he didn't and would need to be up and out sharpish, so he reluctantly pulled back from her.

'What do you fancy for breakfast? I could do you a quick poached egg if you like?'

Her face took on a green tinge.

'I'm not hungry just now,' she said, as she quickly made her way to the bathroom.

'You look a bit washed out sweetheart. Have you had a rough week?' he said, taking her in his arms when she came back from the toilet. He knew that her work with refugees could be emotionally draining as well as physically tiring.

'Not too bad,' she said, snuggling into his arms. 'I must have an upset tummy. I felt a bit queasy at the idea of a yoky egg and thought I was going to throw up there.'

'You go back to bed and I'll bring you a nice cup of camomile tea.'

'I love you Ewan,' she said, turning back towards him as she climbed into bed. When he took her tea in she was fast asleep again.

While waiting for the others to come in, Ewan sat at his desk swinging back slightly in his chair surveying his new office. In pride of place was a photograph in a shiny new frame of Suzie, his son Jamie and himself taken in Spain. It was the first photograph of them together taken by Suzie's friend Melanie outside her café in *L'Aldea*. Who would have guessed that they would end up together? At that time, he had suspected that Suzie might be involved in people smuggling although he had to admit he had never been convinced of her or Andy's guilt. And, of course, he had been proved right. Josh, who had been in the army with Andy, had been the guilty one and was now serving a five-year sentence for selling fake passports.

On his desk were some typed up notes. Jamie and Molly had gone up to see the estate agent, John Crosby, last night while he was at the post mortem and had written up their notes. They had found out that John and Jessica's parting had not been amicable as had been suggested by the cleaner.

'I was fucking raging with her. She was all "it's not you it's me" crap thinking I would feel sorry for her because of her past. Well the only person I feel sorry for is me. I'm now on my own having to pay for a house that I can't live in and support a wife and two kids who hate my guts. I wish it was her that was dead and not that poor sucker that she went with after me.'

'So, you felt sorry for her new boyfriend, not jealous that he had replaced you.'

'What are you suggesting? That I had a motive for killing him. No way.'

'Do you have any idea where Jessica might be? We are concerned for her safety.'

'I've no idea where she could be. All I know is that sometimes she would go to a cottage near Pitlochry when she was stuck or wanted to finish a book, but I don't know where.'

Molly and Jamie had felt that he was an angry man and even although his anger appeared to be directed towards Jessica, he could have been jealous so was worth keeping in the frame for the moment. His alibi was being checked so they would know shortly if he could possibly have been involved.

A knock on the door made Ewan look up from his notes. It was Molly.

'That's Jamie and me in. Flinty's on his way and will be here in five. I brought you a quick cuppa,' she said, placing a milky coffee in front of him. 'There's also a biscuit from a packet I found in the kitchen.'

'You spoil me,' he smiled.

He noticed her looking at the scar on his hand as he picked

up his cup. She probably didn't know about his volunteer work in Syria where Andy was killed while they were on a mercy mission and he decided not to enlighten her. He didn't know much about Molly. She had moved up from Liverpool to join Glasgow's MIT at about the same time as he had joined it. She seemed bright and keen which was always a bonus and didn't seem to have any domestic responsibilities as she was always up for a drink after work if it was suggested. She had a few more years' experience than Jamie so he was hoping that she would mentor him during the course of this investigation.

'Looks like you're settling in okay sir,' said Molly sweeping her arm around the room and he assumed she meant the photograph on his desk and the painting on the wall.

'Yes, they're presents from my partner Suzie. The photograph is of the two of us with my son. He's called Jamie, the same as our young Detective Constable. Suzie does art therapy with refugees and the painting is one that was put on at an exhibition to raise funds for the charity she works for.'

'Sounds like an interesting job.'

'Yes. She gets a lot of satisfaction from it. See you in a mo.'

35

Superintendent Flint arrived just as Ewan got into the briefing room. The Superintendent's name was onomatopoeic. Like his name, Flint was steely and unemotional, and his team had tried to quell their fear of him by giving him the nickname Flinty. It made him sound benign although he was anything but according to the rumours. Ewan was only becoming acquainted with him and hoped that in time he would be able get to know his superior better and perhaps find a heart under that cold exterior.

He remembered the first time he had met Inspector Flint. The injury he had sustained in Syria had left his hand weak and when Flinty grasped it in a firm handshake, he could see by his face that he judged Ewan to be as limp as his handshake.

'So, what's the latest?' Flinty asked in that cold brisk voice of his when he came in. No good mornings or how are yous.

'Well,' Ewan began, 'a knitting needle was stuck through his eye, but it wasn't the needle that killed him. He was bludgeoned to death with the prosecco bottle found at the scene. There were blood splatters on the wall but they came from the deceased so no help there apart from telling us that the body was moved to allow the needle to be pierced into his eye. The killer must have decided to make doubly sure that he was dead.'

'Why the eye?' asked Molly. 'It's a bit extreme.'

'It's one of the only places where a knitting needle will be effective in killing someone. The other place is the ear.'

'So does that mean they had some medical background do you think if they knew that?'

'Excuse me Sergeant, would you mind letting the Inspector get on with his report please. I don't have all morning to listen to your speculations.'

Ewan felt sorry for Molly at Flinty's intervention. Her face burned bright pink with embarrassment.

'Surprisingly,' he continued, 'given that there was alcohol in the vicinity, the toxicology report showed that the deceased had no alcohol or drugs in his system.'

'I wonder who was drinking then and if they were the killer how come they were able to aim the needle so accurately? Perhaps it was Jessica who had been drinking and the killer has kidnapped her,' said Jamie, looking excitedly at his colleagues. He obviously hadn't got the message from Flinty not to interrupt or speculate.

'Don't get carried away now McDougall. We do investigations don't we McDougall. We don't make up fairy tales and make them fit the facts, do we McDougall?'

Ewan could see Molly Smith smile over in sympathy at McDougall as his face became as pink with embarrassment as hers had a few minutes previously. He was pleased to see that they were on side and not laughing at each other's discomfort. He disliked the competitiveness that sometimes operated in the police force preferring people to work as a team. Getting the job done was their priority, not scoring points off one another although if you wanted a good career in the police, sometimes it was necessary.

'What about time of death?' asked Flinty.

'The body wasn't fresh sir. It's believed that death took place at least forty eight hours before the cleaner found him. That would mean that he died sometime between Monday evening and Tuesday evening the pathologist thinks.'

'What about forensics? Anything there to help us?'

'There was only one set of prints on the prosecco bottle that killed him and on the knitting needle. I assume that whoever those fingerprints belong to is the killer. There were several other fingerprints in the house, so we will need to set about establishing who they belong to and whether they can be eliminated from our inquiries.'

'What about the tissue box with the camera. Did it throw up anything?' asked Molly.

'We're still waiting on more information from the Intelligence Analysts about the camera and the victim's phone. I'm hoping we'll get it this week.'

'Anything else?' asked Flinty.

'The pathologist found traces of saliva on the victim's face and is using the DNA from it to try and identify who it belongs to.'

'Right. There's a lot to think about McNeil so I'll leave you to it. Keep me up to date with how the investigation is going. There will be a lot of publicity surrounding the case and I'll probably need to do regular press releases.'

'Yes sir.'

36

When Flinty had gone, Ewan asked for an update from Molly and Jamie.

'Sir, I'm afraid we've not made much progress,' said Molly. 'Jamie talked to Jessica's neighbours but none of them seemed to know her very well and no-one admitted to seeing anything unusual on Monday or Tuesday. We did manage to find out Magnus's surname from the Grosvenor Hotel. It's Nelson, but we haven't been able to trace him yet. We've put his details into the national database, but it will take us a while to check out all possible matches. Luckily, Magnus isn't a common name, so it cuts it down a little.'

Looking through her notes, Molly continued.

'In terms of the teacher's family, we've found out that Mrs Fraser moved away from Milngavie about six months after Paul Fraser died. We spoke to the family who bought Mrs Fraser's house and the two adjoining neighbours. From that we got the name of the solicitor who dealt with the sale of the house and his secretary is checking their archives to see if she can give us any information. According to the neighbours, the Frasers had a son and a daughter. The son was called Sean and was at Manchester University when it all kicked off. Apparently, he didn't come back for his dad's funeral. The girl went off the rails and ran away with some bloke she met. Rumour was she went to Australia, but we need to check it out.'

'What we have managed to do is contact Barbara King and she will give us a list of all those who have attended the knitting circle during the period that Jessica attended,' Jamie continued.

'By the way sir,' Molly interrupted. 'Barbara's husband is that shit hot lawyer Rory King who is being considered for Chair of the Law Society of Scotland. Do you know him?'

'Yes, I do as a matter of fact,' Ewan nodded, and his mind again went back to that party where Sophie had tried to get off with him. Rory King had been at that party too he remembered.

'Also, we got a phone call from Jessica's mother's next-door neighbour and guess what?'

'What?' said Ewan, smiling at his constable.

'The neighbour heard mother and daughter arguing and she reckoned violence could have been involved. She heard something hitting against the wall, followed by a loud smash. She didn't think much about it at the time but when she saw that someone had been found dead in Jessica's house, she thought she should tell us.

'That would certainly tie in with what Mrs Halligan told us happened on her birthday.'

'Oh. you already knew they'd had a fight. I didn't know.'

Ewan felt sorry for McDougall. He had been so excited about that phone call. As he returned to his office, he could hear Jamie complain to Molly.

'Why didn't you tell me about the fight in your report and why does he always put me down? He makes me feel like a complete idiot sometimes. Did you see that superior smirk he put on when I was telling him about Mrs Halligan's neighbour?'

'Perhaps it's because you're too eager and are always trying to impress him. Just relax and do your job. And he wasn't smirking he was smiling. Don't be so paranoid.'

37

It was agreed that Ewan and Molly would visit Barbara King while Jamie would concentrate on tracing Paul Fraser's family and contacting Dorothy Hamilton, Jessica's publisher. It was possible she might know the address of this cottage in Pitlochry that Jessica went to. When he and Molly arrived at Barbara King's blonde sandstone house in the Jordanhill area, she was waiting for them and opened the door straight away. He thought she looked anxious and wondered why.

'Good afternoon. Mrs King?'

'Yes. Please come in. Would you like a cup of tea or coffee?'

'Not at the moment thanks.'

'Please take a seat,' she said, waving her open hand towards the settee and watched as Ewan and Molly sank into the sofa. Sitting on the coffee table was an A4 brown envelope.

'These are the names and addresses of the women who attended the circle,' Barbara said, picking up the envelope and passing it to Molly. 'It covers everyone who has been a member since Jessica joined. Please let me know if you need any further information. I've emailed those I still have contact information for and said that you may want to interview them. I hope that was alright. Evie and Lottie, the most recent recruits to the circle are vulnerable young women and I thought it would be upsetting for them if you turned up on their doorsteps unannounced.'

'So, there were only three people attending the group before it was disbanded?' asked Molly.

'Yes, that's correct.'

'What can you tell us about Jessica, Mrs King?' asked Ewan..

'Well I first met Jessica just over two years ago when she came to me for counselling. She was quite a vulnerable woman despite her success as a writer of crime novels. At the time I didn't realise that she was also the author of a memoir in which she described her childhood experiences including being groomed and sexually molested by her teacher.'

'Why did she come for counselling at that time? She must have been around thirty-five by then and that incident took place when she was fourteen.'

'She didn't come because of that. She came because her father had died, and she was finding it difficult to cope with her grief.'

'But I thought he was an alcoholic and had never been much of a father to her?'

'That's true and it was precisely because of that that her grief was what we term complicated grief.'

'What does that mean exactly?'

'Well, it's viewed by the experts on grief that there is a normal grieving process during which the person bereaved goes through various stages of mourning before reaching some kind of resolution of that grief. In prolonged or complicated grief, it is not so straightforward. So, for example, in Jessica's case, her feelings towards her father would have been ambivalent. Part of her would have been angry at him for abandoning her because of his alcoholism and another part of her would have been in mourning for the relationship she never had with him and because of his death would never have. Also, her own birth was complicated by the fact that her twin was stillborn, and I think this probably caused difficulties for her mother being able to form an attachment to Jessica. All these things can be reasons for complicated grief.'

'And were you able to help her resolve her difficulties.'

'To some extent yes. She was able to function again, but she still had an underlying vulnerability. Also, she became very attached to me. This is what we call transference in counselling. The client transfers their need for a mother/father figure to the counsellor and when I suggested we stop therapy, she became distressed. That was the reason I suggested she join my knitting circle. It meant that we would still be in contact, but our relationship would not be as close as it would be in a one to one counselling relationship. Also, I hoped that she might make friends in the circle. Unfortunately, she never did.'

'Why was that do you think?'

'Well, she could be a little...' Barbara looked down at her hands trying to think of the right word, 'abrasive. She just said what she thought. She was sometimes insensitive to the needs of the other women in the group.'

'Was she ever aggressive?'

'No.'

Ewan wasn't sure that she was telling the truth as she didn't look at him or Molly when she said this. Again, he wondered why. She glanced at the clock and Ewan sensed that their time was up.

'I'm sorry I have a client to see in half an hour.'

'That's fine Mrs King. We'll get back to you if we need any further information and if you think of anything else that's relevant, here is my card. Give me a call.'

'Goodbye Superintendent, Sergeant,' Barbara said, as she shook hands with them.

When they got into the car Ewan could see that Molly was itching to say what she thought of Barbara King.

'Go on Molly. Tell me what you think,' he said.

'Well I thought she was hiding something or not telling us everything perhaps. She seemed on edge. I thought she might not have told us much about Jessica and what she had come to see her about because of the rules on confidentiality but she was quite open.'

'Trying to lull us into thinking she was giving us good information when in fact she was just trying to cover up other things.'

'Well it's possible isn't it sir?'

'Yes it is possible and I think you're right. There is something or several somethings she's not telling us.'

38

Ewan and Molly decided to go and visit the two women who had been members of the circle with Jessica over the last few months. As this was the timescale that she had known Magnus for, they were interested to know if Jessica had shared any information about Magnus with them. If necessary they could interview the others later.

Charlotte MacGregor was closer to Jordanhill than Evie Boyle, so they visited her first. She lived with her dad in Scotstoun and he didn't look best pleased to have the police calling on him and interviewing his daughter. Ewan was surprised when he took them through to the living room to meet her. He seemed very conventional and uptight while his daughter was covered in tattoos and had her hair dyed blue.

'Good evening Ms MacGregor,' Ewan said, introducing himself and Molly.

'As you may have read in the papers a body was found in the home of Jessica Aitken, the novelist and I believe that you attended a knitting circle with Jessica.'

'Yes, that's right. I didn't know that Jessica was famous until I saw it in the papers. I never read murder novels so had no idea.'

'We're wondering whether she spoke to you about her boyfriend Magnus Nelson.'

'Not directly. She mentioned him in the circle in passing but nothing specific.'

'Did you notice any change in Ms Aitken's behaviour over the last few months.'

'Well I think if anything she became softer, more vulnerable.'

'In what way?'

'Well she was really upset when she was telling us what had happened to her when she was a young teenager. I felt sorry for her. And then when my mum died, and my dad took me back to live with him she seemed genuinely pleased for me. She also told me that she was receiving hate mail and was worried about it.'

'Hate mail?'

'Yes, but she didn't tell me any more than that, so I don't know what the mail was about.'

'Was she ever aggressive?'

'Not that I saw but on the last circle meeting I was at, it looked as if her and Barbara had fallen out. I went back as I had left something I had knitted for Evie and I found Barbara sitting looking scared and she had a gob of spit on her face.'

'You think Jessica did it?'

'Yes.'

'Thanks very much Ms MacGregor. This is my card if you can think of anything else please give me a ring.'

'Well, well,' said Molly. 'Mrs King definitely didn't tell us everything.'

'Indeed. Let's go and see Evie Boyle and see if she can give us anything interesting.'

They made their way to Maryhill, where Evie lived. She was obviously not long after having a baby and the house was full of baby paraphernalia, mostly pink. She was cradling the child in her arms when they arrived and proudly introduced them to Charlotte. However, she was clearly ill at ease at being interviewed by the police so Molly asked her if it would be alright to make them all a cup of tea. She nodded her head vigorously. When they began asking questions about Jessica, it was like drawing teeth. She only answered their direct questions and didn't volunteer any additional information but from the facts they did get, it seemed clear that she wasn't Jessica's biggest fan. They were just about to leave when she volunteered some information for the first time.

'I wish my support worker could have been here with me just now. Greer's been a great support to me in the circle. She showed me how to knit this baby hat.'

'Your support worker went to the circle meetings with you?'

'Yes.'

'Can you tell us her full name.'

'Greer Gibson'

Ewan and Molly were delighted to find out that as they suspected Barbara King hadn't told them everything.

39

When they got back to the office Jamie was beaming and almost jumping up and down with excitement. Ewan couldn't help but smile at his youthful exuberance. He liked his eagerness but he did make a bit of a twit of himself sometimes being so openly enthusiastic. Cynicism was more respected in the MIT and he wondered how long it would take him to become like the rest of them; hardened by their experiences of working with *man's inhumanity to man.*

'Go on then Jamie, what have you got for us.'

'Well sir, I've manged to trace Paul Fraser's wife and son. The son was easy. He hadn't changed his name and as he's a doctor he was on the GP Register. He lives in Manchester. I phoned him and he confirmed that he was Mr Fraser's son but that he had never heard of anyone called Magnus Nelson. He also told me that he didn't know where his sister lived. He hadn't seen her for over twenty years. Mrs Fraser was a little more difficult as she had changed back to her maiden name. But the solicitor who sold her property also acted on her behalf for the purchase of another property and we found through the census records that she is still there but that she's now called Greer Gibson. I also contacted her and have arranged for you to visit her tomorrow.'

'OMG sir shall I tell Jamie our news?' asked Molly, smiling widely.

'I think you'd better.'

'We found out that someone called Greer Gibson is the support worker for Evie Boyle and that she also attended the circle meetings. Not that Barbara King told us that. We think there's something dodgy about her don't we sir.'

Ewan nodded and smiled when Jamie joined in excitedly.

'Wow! That's a bit of a coincidence isn't it, sir?'

'It sure is,' said Ewan, feeling like he was in a super hero movie with all the Wows and OMGs being bandied about. 'Anything else Jamie'

'Yes sir. I got a report back from the Intelligence Analysts. The techies discovered there were two of those cameras that allow you to see what's going on in your house when you're out. One in Jessica's living room and another in her bedroom. They were in two tissue boxes so were well hidden.'

'Yes,' said Molly. 'I remember when I arrived at Jessica's house one of the scene of crime officers had just discovered the one in the living room. Do you know how they work?'

'You download an app on your phone so wherever you are you can keep an eye on things. It also allows you to speak to whoever is in the house. So, for example a friend of mine, who has a young family, works away from home a lot and he enjoys checking in while he's at work so that he can see them, and they can hear his voice talking to them.'

'Sounds like spying to me,' said Molly. 'What's wrong with WhatsApp or Skype?'

'And how is it relevant to this investigation,' said Ewan, before they got into a debate on the pros and cons of this device.

'Guess what they discovered on the phone that was found on the body?'

Not waiting for them to reply, Jamie continued on with his guess what.

'It was linked up to those cameras. It looks like Magnus Nelson wasn't what he appeared to be. He had an app on his phone that was linked up to cameras that were found in Jessica's house. He also appears to have been trying to blackmail her. He had sent three emails to Jessica under the name of IamMia. The first accused her of lying about what happened with the teacher and saying she would make her pay. The second email warned her that if she didn't confess to lying or paying £50,000 the photographs that had been sent would be published. The SOCO'S didn't find any photographs in Jessica's house so I'm not sure what the nature of the photographs were. The final email sent a very compromising video of Jessica and warned her that if she didn't pay up, it would go viral. They also found another email to Jessica sending a link to a suicide site purporting to be from,' he looked down at his notes, 'Mocking Bird and Avenging Angel. It also looks like Jessica was in a state as there was a rambling voicemail asking Magnus to come home, that she would pay the money, do anything he wanted.'

'Were they able to download anything from the camera?'

asked Ewan.

'No sir. Both pen drives were missing.' said Jamie.

'I suppose it would have been too good to be true to have a live video of the victim being killed,' said Ewan, smiling ruefully. 'What about the phone? Anything that helps us identify who he is?'

'It was a pay as you go sir, but they managed to trace from the GPS history that he was in Belfast at the weekend.'

'Belfast? That's interesting. We'll contact the Belfast Police Service Northern Ireland in the morning. Well done team. I think it's time to head home now. Enjoy your evening.'

40

Ewan was surprised to find Suzie waiting for him when he arrived home. Hadn't she said she was going home to her own house tonight?

'Hello, you,' he said, giving her a lingering kiss. 'I wasn't expecting to see you tonight.'

'I know but after you left this morning, I got thinking about something. I didn't want to tell you over the phone so that's why I'm here.'

'Okay. I'm intrigued. Just let me get something to eat. I'm starving.'

'I've made some lasagne. It should still be warm. You sit down and I'll bring it through.'

'So how are you feeling tonight Suzie. You didn't look too clever this morning.'

'That's what got me thinking.'

'Hmm.'

'Well what does feeling sick in the morning generally signify I thought and what does having a late period generally signify I thought.'

Ewan almost choked on his pasta.

'You're pregnant,' he gasped.

'Well I don't know yet. I went out and bought one of these,' she said, waving a pregnancy testing kit in the air. 'I thought I would wait and do it when you got home.'

Ewan felt a lump in his throat and thought he was going to cry. He never thought he would become a father again. As they waited for the pregnancy testing kit to do its job, they sat holding hands and as if for the first time Ewan noticed how pale she looked and that she had lost some weight. It reminded him of the way she had looked when they met in Spain after Andy had died. She had been so vulnerable, and that bastard Josh had taken advantage of her. He hoped he was still rotting in jail and hadn't got out for good behaviour. The ten minutes that the kit took seemed like two hours. Gradually the little window began to change. *Pregnant* it read.

'Wow Suzie we are going to have our own little baby. Wow.'

Ewan laughed at himself and thought that he sounded just like his excitable young constable.

'Ewan are you sure you want this? We didn't plan to have a family did we?'

'Am I sure I want this? Of course. It's the most fantastic news you could give me.'

'I want to go and see the doctor Ewan before we tell anyone. I know these things are quite accurate, but I don't want to tempt fate. Also I'm no spring chicken so I would like the doctor to check me out and do any necessary tests for a women of my age.'

'You're not that old. You hear about women in their forties having babies all the time.'

'I know, but I don't want to take any chances.'

'I'm sure everything will be okay, but I get it. We don't want to tell everyone our good news without knowing for definite.'

'How do you think Jamie will react to having a new brother or sister?'

Ewan grinned thinking about his son who just loved Suzie.

'I'm sure he'll be delighted. He probably thought he would always be an only child because me and his mum have split up. I can't wait to tell him.'

Most of the remainder of the evening was spent in tears. Ewan hadn't imagined that such happy news could also be a source of such sorrow. Sorrow for Andy who would never experience the joy that they were experiencing now. Suzie and Andy had been together for ten years, yet Suzie had never become pregnant, so she had given up hope.

'I remember feeling so sad that first time I went to the market in *L'Aldea* after Andy died and it was full of baby clothes. My sadness turned to anger when Joy asked me why we had never had children. I blamed Andy and wished that I had stood up to him rather than just going along with what he wanted.'

'You were grieving Suzie; anger is one of the classic symptoms.'

'I know, but I feel so guilty now and so sad for Andy. All the things that he will miss out on. It just seems so unfair.'

Ewan felt grief sweep over him for his friend and all the

life experiences he would never know, but he recognised he couldn't let it take over. His survivor guilt after Andy died had led him to a very dark place which he had only managed to escape through the help of a therapist. Somehow talking about Andy and remembering the man they had both loved so much helped. But it was late when they went to bed and Ewan knew he wouldn't be at his best in the morning.

41

Ewan wasn't quite with it when he reached his workplace the following morning. He felt like he was floating and wondered if that was what addicts felt like when they took a hit. He had heard it made them feel euphoric and that was the only word he could think of right now to describe how he felt. He knew it was a mixture of the emotional evening they had spent talking about Andy but also because Suzie was pregnant, and he was going to become a father again. They had decided not to tell anyone yet and it would be another six weeks before he could tell his team even although he was bursting to share his news with them. The doctor had still to confirm that Suzie was definitely pregnant and if she was they wanted to wait until after the three month scan.

'You alright sir?' said Molly. 'You look a bit washed out.'

'Yes. I had a late night that's all. So what have we got on today team.'

'A visit to Greer Gibson, contacting the Belfast PSNI, contacting Jessica's publisher, Dorothy Hamilton, and I think a revisit to Barbara King.'

It was agreed that Jamie would go with Ewan to visit Greer Gibson since it was he who had found her. She lived in a ground floor flat in Partick and buzzed them in immediately as if she had been waiting for them. She was standing at her front door when they reached her flat. The close must have been smart at one time but was now looking tired and in need of a clean-up. Graffiti and cigarette dowts adorned the close entrance.

'Hello, I'm Greer Gibson,' she said. 'Come in.'

The living room was homely and cluttered. There were a couple of bookcases and Ewan spotted some of the same Jessica Aitken novels that sat on his bookshelf. He also noticed a cylinder type container of knitting needles and a rattan box beside it with knitting patterns. There was a photograph on the mantlepiece of Greer at a much younger age with two teenage children by her side. He recognised one of them as Sophie.

'Would you like a cup of tea?'

'Thanks,' said Ewan, wanting a little more time to take in his surroundings.

When she came through with the tea, she sat down in one of the well-worn armchairs and indicated the sofa for them to sit on. She sat silently waiting for them to start.

'So, Mrs Gibson, perhaps you could tell us what you know about Jessica Aitken.'

'Well I don't really know her as such. I became a fan last year after seeing her talking at *Aye Write* and I was thrilled when I went along to the circle meeting with Evie and found out she was there. I had bumped into her outside Waitrose only the previous week. She was so lovely.'

'Lovely. That's not what we've heard. We've heard that she could be prickly, outspoken.'

'Well she could sometimes be a little unkind I admit.'

'How did this manifest itself?'

'Well one example was that she wound up my client, Evie, about the father of her baby. It turns out she may have been right though.'

'Right about what?'

'That he would want custody of little Charlotte. Evie thought he wanted to have a relationship with her and the baby, but it looks as if it's the baby he and his wife want.'

'Was Jessica ever aggressive at the meetings?'

'No. Having said that I got the sense she was agitated as if something was worrying her.'

'So, would you say Jessica had enemies in the circle?'

'No. But I don't know why you are asking that. The papers said it was a man that was found dead in Jessica's house and that Jessica was missing. I assumed from what the papers reported that Jessica had committed the murder. But now you're asking about enemies. Do you think she's in danger too?'

'Until we find her, we must assume that it's a possibility. And what about you?'

'What about me?'

'Were you and Jessica enemies Mrs Fraser?'

Ewan was observing Greer's face closely, but she didn't look surprised by the use of her former name.

'You must have felt pretty upset at Jessica Aitken.'

'I was upset but not in the way that you mean.'

'What do you think I mean?'

'Well that I lost everything because of her. I've ended up in this grotty area when I could still have been in my house in Milngavie. You think that I'm upset because of that and might have wanted to punish her.'

'But that isn't how you felt?'

'I didn't connect Debbie Halligan with Jessica Aitken when I met her. I never met Debbie and had only seen a picture of her in the paper. It wasn't until she was talking about what had happened to her in the circle that I put two and two together. I was upset as hearing her tell her story was distressing. Paul had always denied her accusations, but by killing himself he left a huge doubt in my mind. Jessica seemed so sincere that I found it hard to disbelieve her. And if it was true she was to be pitied rather than hated.'

Ewan decided it was time to find out where Greer had been on Monday and Tuesday.

'I was at work then here. I also visited Evie to see how she was getting on with the baby on Monday evening.'

'Do you live on your own Mrs Fraser?'

'Yes, I live by myself.'

'So no-one can confirm when you were at home on those two days?'

'No, I'm sorry. But surely you don't suspect me of anything?'

'Until we know more, I'm afraid we have to keep an open mind about everyone involved.'

42

When Ewan and Jamie got back to the office, Ewan went into his room to catch up on mail while Molly and Jamie got on with their search for clues. He was sitting in his office in a reverie about the future and how he would break the news of Suzie's pregnancy to his son when there was a knock on his door. He looked up and was surprised to see Jade and wondered what could have brought her into the office today. Normally she would just have phoned him or got him to go to her office.

'Hi Jade, this is a surprise. To what do I owe the pleasure?'

She ignored his remark and threw a file down on his desk.

'I thought you would want to see this. It's a report from the SOCO's on the DNA I provided to them from the deceased.'

'How come you've got the report? It should have come to us.'

'Well I was over at their office and they told me what they had discovered so I offered to bring the report over. Hope that's okay with you.'

'Yes of course. I was just wondering.'

'The DNA was put on the national database to see if it revealed anything and it turns out he is known to the Belfast police. His name is Kevin Cooper.'

'That would tie in with what the techies found from his phone. What do they have on him?'

'Domestic violence. Apparently, his wife Sophie was seen in A and E several times and the police were called by the nursing staff but when it came to it she didn't press charges.'

'Did you say Sophie?'

'Yes. Is it significant?'

'You bet it is. That's the name of Paul Fraser's daughter.'

Jade looked puzzled.

'The teacher who groomed Jessica Aitken when she was a teenager. I've been looking for a connection and here it is. I'll contact the Belfast police and see if we can find his wife. We need someone to identify him. Thanks for coming in Jade. It was good of you.'

'No problem,' she said, turning to leave and Ewan wondered why she hadn't just left it to the SOCO's to let him know. It wasn't like her to be helpful but the reason for her altruism soon became clear.

'Oh, by the way, I bumped into your ex the other day.'

'Maggie?'

'Yes. I was in the ante-natal unit at the Queen Elizabeth with my sister who was having a scan and I met her and her 'friend' Fiona there. Have you three got some good news to announce?'

His jaw dropped. Was Maggie pregnant? It was the last thing he was expecting Jade to tell him. He had learned over the years not to react to criminals when they wound him up and he had found it useful in his personal life too, but he couldn't disguise how he felt. Jade got just what she wanted.

'Sorry Ewan didn't you know? I just assumed that since she's now married to a woman, you had donated your sperm to make their little family complete.'

With that bombshell, Jade continued on her way out of his office leaving a hiss of triumph hovering in the air. Ewan didn't know what to think. Why hadn't Maggie told him? Perhaps her and Fiona were being like him and Suzie, waiting before sharing their good news. He wondered how Jamie would take it. He was now going to have two half siblings to get used to in his life.

'Everything alright sir?' asked Molly.

He hadn't noticed her coming in and looked up surprised.

'Eh yes, thanks.'

'What did Jade want?'

'She had some information on Magnus Nelson. His real name is Kevin Cooper and he is in police records in Belfast because of accusations of domestic abuse but there are no criminal charges as they were dropped before he got to court.'

'So it looks like he was up to no good with Jessica if he was using an alias.'

'Looks like it. But the thing is I think I know what his connection to Jessica was.'

'Well tell me sir, don't keep me in suspense.'

'His wife's name is Sophie.'

'Wow, Paul Fraser's daughter.'

'Yes. Can you get in touch with Belfast and ask them to

contact her. In the absence of Jessica, we'll need her to identify the body.'

'Will do.'

'Oh and check with the airlines flying from Belfast to Glasgow whether Kevin Cooper was on a flight this week.'

'Shall I check the car hire people too sir? See if he picked a car up at the airport.'

'Yes. Good idea.'

43

Ewan decided he needed a break to digest this news that Jade had given him so decided to go home for an hour before visiting the Kings that evening. The flat seemed empty without Suzie waiting for him. Joy, Andy's mum, had made a flying visit over from Spain where she ran an art retreat in El Paraiso, so Suzie had taken the opportunity to meet up with her so that she could tell her their news face to face. They had agreed that it would be better coming from Suzie only rather than the two of them. Joy had recovered well from her cancer treatment, but she could still be volatile at times and he supposed she might feel resentful that Ewan was going to be a father with her son's widow.

He decided he would phone Maggie and just check that what Jade had told him was true. He was sure it was. Jade could be malicious, but he was sure she wouldn't lie about something like that. He heated up some leftovers from the day before and sat down in front of the TV, which was showing the latest news. There was the usual Brexit disagreements and hints that Theresa May was about to resign. He felt relieved to see something different when a familiar photograph appeared on the screen. Jessica. She was one of the highlights on the Scottish news. He turned up the volume and waited with interest to hear what Flinty was about to say.

'A body was found this week in the home of Jessica Aitken, the Glasgow crime writer. The body has not been identified but we can confirm that it was not Jessica. She is not a suspect at this time, but we would like to hear from her to help with our inquiries. So if anyone has any idea where she might be, please ring the number on the screen.'

Short and sweet. Nothing about Jade's discovery. Ewan realised he hadn't told Flinty yet and would need to update him asap. He didn't want to get on the wrong side of his boss this early in their relationship. He felt excited at the thought of Kevin Cooper's wife coming over to identify the body. It would give him an opportunity to interview her and perhaps get to the bottom of what had happened. As far as he was concerned, Jessica wasn't the only one in the frame anymore, but he hoped she would turn up soon. It looked like she was involved one way or another.

When the news finished, he switched off the TV and decided to telephone Maggie. Fiona picked up on the third ring.

'Hi Fiona, it's Ewan.'

'Yes, I know it's you Ewan,' she replied. He always felt an undercurrent of dislike from the woman but perhaps he was just projecting his own feelings.

'Is Maggie there?'

'No, I'm sorry. She's taken Jamie to his football practice.'

'Oh yes, I forgot it was today.'

'Is there something I can help you with?'

Ewan considered whether to raise it with her or wait until he could speak to Maggie. He decided to bite the bullet.

'I wondered if you and Maggie had some news to share with me.'

'News? What do you mean?'

'Well I heard from a friend that you and Maggie were in the ante-natal clinic at the Queen Elizabeth today.'

'You mean that Jade Scott. I thought she would have problems keeping her mouth shut. She's such a cow.'

'So what she told me is true. You and Maggie are going to have a baby.'

'Not that it's any of your business, but yes we are.'

'I think it *is* my business. It will affect my son and anything that affects him is my business.'

'Look I think you better speak to Maggie before we both say something we'll regret. I'll get her to phone you when she gets home.'

Ewan felt outraged but then realised that he hadn't told Maggie about Suzie being pregnant and Jamie would be as affected by that birth as by Maggie and Fiona's baby.

44

By the time Ewan picked up Molly and got to Barbara King's house, it was after 6pm. Barbara had told Jamie that they would be home by then, so Ewan was surprised to see the house in darkness. He hoped they hadn't done a runner as well. However, he had no sooner switched off the engine of his Nissan Qashqai than a Volvo Estate drew up and the family got out. They either didn't notice them or pretended not to see them as they made their way up the path to their house without casting a glance in their direction. Normally he would have let them get settled before knocking but he wanted to catch them by surprise if possible. It would put them on a weaker footing when he was questioning them.

Rory King was just opening the door when Ewan called out to them. Barbara and Rory's faces were a picture of disappointment when they saw him and Molly approaching them.

'Your constable said you wouldn't get here until after dinner,' said Barbara.

'Sorry is that what he said? I meant around 6pm and here it is 6.15pm,' he said, casually looking at his watch. 'I won't keep you long.'

The family jostled their way into the house with him and Molly following on behind them so that there was a crush at the front door as they removed shoes, hung up coats and deposited bags despite the generous size of their hallway.

'I'm starving Mum,' said the boy.

'Sorry Ben you'll need to wait until the police have finished with us before you can get your dinner. Why don't you grab a snack just now to keep you going.'

She gave him a smile, but he didn't smile back just glared at her before going through to the kitchen.

'Coming Ella?' he said, looking at the girl who followed meekly behind.

Rory King's face was like thunder and anything but welcoming at this intrusion to his home. Ewan wondered if he would recognise him from their school days, but if he did he didn't say anything.

'What can we help you with? I believe my wife gave you

the information you were looking for yesterday.'

'It appears that she didn't tell us everything Mr King.'

He was running his fingers through his hair and his face was almost puce. His wife went over and placed her hand on his back and when he looked at her she took a deep breath as if suggesting that he follow suit. He shrugged her hand away and went to the drinks cabinet and poured himself a large whisky.

'I won't offer you one as you're on duty.'

'Perhaps a tea or coffee?' said his wife, more reasonably.

Ewan decided to give her something to do.

'Coffee please milk and no sugar for me thanks,' said Ewan.

'And the same for me,' said Molly.

While Barbara made the coffee, her husband sat nursing his whisky taking little sips from time to time and completely ignoring Ewan and Molly. When Barbara came in with the coffees, the rich aroma made him glad he had got her to make some.

'Have you found Jessica yet?' she asked. 'I'm really worried about her. She was rambling about hearing voices the last time she phoned me. I hope she hasn't done anything silly.'

'Silly. Like murder someone do you mean?'

'No, I didn't mean that, although it's possible given her state of mind. I meant like taking her own life.'

'Was she prone to suicidal thoughts?'

'No but then she never normally drank much and whatever was happening to her was obviously making her self-medicate with alcohol.'

'Why do you say that?'

Ewan wondered how she knew Jessica had been drinking and speculated fleetingly if she had been to Jessica's house.

'It was her text. Jessica is very articulate but she was rambling and there were lots of typos.'

'Do you have that text?'

'No sorry. I'm afraid my phone packed up and I had to buy a new one.'

How convenient he thought.

'From our investigations, it would appear that you and Jessica had a falling out. Is that correct Mrs King?'

She swallowed and blinked before answering.

'Who told you?'

'It doesn't really matter does it? Can you just answer the question.'

'Yes.'

'Why didn't you tell us this when we saw you earlier?'

'I didn't want Jessica to get into any more trouble than she was already in.'

'So you think Jessica's in trouble then?'

'Well she must be if there's a dead body in her house.'

Barbara was beginning to lose some of her composure Ewan noted happily.

'What happened Mrs King? Why did you and Jessica fall out?'

'I was having to wind up the group and she wasn't happy about it. I think I told you earlier she became quite attached to me. She reacted badly.'

'What did she do?'

'She spat in my face and called me a prostitute. Said I was selling my love for money.'

'When was that Mrs King?'

'It was Monday. After the last circle meeting.'

'So it's fair to say Jessica was pretty upset when she left you that day.'

'Yes.'

'Have either of you ever heard of someone called Kevin Cooper?'

Barbara and Rory looked at each other and then said no jointly. Ewan wasn't sure whether they were telling the truth.

'Who is Kevin Cooper?' asked Barbara.

'We believe he is the man who was found in Jessica's house.'

'So it wasn't Jessica's boyfriend Magnus who was found dead.'

'We believe they may be one and the same.'

'Oh that's awful. Jessica would have been devastated to find out that he was lying to her. She was deeply in love. I had never seen her like that before.'

'Do either of you know anyone called Mia?'

'No,' they said in unison, a bit too quickly for Ewan's liking. He felt there was some kind of undercurrent between them that he wasn't getting.

'That was the name that Kevin Cooper used on his emails to Jessica and we wondered why he had used that name.'

'Sorry, we can't help you Inspector,' said Barbara.

'He also sent an email to her under the names Mockingbird and Avenging Angel. Any idea who they might be?'

Rory King began coughing and spluttering and his wife looked over at him with a worried frown.

'Sorry. The whisky went down the wrong way,' he said, lifting up his glass. Ewan didn't believe him but was at a loss as to why he would have a reaction to those names.

'Finally, Mrs King. When you gave us the list of people who attended your circle meeting, you didn't tell us that Evie Boyle's support worker also attended.'

Barbara's face turned pink and then she put on a puzzled expression.

'I'm sorry Inspector, I thought you only wanted the names of the members of the circle. I'm sure that's what your constable asked me to provide.'

'You didn't know that Greer Gibson was the wife of the teacher who groomed Jessica?'

'What? Are you sure? She never said anything,'

Ewan was sure she was lying.

'Although I remember now that she had to leave the room when Jessica was talking about what had happened to her. How awful.'

'Right well I think that's us finished. We'll let you get on with your dinner. Sorry to have disturbed you.'

Ewan could see their tension physically leaving them and felt sure that there was more to them than met the eye. What else did they have to hide?

45

It had been arranged that Sophie Cooper would be flown over to identify her husband, so Ewan made his way to Glasgow Airport to pick her up. He stood waiting outside the arrivals area for flights from Belfast. The plane was on time, so he didn't need to hang about too long. He was surprised that he recognised her straight away. She hadn't aged well but there was still something of her youthful self remaining. He wondered if she would recognise him. They had been friends back in the day and if truth be told he had hoped it might become more but he had given her a body swerve when she got into drugs. They had obviously taken their toll on her and he wondered what kind of life she had been living for these past twenty odd years with Kevin Cooper.

'Sophie Cooper?' he asked quietly.

'Yes,' she said, 'you must be Detective Inspector McNeil. They told me you'd be waiting for me.'

She didn't look directly at him and he got the impression she was feeling awkward. He wondered if it was because she recognised him, but she didn't say anything, and he decided it was best to do the same.

She didn't speak on the way to the mortuary and he wondered how she was feeling. It must be difficult going to identify someone you had loved. She looked vulnerable so he decided to ask her if she would like her mum to go along with her to identify her husband.

'My mum?'

'Yes I could phone her and pick her up.'

'How do you know my mum?'

'She's been involved in our investigation.'

'I haven't seen my mum for over twenty years.'

'So would you like me to contact her?'

She nodded and Ewan phoned Molly to pick up Greer Gibson and bring her to the mortuary. She was waiting for them when they arrived and flew towards her daughter with arms open wide. Twenty odd years was a long time to be separated from your child. The two women intermittently hugged and sobbed and gazed at each other for what seemed a long time.

Ewan felt a lump in his throat when he looked at them. They made him think of Andy and what it must have been like for him to become reconciled with his mum, Joy, after all the years of separation.

When they had calmed down a little, Ewan went up to Sophie.

'Are you ready Mrs Cooper?'

She looked at her mum and then at Ewan.

'Can Mum come in with me.'

'Yes, of course.'

The identification was a difficult one. When the three of them got in, Sophie looked at her husband's body lying on the table. He looked better than the last time Ewan had seen him, peaceful even with his eyes closed covering the damage the needle had done.

'Is this your husband, Kevin Cooper, Mrs Cooper?'

'Yes that's him. That's Kevin,' said Sophie.

Suddenly, she began to scream and bent over the dead man weeping and shouting at him to such an extent that Ewan thought she was going to hit him. Her mum did her best to calm her down and pull her back from the body but to no avail. He decided he better intervene.

'Thanks Mrs Cooper. Let's get you out of here now,' he said, taking her arm firmly and escorting her from the room.

She was still crying when they got outside into the hospital corridor and Ewan was reluctant to tell her she would need to come in for an interview, but he had no option. She might hold the key to all of this.

'I can see how distressed you are, but we'll need to ask you some questions Mrs Cooper.'

'She's just identified her dead husband. Do you have to do it now?' said Greer, taking her daughter's hand and giving it a rub.

'I'm afraid we don't have much time. Her flight back to Belfast is at 7.30pm and we really need to find out more about Kevin.'

'Alright Inspector. Let me take her back to mine for a cup of tea and then I'll bring her along to the Police Station.'

46

As promised, Greer brought Sophie back to the station and he was pleased to see that she seemed much calmer.

'This is an informal interview Mrs Cooper. You are not a suspect for the murder of Kevin Cooper as the alibi which you provided has been confirmed by the police in Belfast. However, it would help us immensely if you could give us a picture of who Kevin was. Perhaps you could begin by telling us how you met him and when.'

'I met Kevin when I was sixteen. I ran away from home with him hoping that he would take me to exciting places but the furthest we got was Belfast where his family lived.'

She paused and Ewan stopped himself from filling the silence. He had been taught that the best way of interviewing witnesses or suspects was to initially let them talk freely without intervening and then picking up on relevant details. One of the most important lessons he had learned on the course was to ask open questions and refrain from leading the witness. Too many police officers had a theory and framed their questions in such a way that witnesses confirmed that theory.

'I realised I was pregnant when I got to Belfast, so Kevin and I married fairly quickly after that. We had a daughter. I was a mess at that time and unfortunately having Mia didn't help nor did having Kevin as a husband.'

Ewan sensed Molly sitting up at the mention of the name Mia.

'I suffered post-natal depression and Kevin stepped in and took over. It meant that Kevin and Mia became close to each other in the early years. He was daddy of the year as far as she was concerned.'

She sighed and took a gulp of her tea.

'Kevin was controlling Inspector. He used my problems to undermine me in any way he could. By the time he was finished with me I thought I was the worst person in the world; a person who couldn't even look after her own daughter. I self-soothed with prescribed drugs and alcohol. This only perpetuated my problems and gave Kevin an excuse to blame me when he lost his temper. Of course he would always ask for forgiveness afterwards and I always gave it because I blamed myself. I constantly tiptoed around him and was terrified that he would one day turn on Mia. Fortunately, he never did.'

She took another gulp of her tea and continued without looking at them.

'As Mia grew up she could see what was going on. She wanted to study Psychology and only applied to Queen's University so that she could continue to live at home. She tried to get me to leave him, but I couldn't. I had no way of supporting myself. I had never worked and at that time was still drug and alcohol dependent. Even when I became clean, it just seemed impossible. I had made my bed.'

She looked up at them and smiled.

'You have no idea what it felt like today looking at his body. To know that he would never hurt me again. To know that I was free. Thank God he was murdered in Glasgow and I had an alibi or I'm sure I would have been your prime suspect.'

Ewan thought she certainly had a motive but what he had to remember was that it didn't matter that the victim was a bastard, he was still dead, and it was his duty to get justice for him.

'You mentioned you had a daughter, Mrs Cooper. Mia I think you said her name was.'

'Yes that's right.'

'Where is Mia now?'

'She's gone travelling. After she graduated she decided to take some time out before looking for a job. I'm not quite sure where exactly. All I know is that she's in Europe somewhere. You know what young people are like. They go off radar and then come back when they need something.'

'So she had stopped worrying about leaving you alone with Kevin?'

Sophie looked nonplussed by this question.

'I hadn't thought but I suppose she must have decided that she couldn't do anything as I refused to leave him.'

'So she doesn't know her dad is dead?'

'No. I've texted and left a message on her voicemail to contact me urgently, but so far she hasn't responded.'

'Perhaps we could help you with that.'

'Could you? I didn't realise.'

'Mia was the name that Kevin used to send emails to Jessica Aitken. He was blackmailing her you know.'

'Blackmailing her? I thought they were in a relationship.'

'What made you think that?'

'When the local police told me he had been found dead in this woman's house I just assumed. Why was he blackmailing her?'

'Do you know who Jessica Aitken is?'

'Not really. I know she's an author that Kevin liked. He had a few of her books but other than that no.

'Jessica Aitken is Debbie Halligan.'

'Debbie Halligan, the girl that my dad groomed.'

'Yes. Kevin was trying to blackmail her. He accused her of lying about what your dad did and said that if she didn't fess up to it or pay £50,000 he would go to the papers and put compromising photographs of her on the internet.'

'Poor woman. She must have been so distressed. No wonder she killed him.'

'Well we don't know for sure that she did yet. But what I'm interested in Mrs Cooper is whether you knew anything about what Kevin was up to.'

'No.'

'Where did you think your husband was every Friday for the last five months? We have on record that he caught the Friday afternoon flight from Belfast to Glasgow and returned on Saturday afternoon almost every week from the beginning of the year.'

'I was obviously aware that he had changed his routine, but I didn't know he was coming to Glasgow. He told me he was working. I had no reason to disbelieve him as he travelled a lot in his job. I never questioned Kevin on what he was doing Inspector. He wouldn't allow it and I learned over the years not to rock the boat.'

There was a knock on the door and an officer popped his head round.

'Phone call for you sir.'

It was Jamie.

'Sorry to disturb you sir but I managed to get a hold of Jessica's publisher, Dorothy Hamilton. She's given me the address of the cottage in Pitlochry that Jessica uses. She also said something interesting sir. She said that a woman had phoned Jessica purporting to be Nancy Gardener from True-Life Magazine. However, when she contacted Ms Gardener she denied getting in touch with Jessica. I just wondered if it might have been Kevin's wife who made the call.'

'Good work Jamie. Get on to the local police at Pitlochry and get them to check out that cottage.'

47

When he and Molly finished interviewing Sophie Cooper, they dropped her off at Greer Gibson's flat. It was agreed that Jamie would pick her up for her flight from Glasgow Airport back to Belfast. The local police had confirmed that Jessica was at the cottage in Pitlochry and were bringing her in. It would take them approximately an hour and a half to get to Glasgow, so they decided to go and have something to eat rather than go back to Osprey House as they probably wouldn't have time for dinner yet again.

'What did you think of Sophie Cooper sir? Did you believe her when she said she hadn't made that phone call to Jessica Aitken,' asked Molly, tucking into her meatballs and pasta. Ewan had opted for pizza and salad.

'To be honest I couldn't make a call on that. She's been controlled by that man since she was a young girl so who knows what things he made her do over the years.'

'But why would she lie now sir when he's dead? She doesn't need to protect him.'

'No, but she may feel she needs to protect herself or someone else.'

'You mean her daughter Mia? Could she have been involved? It was her name that Kevin used in those emails.'

'I think it's a possibility. He could have threatened to hurt her mum if she didn't. We need to try and find out where she is. It's strange that she's gone to Europe when she stayed at home during her years at university. I wonder why she stopped worrying about her mother's safety.'

His mobile rang as they were finishing their meal. It was Maggie. This wasn't the time for baby talk, so he hit the reject button. He would phone her later. Interviewing Jessica Aitken was his priority just now. They made their way back to the station and it wasn't long before Jessica arrived. She was a mess. Her hair looked as if it hadn't been washed for days and her eyes were dead. Ewan wondered if she was on something. He thanked the local police for bringing her through and then moved on to the formalities.

'Deborah Halligan, I am Detective Inspector Ewan McNeil

from Police Scotland's Major Investigations Team. We would like to speak to you in connection with the murder of Kevin Cooper. You do not have to say anything but anything you do say will be written down and may be used in evidence against you.'

'I'm Jessica Aitken, not Deborah Halligan. She died a long time ago.'

'Did you hear what I said Miss Aitken? We want to talk to you in connection with the murder of Kevin Cooper.'

'Who's Kevin Cooper? What are you talking about?'

'It's possible that he and your boyfriend Magnus Nelson are the same person.'

'I don't understand. You're telling me that Magnus wasn't called Magnus.'

'His body was identified today as Kevin Cooper.'

'Are you arresting me Inspector?'

'Not yet. We just want some help with our inquiries. You are aware that we have been looking for you?'

'No. There's no television in the cottage.'

'Do you know that a man was murdered in your apartment?'

'Yes, of course, it was me who murdered him.'

'You murdered him? You're confessing?'

'Yes it was me. But I thought I had murdered Magnus. I don't know anyone called Kevin.'

Given that Jessica had confessed, they formally arrested her and told her she could have legal representation. He was surprised when she asked for Rory King as he assumed she would have her own solicitor that she could call on. But he supposed the legalities in the publishing world were vastly different from that of the criminal world. It was late by the time Rory King finished talking to his client, so it was agreed to keep Jessica in a holding cell and carry out a formal interview in the morning. Rory King was looking almost as pissed off as he had been when they had gone to his house, but he told them he was concerned for his client and suggested that Jessica should be put on suicide watch.

48

When Ewan caught up with Suzie that night she was upbeat. Joy had taken the news of her pregnancy well and Suzie felt it had drawn them closer. Like her and Ewan they had talked a lot about Andy and what it would have been like for him to become a father.

'I've got something to tell you Suzie.'

'What is it? Something good I hope.'

'I suppose it depends on how you look at it.'

'Tell me then,' she said.

'Jade came into my office yesterday. You know Jade,' he said, hoping he didn't need to tell her.

'Yes I know Jade. You had a brief fling with her when you split up from Maggie. Is she working on this case with you then?'

'Yes. So she came in to tell me that they had discovered the identity of the murder victim. I did wonder why she had come to tell me rather than just phone or leave it up to the SOCO's to let me know.'

'Maybe she still fancies you.'

'Don't be silly. Hates me more like.'

'Hates you?'

'Well because of what happened between us.'

'And what did happen between you?'

'It was only ever a casual thing, from my side anyway. But she took it badly when I told her I didn't want to become more serious. I think perhaps she was hoping it might have gone somewhere but I wasn't in the right place. She was transitional. I needed Jade or someone like Jade to help me get over what had happened with Maggie.'

'So you used her?'

'I suppose but don't we all use people from time to time to get our needs met. You used Josh in a way.'

'Josh? Eff off Ewan. He used me that was for sure. He took advantage of me when I was vulnerable, and it sounds like you took advantage of Jade at a time when perhaps she was vulnerable.'

'Why is it always the woman who is vulnerable. I was vulnerable. I had been dumped by my wife for her best friend and *my* best friend had just been killed. I needed something or someone at that time and Jade was it. She threw me a lifeline in an emergency situation and I will always be grateful to her for that but surely it doesn't mean that I should have to spend the rest of my life with her.'

'You can dress it up anyway you like Ewan, but you led her on by the sounds of things and I am really disappointed in you. I thought you were better than that.'

She flung herself down on the couch and burst into tears.

'Suzie, Suzie, come here darling. Why on earth are we fighting. This is all in the past and we are giving Jade what she wants. She was trying to create mischief and she has succeeded. Please, please don't let her come between us.'

Suzie sobbed and pulled tissues out of the box in handfuls throwing them on the floor as she finished with them until it looked like a snowstorm had landed. Suddenly she started to laugh. He didn't quite know what to do but thought he would laugh too.

'Why are you laughing?' she asked.

'I don't know,' he confessed. 'Just hoping it will ease the tension. Why are you laughing?'

'Hormones I guess. The nurse did say that my moods might be up and down as my body adjusts. Sorry Ewan. I know you didn't mean to take advantage of Jade but just because you didn't mean to doesn't mean that you didn't. The difference with Josh was that he did want to take advantage of me and succeeded.'

Now that Suzie had calmed down, Ewan decided this wasn't the best time to share his news about Maggie and Fiona. He didn't want her to get wound up again.

'Let's sit down and watch a movie and try to calm ourselves,' he said instead. 'I got some sushi from the deli so shall we have that?'

'I don't know if I should be eating raw fish.'

'I didn't think. Sorry. I'll need to read up on what pregnant woman can and cannot eat,' he said, sitting down beside her and giving her a cuddle.

49

Ewan had no sooner got into his car to go to work than his phone rang. It was Maggie. He decided he better answer as she had tried several times to get him yesterday.

'Good morning Maggie.'

'Morning. I tried to get you all day yesterday Ewan. Why haven't you picked up?'

'Sorry I've been on a case and couldn't answer. Thanks for phoning me back.'

He decided he would try to sound reasonable in the hope that it would avoid an argument. It must have worked as Maggie sounded quite calm and reasonable when she spoke.

'Look Ewan, I'm sorry you had to find out from Jade that Fiona was pregnant.'

'Fiona is pregnant. I thought it was you from the way she spoke.'

'Does it make any difference? We are still having a baby and it obviously has implications for Jamie.'

'Yes, of course it does. Can I ask who the father is, and will he be involved in the child's life? I'm only asking as obviously that would affect Jamie too.'

'It was donor sperm if you must know so you don't need to worry about any other *man* coming into Jamie's life.'

He could feel his hackles rising but took a breath while he waited for her continue.

'The thing is though that Fiona and I have decided to change our childcare arrangements. We've decided that once the baby is born I'll go back to work, and she'll become a full time mum.'

'I see.'

'That's why I think it might be better if we reviewed our current custody arrangement.'

'You know I'm always as flexible as I can be within the confines of my job Maggie.'

'But you won't be the only one with a job Ewan. What Fiona and I would like is for you to have prime custody of Jamie and for me to have visiting rights.'

Ewan was stunned. He hadn't been expecting this. What

on earth would Suzie say? He knew she loved Jamie, but would she want him living with them 24/7 when she had just had a baby of her own for the first time.

'Are you still there Ewan?'

'Yes.'

'I know you will need time to digest the implications but I know that Jamie loves Suzie and that she loves him so I didn't think it would be a problem.'

'I'm just wondering why the current arrangement can't continue if Fiona is going to be a full time mum.'

'It's her first time having her own baby Ewan, so she wants to have quality time to concentrate on her rather than have a ten year old needing attention too.'

'I'll obviously need to talk it over with Suzie, but my priority will always be what's best for Jamie. I wouldn't like him to feel that you didn't want him because you and Fiona were having a baby of your own.'

It was the wrong thing to say. Her calmness left her.

'What's best for Jamie is my priority too, you sanctimonious prick. Jamie knows how much I love him. Times are changing Ewan and you'll need to adjust and change with them. Phone me when you've had a chance to speak to Suzie.'

She hung up and he couldn't help wondering if he was being a sanctimonious prick.

50

Ewan didn't have a lot of time to think about the implications of what Maggie had told him as Jessica's solicitor had arrived by the time he reached Partick. Rory King had been replaced by Steven McIntyre who was more experienced in dealing with criminal work and Ewan found himself relieved that he didn't have to look at Rory's permanently irritated expression. He and Molly made their way to the interview room and Ewan wondered how it would go. Jessica looked the picture of vulnerability. She sat with her eyes staring at the table not looking up when they came in.

'Interview with Deborah Halligan otherwise known as Jessica Aitken in Partick Police Station,' began Ewan. 'Present at the interview, Ms Aitken, her solicitor Steven McIntyre, Detective Sergeant Molly Brown and Detective Inspector Ewan McNeil.'

Jessica was still staring at the table, so he began his questioning. His voice was gentle.

'So Ms Aitken, perhaps you would tell us in your own words what happened.'

She didn't look up.

'I killed him. I thought he loved me, but I found out that night that he had been using me and messing with my head. He succeeded. That's all there is to it.'

'Tell me how he messed with your head as you put it. Maybe start from when you first began going out with Magnus.'

She told them most of what they already knew but it appeared that she had been trolled by Mockingbird and Avenging Angel before Kevin began sending her emails Ewan took a note to get her phone checked by the Intelligence Analysts. It might be relevant, or it might not.

'Tell me how you killed him Ms Aitken.'

'I hit him first with a prosecco bottle and then stuck a knitting needle in his eye. I had researched how to kill someone with a knitting needle for one of my books and for some reason it came back to me when I saw my knitting lying on the settee.'

'What made you hit him.'

'When he realised I knew what had been going on he gave up all pretence. He said the most horrible things and I could see he was enjoying it. Sneering at me, telling me what a gullible bitch I was, how he had never loved me. He even put on the voice he had used to make me think Darren was speaking to me.'

She paused and for the first time Ewan thought she was feeling something. Until now everything had been said in an expressionless voice.

'Who is Darren?'

'He's my twin. He died at birth.'

'What made you think Darren was talking to you?'

She looked at Ewan and he thought he could see rage in her eyes despite her flat demeanour.

'A voice that told me it was Darren. What do you think made me think he was talking to me?'

'And then what happened?'

'He grabbed me and said that if I didn't pay him the £50,000 he had asked for in the emails he sent me, he would go to True-Life Magazine.'

'Was that the emails from *IamMia*?'

'Yes, apparently he wanted to put me off the scent by calling himself by a woman's name.'

'Go on.'

'I spat in his face and screamed that I would never pay him. He could do his worst.'

Ewan could imagine the scene. Jessica was obviously good at spitting as it was her weapon of choice against her therapist and it confirmed why there was saliva on the dead man's face.

'That's when he lost it. He pushed me towards the wall but as he did so, he stood on the prosecco bottle, lost his balance and we both went down. I was screaming and trying to get away, but he was too strong. His hand was over my mouth and I couldn't breathe. His cruel, horrible words were still ringing in my ears, so when I felt the bottle I knew I had to hit him with it; hit him for all the bad things he had done to me. I just kept hitting and hitting him until he went limp.'

'And the knitting needle? Magnus was already dead when you stuck that in his eye. You must have deliberately turned his body over to do that.'

'Must I? I don't remember. All I know is that when I saw my knitting lying on the settee, I pulled one of the needles out and stuck it in his eye. I don't know why. I thought he loved me.'

She began to sob, and Molly pushed the tissue box towards her.

'It was like Mr Fraser all over again. He led me on and then told me it was all a mistake. It was all in my head. I couldn't let Magnus do that to me too. So, I killed him.'

'I think we should have a break Inspector,' said Steven McIntyre, speaking for the first time. 'My client is clearly distressed.'

51

Ewan and Molly made their way along to the canteen for a coffee. Jamie was waiting for them.

'How's it going sir,' he asked.

'Her description of how she killed Magnus ties in with the evidence and her motivation is clear. Kevin Cooper had been messing with her head.'

'But she hasn't explained how she knew what he was up to. What it was that gave the game away,' said Jamie.

'What I don't get,' said Molly, 'is why he was blackmailing Jessica. From the way Sophie spoke during her interview, she believed that her dad had acted inappropriately towards Jessica.'

'Yes that was strange. And who was the woman who phoned Jessica if it wasn't Sophie?' said Jamie.

As his colleagues discussed the ins and outs of the case, he thought back to last night. He hadn't managed to tell Suzie that Fiona was pregnant and now he had the added news that Maggie was going back to work and wanted him to have full time custody of Jamie. He wondered how Suzie would react.

His thoughts were interrupted by the announcement that Jessica was ready to continue the interview.

'You said Ms Aitken that Kevin gave up all pretence when he found out you knew what he was up to. How did you know.'

'It was those ugly tissue boxes he gave me. I knocked one over at the same time as I knocked over the prosecco bottle and it fell open to reveal a pen drive. I knew what it was because I had used something similar in one of my stories. It was the only explanation of how the blackmailer had taken those photographs and video. I didn't want to believe it. I loved Magnus, I thought we were going to be married.'

She began sobbing again. Ewan suggested that Molly get her a glass of water before they continued. He didn't want the solicitor to call another break in the interview. They would be here all night. When she had recovered, he began the questioning again.

'What happened to those pen drives Ms Aitken? They

weren't in the boxes.'

'I took them out and threw them into Faskally Loch. I didn't want anyone to see what was on them. I was ashamed.'

'Can you tell us what connection the man you knew as Magnus Nelson had with Paul Fraser? It appears that he was trying to punish you and extort money from you because of what had happened with Mr Fraser when you were a teenager and I'm wondering why.'

'I don't know. Maybe when we started corresponding on Facebook, he did some research into my writing career and found my memoir and that gave him the idea of blackmailing me. I don't know.'

'You didn't ask him that night when he was tormenting and taunting you.'

'I begged him to tell me why he was doing it Inspector, but his only answer was *because he could.*'

'He didn't mention his wife Sophie Cooper or his daughter Mia Cooper?'

'Mia Cooper. You mean there is someone called Mia?'

'Yes. It turns out that his wife Sophie Cooper is Mr Fraser's daughter and Mia his granddaughter.'

'Well he never told me.'

'Why did you run away after you killed Magnus?'

'I don't know. When I realised what I had done I was horrified and frightened. I wasn't thinking straight. Remember I had been drinking so although it had begun to wear off I wasn't my usual self. I needed time to take in everything and I did what I always do when I need time alone, I went to the cottage in Pitlochry. It's a safe haven for me.'

'When were you planning to hand yourself in?'

'I wasn't. I was planning to take pills that Magnus had put in the bathroom cabinet for me in case I couldn't sleep. He had plenty being in the trade you understand.'

'Were you worried about going to prison? Is that why you contemplated taking your own life?'

'Not that Inspector although I don't relish the thought of spending my life in jail. It's because I have nothing left to live for. No Magnus, no Mum, no Barbara, no friends and, if those photographs and the video go viral, no reputation. My career as a writer will be over.'

She began to sob again, and Ewan decided she had had enough. He still wasn't convinced that she was telling him the whole truth. There were some issues with forensics, and he felt that they needed to find this Mia Cooper. He would need to speak to Flinty.

52

It had been a long day and normally he would have looked forward to going home, having a glass of wine and snuggling up with Suzie but tonight he was reluctant. Maggie had plans that would affect him and Suzie and he didn't know how he would tell Suzie or how she would react. They had been in their own little bubble, looking forward to having a child together and living happily ever after. But life wasn't like that. It threw you a curve ball every now and then.

'Hi Suzie. That's me home,' he called, and as he turned from hanging up his jacket, there she was looking beautiful.

'I've saved you some food. Come on through when you're ready.'

'Suzie I've something to tell you,' he said, when they were sat at the table. She looked at him expectantly but didn't say anything.

'Remember when we spoke about Jade the other night, well I didn't get around to telling you why I had brought her up.'

She laughed.

'No, I didn't give you much of a chance did I? So why did you bring her up?'

'She told me that she had seen Maggie and Fiona in the antenatal clinic.'

'The antenatal clinic?' her smile had become a puzzled expression.

'Fiona is going to have a baby,' Ewan said, deciding to get to the point, 'and Maggie is going back to work to support them. Maggie wants me to have full time custody of Jamie so that Fiona can have quality time with the new baby.'

Suzie was silent. Ewan's stomach was in knots as he waited for her to respond. Would she say she wanted quality time with her baby too? Would it mean their plans for moving in together wouldn't happen?

'Don't look so worried Ewan. I know this is a big change for you and you'll need to think about your hours and everything, but I've decided I'm going to take time out to look after our baby and having Jamie around to help me will be an added bonus. But we'll need a bigger house, of course, and preferably one with a garden.'

'Oh Suzie. Thank you. Thank you. I don't know why I was so worried. You're an angel. You do know that don't you?' he said, taking her in his arms and hugging her tightly.

'Of course, watch you don't squash my wings.'

53

The next morning Ewan, Molly and Jamie met with Flinty at Osprey House to decide the way forward. The Procurator Fiscal had looked at the paperwork and felt they would have a good chance of conviction so their boss was of the opinion that they should go ahead with the case, but Ewan was still uncertain.

'Look she's confessed, and the Procurator Fiscal believes we have sufficient evidence to charge her. What more do you want?' asked Flinty.

'I know sir, but the forensics don't totally add up and we don't know why the deceased was blackmailing Jessica into confessing that she lied about what happened between her and Paul Fraser. Although he was married to Sophie Fraser, she appears to believe that her father was guilty.'

'Does it matter? It sounds to me that he was more interested in getting the money than getting her to confess. Why else would he have got close to her and taken those photographs and that video. When people have reputations to lose they can be blackmailed.'

'And we still haven't had the chance to interview Mia Cooper. All we know is that she's in Europe somewhere. We could try and get Europol to trace her.'

Flinty blew his cheeks out in frustration.

'That could take a while and it seems unnecessary given Jessica's confession, but I want each of you to put your case and I'll hear you out. If you convince me then we'll get onto Europol but if you don't I'm going to go with the Procurator Fiscal and I want you to charge her. Who would like to go first?'

'Can I go first sir?' asked Jamie. 'I believe she did do it so I'm kind of with you Superintendent.'

'I don't know if you *can* go first but you *may* go first,' said Flinty sarcastically, reminding Ewan of his old English teacher at Boclair Academy.

Jamie took a deep breath and jumped in feet first. Ewan couldn't help but admire his gumption.

'I feel there is a compelling motive for her doing it. There is evidence that who she thought was her future husband was deliberately manipulating and blackmailing her. Anyone would have been devastated to find out the extent of his behaviour but for someone like Jessica who we understand from her psychotherapist was a damaged and vulnerable individual it would have been extra devastating. The knitting needle is Jessica's. It matches the one we found in a man's jumper that she seemed to be in the middle of knitting and her fingerprints are all over it. The murder took place in her apartment, so she had opportunity as well as motive. There are no other credible suspects.'

'Thank you constable. Who wants to go next?'

Ewan was surprised that Flinty hadn't questioned or made any disparaging remarks. He hoped this meant he was genuinely interested in what they had to say and wasn't just humouring them. Molly indicated that she would like to go next.

'Well sir, I'm kind of in the middle. I agree wholeheartedly with what Jamie has said but I feel the forensics don't add up. She would have had to move the body in order to stick that needle into his eye and although she's fit, it would have been difficult for her to move a dead weight on her own. Jessica threw the pen drives away. She says it was because she was ashamed, but she must have known we would see the video once we went through Magnus's phone. It would have made more sense to preserve it to support her version of events. Also the prosecco bottle had no fingerprints other than Jessica's. Normally, there would be other fingerprints on it from the assistant who put it through the checkout or other people who had handled it so unless Jessica was OCD and wiped all her bottles before putting them in the fridge it doesn't make sense. Also the tissue box in the living room appears to have been wiped clean too. Again only Jessica's prints were on it. There were other prints in Jessica's apartment that we haven't been able to identify. In terms of the knitting needle, you told me sir,' she said, turning to Ewan, 'that Greer Gibson had a whole tin full of knitting needles sitting in her living room and presumably Barbara King has a supply as well given that she runs a knitting circle. Also there's something supicious about the Kings. I feel they're hiding something.'

'Have you checked whether Jessica has a compulsive behaviour problem?'

'No sir. Her counsellor didn't mention it and to be honest it just occurred to me as I was talking.'

'What about the knitting needle. How did Jessica's prints get on it if it belonged to Mrs Gibson or Mrs King?'

'I don't know sir. I suppose they could have swapped one of their needles for Jessica's needles at the circle and kept the one with her fingerprints on it to plant in the body later.'

'Motive?'

'Molly shrugged her shoulders and Ewan knew it was now his turn to try to convince Flinty to do a more thorough investigation.

'Sir, I think there is so much we don't know about Kevin Cooper that it's impossible to know whether anyone else had a motive. Clearly Jessica did but she may not have been the only one. Police records indicate that he was violent towards Sophie and we haven't got Mia Cooper's side of the story. We know that he had a female accomplice as a woman phoned Jessica telling her that she was the editor of True-Life Magazine, but we know that she was an imposter. Also, Kevin had access to Jessica's garage yet the car he had hired was found in the street and it had been wiped of fingerprints. I get the feeling that Jessica is taking the blame, but I'm just not convinced that she did it. Call it a hunch or intuition.'

'I thought you were like me Inspector, not keen on hunches or intuition. I thought you preferred facts. What facts have you got that would merit us continuing the investigation? My understanding is that the local police have been able to corroborate Mrs Cooper's whereabouts on the night that he was murdered and for the week prior to it. She was nowhere near Glasgow and if the daughter has been travelling then she would be in the same boat.'

Ewan couldn't argue with that. It was he who had got the local police to check Sophie out, but he just felt that they were missing something. But what? Jessica was displaying all the signs of someone who had killed another person and in fact he was so worried about her he had agreed with Rory

King that she be put on suicide watch. He could see Flinty wasn't convinced. He was snookered.

'I'm sorry McNeil. I'm going with the PF. Charge Jessica.'

And that was that. Ewan read her the usual statement and she was remanded in custody until a pleading diet could be arranged.

54

When Ewan got home, he felt deflated and exhausted, but his spirits lifted when he smelled Suzie's signature dish of Spanish stovies made with chorizo. She had improvised when she lived in El Paraiso and it was one of the first dishes she had cooked for him during his many visits. Whenever she cooked it, it reminded him of the first flush of his love for her.

'You look washed out Ewan. Bad day?'

'Yes. We've charged Jessica Aitken. It will be in all the papers tomorrow so I can tell you without breaching any confidentiality.'

'Aren't you pleased? You've managed to arrest a murderer in less than a week.'

'I know I should be but there is just something not right. I feel we haven't done a thorough enough investigation. We've just accepted Jessica's confession and taken the evidence at face value.'

'Here, have a drink,' she said, pouring him a glass of Merlot. 'The food will be another fifteen minutes. Sit down and relax.'

'You're the best,' he said, taking her in his arms. 'I love you Suzie. When we get married where would you like to live?'

'Is that a proposal?'

'I guess it is.'

'I fancy Milngavie, maybe somewhere not too far from your mum and dad. What do you think?'

'Is that a yes then?'

'I guess it is.'

PART THREE
MAKING UP

'You can't go back and change the beginning, but you can start where you are and change the ending.'
CS Lewis

55

I sit in the holding cell hoping that I've done enough to get my sentence suspended or at least reduced. It's almost twenty five years to the day since Mr Fraser drove me home from the Christmas Dance and I think back to that winter night all those years ago and wonder what my life would have been like if Mr Fraser hadn't committed that act of kindness. Perhaps I would have ended up in prison anyway – a girl with alcoholic parents, a no-hoper. I knew that's what the other teachers thought of me but not Mr Fraser. He had been the only person in my whole bleak world who had seen underneath the grubby looking girl with chipped nails and streaky blond hair. He had been the only one who had encouraged me at school, who had told me that my writing was good, that I could go to university if I worked hard. So why had I done what I did. Why had I lied about him.

I think back to the girl I was then, so different from this successful writer that I've become; fit, healthy, and clean now. Mr Fraser's death had been instrumental in that transformation. I hadn't realised that what I accused him of would affect him so much. As a girl of very little influence, I hadn't realised that what I said would be taken seriously. He was a teacher after all and teachers were like Gods in those days, at least it felt like that to me.

I had got the idea from reading *Bliss* I think it was. There was a problem page and a girl had written in saying that she had accused her teacher of kissing her, but no-one had believed her. I thought no-one would believe me, but I was so angry I wanted to hurt him as badly as he had hurt me. He had never intentionally hurt me of course. He had always been kind.

Even on that morning after the Christmas break when I had lingered on after class. I pretended I was looking for something in my bag as the other pupils trooped out and I had no friends calling to me to come on. After the last kid had left I closed my bag and made my way to the front of the class.

'Happy New Year Mr Fraser. Did you have a nice break?'

'Oh, hello Debbie. Yes, I did thanks. And you?'

He didn't look directly at me and kept on sorting through his papers.

'Yes. It was lovely thanks. I just wanted to come and thank you for taking me home after the school dance and for my present.'

'Present?'

'Yes, the little earrings you gave me.'

I pointed at the sparkling spots in my ears.

'Oh yes. I remember. I'm glad you liked them. I got my daughter a pair too.'

My stomach clenched a little at that. I didn't like to think of him having a daughter for some reason or to think that he had given her the same present as me. I wanted to be special, unique.

'I've written something sir and wondered if you would mind having a look at it.'

Mr Fraser and I had spent many hours together going over my school work and stories I had written. He was always so encouraging and helped me look at my work in a different way.

'Yes, of course, Debbie. Just put it on my desk and I'll have a look later. I'll give you it back with my written comments.'

'But sir, can't we do it just now?'

He turned from whatever he was busying himself with and for the first time looked me straight in the face.

'I'm sorry Debbie. After what happened at Christmas I'm afraid I'm not going to be able to give you individual tuition any longer.'

'But why?' I could hear the whine in my voice. 'We didn't do anything wrong.'

'*I* didn't do anything wrong Debbie, but I'm afraid you did. Trying to kiss me was totally inappropriate and I fear that I may have encouraged you to think this was acceptable behaviour by giving you the extra tuition. You're a bright girl Debbie and I'm sure you know that I could get into trouble if it was thought there was any inappropriate relationship between us.'

'So, you're not going to give me any more help with my work all because of a little kiss.'

I moved closer to him and fluttered my eyelashes in what I thought was a provocative manner and hoped that he would succumb to my charms. I laugh at the naivety of that girl. He stepped back in horror and I was reminded of how he had looked at me that night after the dance. I had been dreaming of him constantly, fantasizing about him kissing me and more. I had completely blanked out the look on his face, but it hit me like a blow from his hand now. He hadn't wanted to kiss me then and he didn't want to kiss me now. He didn't love me. I began to cry, and he just stood looking hopeless. Didn't try to put his arms around me or anything.

'I hate you,' I cried, reminding myself of the times I had shouted this at my mum and dad.

He was just like them. No-one loved me. I couldn't bear it. Mr Fraser had been the one light in my life. I ran out of the door and almost bumped into Mrs Crane.

'Debbie are you alright?' she asked, putting her hands on my arms her face all concerned.

'Leave me alone,' I screamed, pushing her hands off me. 'Don't touch me.'

And I ran out of the building and all the way home.

When I got there, Mum was in the kitchen.

'What's wrong with your face?' she said, in her usual caustic way.

'It was that Mr Fraser, he tried to kiss me, and I know that's not right Mum. He shouldn't have done that.'

As usual she didn't believe me or take my side.

'Don't be daft Debbie. He's a teacher why would he want to get involved with a girl like you. Have you looked in the mirror recently?'

'Why do you never take my side? Why don't you believe me?' I screamed at her.

It was Dad who phoned the police. He had been lying sleeping in the living room but my screams at Mum must have penetrated through his alcohol induced afternoon nap.

'What the hell's going on in here, what's wrong Debbie?'

'It's Mr Fraser Dad, he tried to kiss me. He's been giving me extra tuition and he gave me these earrings as a present at Christmas. I think he wanted to have sex with me, Dad.'

And that was how it started. People did believe me. The evidence was there for all to see: the extra tuition, a witness to me getting into his car after the dance, Mrs Crane seeing me run out of Mr Fraser's room. I even started to believe it myself so when Mr Fraser came to see me to try and get me to change my version of what had happened, I couldn't understand what he meant. In fact, I became so upset that Dad had to throw poor Mr Fraser out of our house. But when he jumped from the Erskine Bridge, just like his body had ended up battered and broken, something broke inside me and I promised myself that I would do anything to make him proud, to not let his death be for nothing. What I was doing now was for him.

56

I had received bail after my pleading diet as the judge decided that I didn't appear to pose a threat to the public, which meant I was free to go home until the date of my trial. I chose not to go home, however, as it felt too difficult going back to the place where Magnus had died. I stayed in a hotel for a few weeks but Cathy helped me to see that this wasn't a long term solution. I would either have to sell or move back in. I decided I would sell up once this was all over but there was too much media attention to put it on the market just yet. I would need to move back in. So Cathy organised for her husband, who was a painter and decorator, to give the place a full makeover and by the time I took up residence again you would never have known that a bloody murder had taken place.

I took a taxi to the high court on the first day of my trial. It is a beautiful building. What a shame it's beauty is marred by what goes on inside its rooms and corridors. All those violent offenders and their victims fighting for justice. I made my way through the airport type scanning procedure and was directed to the room where I was to meet with my solicitor and advocate. I could hear my heels clicking on the tiled floor, not too high. Didn't want to give the jury the wrong impression. I chose carefully what to wear for my trial. I know how important appearance is. What is it they say about first impressions, people make their mind up about you in the first seven seconds. This fact is especially important in a court of law. Although the Advocates for the defence and the prosecution use their verbal skills to convince the jury of the guilt or innocence of the accused, this bias of the eye is much more important in terms of what sways the jury. I have therefore chosen a navy blue dress with a lacy cardigan that I knitted in the circle last year and my curls are tied back with a clip. I'm hoping it will make me look pretty and jejune. I want to create the appearance of a woman who is honest and vulnerable, someone who could become a victim of coercive control. This is my defence. My mitigation for murdering Magnus.

Steven McIntyre, my solicitor, and Advocate Flora Fleming

were waiting for me when I arrived.

'Good morning Jessica,' began Flora, taking my hand.

Although I am being tried as Deborah Halligan, I am not her. I am Jessica Aitken and I have asked Flora to call me that.

'The jury will be deciding on your guilt or innocence so remember to look at them when you're talking. That won't be today, so you don't need to be nervous.'

'I'm not nervous Flora. I know what Magnus did to me.'

'Yes, of course you do but try not to be too sure of yourself. Remember the jury must believe you are a person who can be gaslighted. That you were a person of unsound mind on the night of the murder.'

'I know what I must do.'

'Okay. Let's go for it. See you upstairs.'

'By the way I've heard it's Judge Margaret Garrity so that will work in our favour. A woman judge is more likely to be sympathetic to coercive control than a man.'

I wasn't sure that Flora was right. Afterall, not just men could be controlling.

57

It was day three of the trial and Flora told me it was going quite well despite the evidence of the arresting officer, Detective Inspector Ewan McNeil, and Pathologist Jade Scott. After telling the court about the findings of his investigation and reading out my statement in which I confessed to the killing of Magnus, McNeil began to answer questions from the procurator fiscal and my counsel. His argument was that the killing was pre-meditated, not an unplanned act due to diminished responsibility. If I had known the truth about Magnus before he died then McNeil would have been correct, but I didn't.

'Please tell the court your reasons for believing this Detective Inspector,' began the prosecuting advocate, Keir Parland.

'My primary reason is that in my experience, someone who has murdered another person unintentionally would telephone for help right away but Miss Halligan left the scene and it was only after we discovered from her agent where she was staying that she confessed to the crime.'

I knew that would go against me, but I had no other option. I needed time to get rid of the bloody clothes and the pen drives. I also needed to think things through and decide my next course of action.

'In addition, as you will hear from my colleague, Ms Scott, Mr Pearson was already dead when the knitting needle was stabbed into his eye. This seems like a premeditated act of brutality and not a spur of the moment act such as grabbing the nearest object and hitting out'.

It was a calculated act. The needle linked me with Magnus, but I was also hoping that it would be evidence of my diminished responsibility. Only a nut job would do something like that.

'Furthermore, the camera hidden in the tissue boxes in the lounge and bedroom had no pen drives inside and I believe these were disposed of by Miss Halligan to conceal what happened that night. If her story was true, then it would have been recorded on the pen drive and could have proven it so I can only deduce that she is guilty of murder.'

I knew it would look strange but there was nothing else to do but remove it. It's evidence would have thwarted my plan.

'You will also hear witness statements later that confirm Miss Halligan was herself controlling and of a violent disposition.'

John was one of those witnesses and I wasn't surprised. Our parting hadn't been sweet. He told the court that if anyone was controlling it was me. He went into detail of how I had lured him into a relationship even although I knew he was married, which was a complete lie. What a job I had done on him getting him to leave his wife and kids and move in with me. And then how I had cast him aside when I had finished with him and wanted to move on to pastures new. He was positively gleeful when talking about what Magnus had done to me.

'She deserved every bit of it,' he said. 'The bitch had it coming. Karma that's what it was. Karma.'

Flora did her best to get over the truth, that I hadn't known he was married when we first met but I think his anger went against him. In general, people and probably juries especially, don't like to see such naked hate displayed in public. Watching John, I realised how important it was to conduct myself with decorum. I would get more sympathy that way.

The other prosecution witness was Barbara. This had been a problem, but we had agreed that she would convey to the jury that she was a reluctant witness for the prosecution, and she managed to do this rather well. In cross examination from my counsel she confirmed that what had precipitated my attack on her could have caused me to become of unsound mind. She went through all the theory on attachment and so on and I could see the jury looking towards me with sympathy. I knew Barbara wouldn't let me down.

The third witness, I hadn't been prepared for. When I found out that Mum was being a witness for the prosecution, I was sure that, like Barbara, she must be doing it reluctantly, but when I heard her testimony I knew she hadn't been reluctant. Like me she was trying to convey an image to the court. She wanted to be seen as an upstanding citizen who had become a victim at the hands of her daughter. She was wearing a black and white checked coat, had obviously had a cut and blow dry at the hairdressers and swore on the bible that she would tell the truth, the whole truth. She had joined AA after Dad died and God had played a big part in her recovery from addiction so I knew that she wouldn't lie but perception is such a personal thing. When she described what had happened on the day of her birthday I had to admit when I heard it from her point of view it did sound as if I was a bitch of a daughter. Flora in her cross examination asked my mother to try and see it from my point of view and in so doing was able to show the jury a different side to my mum's story.

'I ask you to stand in your daughter's shoes Mrs Halligan. There were no family photographs of Debbie on display, you told her you didn't like the cardigan she had knitted for you specially for your birthday and you told her that her birthday wasn't worth celebrating. Is it any wonder she became upset?'

Mum didn't bother to answer but I wondered if Flora had been able to make her see things from my perspective. The fact that my mum wouldn't lie on the stand was actually a bonus for us. When Flora moved on to my childhood, Mum didn't deny what poor parents she and Dad had been. Flora was able to show that their alcoholism had left me vulnerable and seeking love in inappropriate and as it turned out dangerous places. During the whole thing, Mum never looked at me once.

58

My first defence witness was Greer. She was good in the witness box. Looked like butter wouldn't melt. I hoped I would be as convincing. She told the court how she had met me outside Waitrose back in January and how friendly I had been. How delighted she had been when she found out I was a member of the knitting circle that her client Evie had joined. She described in detail what she considered my degeneration almost from the beginning of my relationship with Magnus. I had turned from a beautiful young healthy woman who always had something to say in the circle to someone who was withdrawn and often tearful. She said she hadn't known I had turned to drink but in retrospect remembers that I was increasingly late for the circle meetings and seemed less interested in keeping fit. Even during cross examination when Keir Parland drew the court's attention to the fact that she was the wife of the person I had accused of grooming me, she was very convincing when she said that she regretted her husband's actions and the obvious long term effects it had had on me.

Evie, Lottie, Cathy and Dorothy were my other defence witnesses and they all confirmed how much I had changed since meeting Magnus. I was delighted to see Evie looking more confident. She answered the questions and stuck up for me when Keir tried to diss me. Lottie looked the picture of respectability. Her hair had grown and she had dyed it back to its natural mousy colour. She also wore clothes that covered most of her tattoos so when she spoke in that quiet polite voice of hers there were no surprised looks from the jury. Cathy gave a good account of my difficult childhood and it was obvious how fond she was of me. Dorothy testified to how hard working an author I was and how devoted to my fans I was and mentioned the only piece of the puzzle that the police still hadn't resolved in relation to the blackmail. They never had found out who the woman was who phoned me purporting to be Nancy Gardener.

Their testimony didn't always quite fit in with the image of a vulnerable person who could be easily hoodwinked that

I was hoping to portray to the court, but it was evidence to support what had been found on Magnus's phone and of how much I had changed over the few months that I had been seeing Magnus.

In terms of my defence of diminished responsibility, Barbara's evidence on my vulnerability was supplemented by the testimony of that psychiatrist I had seen when Dad died. Who would have thought that the time spent with him would have come in so useful? Dr Kumar, MB ChB MRCPsych told the court that I had a borderline personality disorder and that what Kevin had done to me could have led to an episode where I would not have been thinking rationally.

My final star witness was Sophie, Kevin Cooper's wife. We heard first-hand what a controlling man he had been all of their married life, the undermining, the controlling, the trips to hospital. She was convincing. There was no doubt that she had been a victim of coercive control and the police records backed up her claims in respect of the hospital visits. There was therfore no need for Mia to come to court to back her mum up. When Keir cross-examined Sophie, he tried to convince the jury that she was part of Kevin Cooper's plan to blackmail me and therefore not the victim she was making out. But his brow-beating of her only made it clear to everyone in the court that she was a victim. Poor woman. I could understand why she hadn't fessed up to making that phone call. There was no way she could have coped with getting done for being an accessory to blackmail.

After all the witnesses had spoken, it was my chance to convince the jury of my innocence. When I was called, I walked up demurely with my head down not looking at anyone in the court room but when I stood in the witness box and read out the affirmation I looked straight at the jury hoping that they would be convinced that I was telling the truth. When I sat down I noticed my mum in the public gallery and felt a wave of hope. Perhaps Flora's attempt at getting over my side of the story on the day of her birthday had got through to her and she had come to show her support. I smiled over at her, but she didn't smile back. I felt my spirits drop just as quickly as they had risen. Mum - the mistress of coercive control.

After stating my name, address and occupation it began. Flora led me through my testimony with great proficiency and I now understood why her fees were so astronomical. She was adept at her job and I could see that she was helping me win over the jury. I even felt sorry for myself by the time she had finished. Then it was the turn of the prosecutor to try and undo all the good work that Flora had done.

'So, Miss Halligan, you have freely admitted that you killed the person you knew as Magnus Pearson. Is that correct?' began Keir.

'Yes.'

'And you say that you killed him because his behaviour towards you had made you of unsound mind at the time you took this action. Is that correct?'

'Yes.'

'When did you come to believe that Mr Pearson was manipulating you.'

'The night that I killed him.'

'So, there was no premeditation on your part, no planning your revenge.'

'No.'

'And yet, these pictures, Production 10 My Lady, show that you not only repeatedly struck the victim's head with a prosecco bottle but that you pierced a knitting needle through his eye.'

'Yes.'

'Weren't the bottle injuries enough? The man you knew as Magnus Pearson was already dead when the needle went through his eye. Why did you stab him with the knitting needle?'

'I don't know. All I know is that when I saw my knitting lying on the settee, I pulled out the needle and stuck it into his eye. I wasn't thinking straight.'

I paused, looking at the jury and then whispered, 'Otherwise I wouldn't have killed him.'

'What did you say Miss Halligan?' asked the judge.

'Sorry My Lady,' I said, looking up pitifully at the judge. 'I said I wasn't thinking straight otherwise I wouldn't have killed him.'

A collective intake of breath arose in the courtroom like the sound of wind whistling through trees.

'Okay Miss Halligan,' said Keir testily. He knew I had scored a point with that one.

'Take us back to that night and what made the penny drop that he was manipulating you. My understanding of coercive control is that victims rarely recognise it as such. What made you recognise it on that particular night?'

'The tissue box.'

'Production 12 my Lady.'

A picture of two tissue boxes was placed up on the screen for the jury to see. They still looked ugly to me and I wondered now why I had kept them.

'Yes. I had been crying and pulled a tissue from the box and it fell on the floor. I thought I had broken it and felt nervous as it was Magnus who had given me it. He was always telling me how clumsy I was.'

'Yes, Miss Halligan. But what was it about the box that made you see the light so to speak.'

'When I picked it up I realised it wasn't broken but had merely fallen open. When I examined it more closely I could see a pen drive inside, and I knew what he had been up to.'

'How?'

'I was planning to use something similar in one of my books and had done some research. The voice I had been hearing, the porn photographs, how Magnus seemed to know what I had been up to; everything became clear. I didn't want to believe it at first. I loved Magnus. We were going to be married.'

I let the tears begin to flow then and didn't try to hold back my racking sobs. They were half genuine. I was still grieving for the life I thought I was going to have with Magnus.

'Have you many more questions for the accused Mr Parland?' said Judge Garrity looking down at me. She was clearly getting annoyed at my blubbing and would call a recess if I didn't pull myself together.

'Only a few more My Lady.'

'Miss Halligan are you able to continue with Mr Parland's cross examination or would you like a recess to compose yourself?'

'I'm happy to continue with the questions, My Lady,' I said, sniffing loudly and wiping my tears. Luckily, I had thought to stick some tissues up my cardigan sleeve.

Keir carried on with his cross examination. He did his best but in my opinion he didn't do as good a job as Flora and I felt he had an air of defeat in his voice when he declared finally that he had no more questions.

59

I sat in the holding cell alone after Steven and Flora went back to wherever in the court they waited for the jury's verdict. Perhaps they just went back home or to their office and were called when the jury were due to return. I realised I didn't know much about the criminal justice system despite all the murder novels I had written. All the evidence, such as it was, had now been heard and the jury was out. Both Steven and Flora seemed to think it had gone well and that I had given a good account of myself. It all depended on whether the jury believed beyond reasonable doubt that I was of diminished responsibility at the time I attacked Magnus. If they didn't, I would be found guilty of murder and would serve a life sentence. I had taken a gamble and I was hoping it would pay off. My debt would be repaid, and I could start over again.

I didn't have to wait very long before the court official came to take me back upstairs to the court. The jury were ready to deliver their verdict. There was an air of repressed excitement as I entered the oak panelled courtroom filled with the wig clad advocates and their assistants, the court clerks, the public and press sitting in the gallery and I took my seat in the dock hoping that they would have believed me and would set me free.

'Court,' shouted the court clerk, as the door opened and Judge Garrity walked regally into the room. There was a shuffling of chairs as we all stood up giving our honour to the judge.

'Ladies and gentlemen of the jury have you reached your verdict?' asked Margaret Garrity.

'We have my Lady,' said the chairperson – a woman in her late fifties with bright red hair and glasses. I felt sure I had seen her at one of my *Aye Write* gigs.

A piece of paper was handed to the judge and she asked whether they had found me guilty or not guilty. I held my breath.

'To the charge of murder, we find the defendant not guilty. To the charge of manslaughter, we find the defendant guilty on the grounds of diminished responsibility.'

I breathed a sigh of relief but didn't smile. I still had to be sentenced and I didn't want the judge to think I was being triumphant. A man was still dead.

'Thank you Madam Chairperson. You may stand down. Thank you for your services to the court today.'

There was some noise from the public gallery as the jury made their way out of the courtroom, their job done, and the press made their way out to phone their editors with their news.

'Order,' shouted the Court Clerk.

'Miss Halligan,' began the judge, 'you have been found guilty of manslaughter which carries a lesser sentence than murder. I propose to seek background reports and to call a sentence hearing for next Friday. You will be retained at her majesty's pleasure in Cornton Vale Prison until that date. Please take her down.'

When I was safely deposited back in my holding cell, I received a visit from Steven.

'So, you got the result you wanted Jessica.'

'Yes, but I could still get a stiff sentence. What do you think the judge will do?'

'I'm not sure. We'll just have to wait and see. As Flora told you at the outset she's pretty woke in the field of coercive control and domestic abuse so I would expect her to be lenient, but you never can tell. The least you will get is community service but if the judge decides on a custodial sentence then the length of time will be at her discretion as there's no statutory amount for manslaughter.'

Not long after he left I was handcuffed and taken in one of those vans you see on the telly to Cornton Vale Prison and provided with a cell after the humiliating admission procedures had been carried out.

'You're just in time for dinner. Aren't you lucky,' said the prison officer.

'Thanks.'

I wasn't going to get into any kind of conversation with anyone. I wanted to be squeaky clean for my sentencing diet next week.

60

I didn't have a lot of time to think that week. I tried to keep myself to myself as the saying goes but it was nigh impossible as word got around who I was; Jessica Aitken, the crime novelist. I was one of their favourites, so I became a kind of celebrity, with the cons offering me treats like chocolate and cigarettes even although I didn't use either. I was even asked to help at one of the therapy classes where women were encouraged to write about their experiences as a way of releasing their guilt and trauma. This also helped them to think about their victims and how what they had done had affected them. I was surprised to find that I enjoyed sharing my talents. Reading their stories made me sad and I realised how lucky I was even with all the bad things that had happened to me.

The night before my sentence hearing, I lay in bed thinking about Magnus and what had happened that night. Everything was a bit hazy to begin with as I had had a lot of alcohol. When I think back I am amazed at how quickly I had succumbed to the demon drink. All I had needed was a little push from someone I thought loved me and I forgot all the resolutions I had made never to drink more than a couple of glasses of wine. I had always worried that having the same genetic makeup as my parents would double the chance of me becoming an alcoholic. It seems that I was right to worry.

When I woke up after my day from hell, the shutters were tightly closed so I was unsure what time it was. I checked my phone and saw that it was 1am. I had only been asleep for a few hours. I wasn't sure when I had gone to bed, but I knew it was earlier than my normal bedtime. I was finding it hard to remember much of the previous night, but I had a horrible nervous feeling in my gut. I wondered where Magnus was as he wasn't in bed beside me. I felt sick at the thought that he might have left me again.

I was a little unsteady as I got out of bed and went to get some water. As I walked to the kitchen, flashes from last night came back. My stomach knotted at the memory of what Magnus had told me. I was gutted at the lengths to which Mr

Fraser's family had gone to take their revenge and to get their hands on my money. But worse than that I was ashamed. I had been just like my parents, drinking too much to deal with the trials of life. What if Magnus decided that he didn't want to marry a potential alcoholic. There would be no wedding and no happy ending. I noticed the light was on in the lounge and wondered if Magnus was still up.

I opened the lounge door and the first thing to hit me was the smell of booze laced with something sickly sweet. I almost gagged. The room was in turmoil like a fight scene from a movie. What the hell. That's when I saw Magnus lying on the floor. My heart was suddenly beating much louder than it should in a healthy thirty something. He was lying on his front and I could see a pool of red gunge on the floor beside him.

'Oh my God, Magnus,' I said. 'What's happened to you?'

I knelt next to him and felt for a pulse but there wasn't one. I looked round the room and saw the bottle of prosecco lying next to Magnus. There was blood and hair on it, hair that was the same colour as Magnus's.

'I don't know what to do. What will I do Magnus? Magnus!'

I began shaking him and shouting his name hoping I could bring him back to life, so I was barely conscious of the noise behind me. When I turned to see what it was, I saw Mia. Her clothes and face were splattered with blood. Her mouth was moving but there were no words coming out. She looked so vulnerable; little more than a girl. The sight of her somehow stopped my own hysterics and I got up knowing I had to calm her down and get her to tell me what had happened. I would then phone the police. Magnus was obviously dead so there was no hurry.

'Okay Mia. Take a deep breath and try to tell me what happened.'

'Kevin,' she gulped, pointing at Magnus. 'Kevin.'

'Whose Kevin? That's Magnus, my boyfriend that I told you about.'

'No, it's not. His real name is Kevin Cooper. He's my stepdad. He, he grabbed me when I was leaving last night and locked me in the garage. I banged and banged but no-one heard me.'

She began sobbing. I didn't know if I believed her. Magnus had told me that he had got those tissue boxes from Sean Fraser and last night I had concluded that Greer and Mia were in on the blackmail as well as Sean.

'I don't understand. Why would he put you in the garage?'

'He didn't want you to know that he knew me.'

'I don't believe you Mia. Magnus told me that he had got the tissue boxes with the camera inside from your uncle, Sean Fraser. He said that you and he must be working together to blackmail me.'

'But I've never met Sean,' she wailed. 'I tell you that man lying there is Kevin Cooper, my stepdad. Look I have a photo of him on my phone.'

She grabbed her phone from her backpack and shakily flicked through it searching for the evidence that would break me. And there it was. A picture of Magnus with his arms round Mia and a woman that I assumed was Mia's mum. They looked the picture of happiness.

'I promise you I didn't know he was blackmailing you. I came to Glasgow to find my dad that was all. I told Mum and Kevin that I was going travelling in Europe so he must have got a real shock when he saw me coming out of your house.'

'But if that's true, why did he have to get close to me and make me believe he loved me? Why didn't he just try to blackmail me by threatening to go to the press or whatever. Why did he have to be so cruel?'

'It's what he does. He's a manipulator. He gets his kicks out of controlling people. My mum has been married to him for 25 years but it's only in the last couple of years that I've realised what he has been doing to her.'

'What has he been doing to her?'

She took a deep breath, trying to steady herself. I realised we were still standing over Magnus's body and decided that the kitchen might be a better place for us to talk. I took her through and made us a cup of tea. A cup of tea always made things better Cathy used to say when I went to her after falling out with Mum and Dad.

'Have you heard of coercive control? Did you read in the

papers recently about the woman who was let out of prison after an appeal against her conviction for murdering her husband. She was released because he was using coercive control and that caused her to have a breakdown and kill him. But the thing about it was her sons weren't aware that it was happening and that's what it was like for me.'

Her voice broke and she hiccupped a sob before continuing.

'Kevin was always nice to me when I was young. I really thought he was the bees knees and we kind of became allies against Mummy. She never worked so it was Kevin who bought me treats and clothes. Mum did the cleaning and the cooking and always tried very hard to please Kevin. Sometimes he was pleased. That was the side of him I saw. He would give her a hug, bring her flowers that kind of thing. But sometimes I would hear them arguing and when I asked Kevin what had caused the argument, he would blame Mum and say that she was in a mood with him. Even when Mummy had bruises or ended up in hospital he told me she had fallen and hurt herself because she had drunk too much. And I believed him.'

'So, what made you realise what was happening?'

'Mum ended up in hospital again and when I went up to collect her the police were there. They were part of a special department that dealt with domestic abuse and they were trying to convince Mummy to press charges. She didn't of course but it opened my eyes. Not long after that Kevin's job changed, and it took him away from home more than before. It gave Mummy and me a chance to be on our own more often. We had the chance to talk in a way that we never had before. We always made sure to stay out of the range of the camera he had rigged up at home to 'deter burglars' he said, but Mum knew it was to keep tabs on her. That was how we got talking about who my dad might be and she told me about Rory King. When I discovered he was a lawyer and quite wealthy I decided to see if I could get money from him. If I was successful it would have meant Mum and I could have left Kevin and perhaps come back to Scotland to live with Nana.'

'So, it definitely wasn't you who sent those photos and the

video.'

'No. I told you that last night.'

My doorbell rang it's little tinkling tune and I looked at Mia in horror.

'It's okay it's my Nana,' she said. 'I phoned her after I killed Kevin. I was so scared.'

That woman again. Since I'd met her at Waitrose my life had turned to shit. I made my way to the door my heart in my mouth. When I opened it, she didn't even look at me just pushed past me and Mia ran into her arms crying and sobbing with relief. What she thought her Nana would be able to do was beyond me.

61

I realised I was starving and made another pot of tea and some toast. After she had been able to extricate Mia from her arms, Greer had gone into the living room to look at the scene of the crime. As we drank our tea and ate our toast she asked Mia to tell her in detail what had happened.

'Just take your time darling. Tell me everything you remember.'

She explained to her what she had already told me about him putting her in the garage and then moved on with her story.

'It was dark when he came for me and took me into the house. Jessica was obviously in bed by that time.'

"What the feck are you doing here in her house? You'll ruin everything," he said.

"I don't understand. Why are you here Kevin?"

"I'm working on Jessica to get her to pay money to your mum to compensate for the lie she told. She's about the cave in. Another week and we'll be sitting pretty.'

"I don't understand Kevin. What lie? Mum never said that girl lied."

"It doesn't matter. When you have a reputation to lose you can be blackmailed. But more to the point why are you here? I thought you had gone travelling to Europe."

'I wondered what to say. I knew because of what had happened to Mum that he could be violent, and I wasn't sure how he would take the fact that I was trying to find my dad. So I decided to make it about money.

"How much have you asked her for?" I asked.

"£50,000."

"That's not much Kevin. I can do better than that."

"What do you mean, better than that? Have you been blackmailing her too."

"No. I've found my real dad and he's minted. I've asked him for £250,000. That's real money."

He was gobsmacked.

"Your real dad?"

"You're not my dad Kevin."

"What do you mean, I'm not your dad. Of course I am."

"No you're not. But it doesn't matter. You'll always be special to me and we'll have all this money to spend."

'That was when he went for me.'

"Money. You think money makes up for finding out I'm not your real dad. I've been with you since you were born. I've brought you up and paid for everything you ungrateful little bitch. If that cow of a mother of yours has been lying to me all these years, I'll kill her."

He grabbed me and went to push me up against the wall, but he stood on the prosecco bottle, lost his balance and we both went down. I was screaming and trying to get away, but he was too strong. His hand was over my mouth and I couldn't breathe. I remembered all the things mummy had told me he had done to her, the way he had controlled every part of her life, even put her in hospital. So, when I felt the bottle I knew I had to hit him with it; hit him for all the bad things he had done to Mummy. I just kept hitting and hitting him until he went limp. I'm scared Nana. I don't want to go to jail. I didn't mean it. I just lost it.'

She was sobbing again and looked so vulnerable. For some reason I thought about Mr Fraser and that's what made me decide. Although Mia would maybe get off on a self-defence plea, going to prison and standing trial would have a traumatic effect on her and who knew how she would end up. I didn't want to be responsible for another lost life. If it hadn't been for me, her mum wouldn't have ended up in a toxic relationship, her stepdad wouldn't have come into my life and she wouldn't be standing here now covered in blood having committed murder. I didn't have anything to lose. No happy ever after with Magnus, no reconciliation with Mum, nothing.

'I'll say I did it.'

Greer and Mia looked at me incredulously.

'Why would you do that? What's in it for you?' asked Greer.

'Redemption,' I replied, for some reason thinking about Lottie and that church she went to.

'Redemption for what?' asked Greer.

'For what I did to your husband. I lied about him trying to

kiss me and have sex with me. It was the other way about, but I got so caught up in the lie I didn't know how to get out of it until it was too late.'

I expected both Greer and Mia to be angry with me and was worried for a minute that I was in the presence of a murderer. What was to stop Mia losing it with me as she had with Magnus? But it was the exact opposite. Greer began to sob quietly and hug her granddaughter. Then she turned to me and took both my hands in hers.

'You don't know what this means to me Jessica. All these years never knowing the truth. Thank you.'

She even gave me a hug before we got down to business. We talked about how it could work, and it took them a while to agree but eventually they did. I could see the relief in Mia's eyes and knew I was doing the right thing.

It was Greer who proposed that we phone Rory and Barbara and I was surprised first of all that they picked up and secondly that they arrived so quickly in the middle of the night. With their help we developed a plan for making it work. It hadn't been easy. Mia's fingerprints were on the bottle as well as other things she had touched while in my flat so we had to wipe as much as we could and then get me to put my fingerprints on the bottle. It was important that there was no trace of Mia being in my flat. It was Barbara's suggestion that I spit on Magnus and stab him with the knitting needle. I felt my face burning when she mentioned spitting, but I supposed it made sense because of what I had done to her and Mia had no link with a knitting group while I did. I must say I took great pleasure in pushing that needle through Magnus's eyeball even although I knew he couldn't feel any pain.

It had been agreed that Rory would represent me and would find out more about coercive control and how I might be able to get off with manslaughter on the grounds of diminished responsibility. Barbara coached me in the psychological effects of a controlling relationship although I didn't really need much coaching as I had pretty much disintegrated because of what Magnus had done and the evidence was there for all to see.

We deliberately left Magnus's phone for the police to find

as it had the emails on it. We also left his car key for the police to find but needed to move Magnus's car out onto the street to allow me to get my car out of the garage and wipe off any evidence that Mia had left in there. I'm amazed that none of my neighbours seemed to hear anything.

We had decided that it would be better to leave the body to be found rather than me reporting it as it would make it more difficult for the forensics to establish an accurate time of death. Also it would give me time to get rid of Mia's bloody clothes and the pen drives and would give her time to go to Europe to lie low. I hadn't bargained on Cathy's zealous need to clean before going on holiday so we didn't get as much time as we had planned.

62

So here I am back in court.

'Court,' the clerk calls in her shaky voice.

Judge Garrity enters, adjusts her wig and sits. Everyone else sits too except for me. I'm required to stand.

'Miss Halligan, you have been found guilty of manslaughter on the grounds of diminished responsibility. I have sought background reports and am satisfied that you do not pose a danger to the community. I therefore sentence you to two years community service and compulsory therapeutic treatment for the trauma you have suffered. You are free to go. Court dismissed.'

I sink down into my chair as everyone else rises for the judge to leave the chamber. I am free to go. I have done it. I look up to the public gallery and see the back of Mum's checked coat as she leaves the chamber. No joyous shouts from her at her daughter being free. I am being abandoned yet again.

Steven and Flora come over.

'Congratulations Jessica,' says Flora, giving me a hug.

'Thanks for everything Flora. Thank you too Steven,' I say, holding out my hand.

The three of us walk from the courtroom and as I suspected the press are waiting, shouting out questions at me.

'How do you feel Jessica?'

'Will you write a book about your experiences?'

'Do you feel Magnus deserved to die?'

As I push my way through the throng, I spot them on the other side of the road, Evie with baby Charlotte in her arms and Lottie. They are waving me over. I hesitate. It has been agreed that Steven will drive me away from the court so I get into his car but as soon as we turn the corner I ask him to let me out. This throws the newspaper hacks off the scent, and I am able to make my way over to Evie and Lottie without the press noticing.

'Congratulations Jessica,' they say in unison when I reach them.

'We thought you would like to meet Charlotte,' says Evie,

putting her precious child into my arms. She is now about six months old and all smiley.

'I can't thank you enough for all you've done Jessica. I wouldn't have been able to fight against Tom trying to get custody of this little one if it hadn't been for your generosity. Do you mind if I give you a hug?'

'Of course not. Barbara isn't here to enforce her ground rules,' I laugh, letting her put her arms around me.

'Actually she is,' says Lottie, pointing to a nearby café and linking her arm through mine. 'Let's go and have a cup of tea to celebrate your release.'

When we get to the café, Barbara and Greer are inside waiting for us. I can't believe it. I thought they had only got involved because they wanted to save Mia but here they are smiling at me and putting their arms out to hug me. All our ground rules are being broken just for me. I like that. It means we are no longer just members of a therapeutic knitting circle, we are friends. How good is that!

The End

ACKNOWLEDGEMENTS

I would like to thank everyone who has supported and encouraged me in writing The Circle. It has been more than two years in the making. I started writing it in January 2018 in Tenerife where my husband Charlie and I had rented an apartment for a month. I foolishly thought I would make good progress being away from home but it was not to be. It took me until the end of 2019 to come up with an ending and I believe I have Bearsden Writers Group to thank for that. I joined it in September and doing their monthly prompts and receiving feedback seemed to get my creative juices going again. So thank you Leela, Palo, and the others.

Although only a small part of The Circle is about the police investigation, I would like to thank Camay Carroll and George Lindop for talking me through some technical issues relating to police forensic procedures. Police Scotland's website was also helpful for this part of the story.

The lockdown brought its rewards in that although my love of reading and knitting seemed to desert me, I was still able to write and the last four months have allowed me to concentrate on finalising and editing, editing, editing! It also gave me time for a new venture - setting up an Author's Page on Facebook as part of my plan to promote The Circle prior to publication. I would like to thank all my FB friends for liking and supporting it.

Having readers you can trust to give honest and constructive feedback is really important so a huge thank you to Liz Findlay, Ian Scott and Jeanne McTaggart for taking the time to read my book and give me feedback. Sadly, Jeanne, a long time friend, died suddenly in October last year and I have dedicated The Circle to her. I am so sorry that she never got to read the final version.

As an indie author, I don't have an editor or proofreader so I would especially like to thank my sister, Catherine Moore, who did an excellent job reading and proofing the final draft. As usual we had a giggle at some of the mistakes she found that I had completely missed.

Emotional support and encouragement is as important as the writing support that I received and I would like to thank Elizabeth Reid and Margaret Scalpello for the Sunday evening Zoom meetings during lockdown that always lifted my spirits.

I also want to thank my amazing husband, Charlie Felvus. I neglected him shamefully during the lockdown but he willingly took on extra cooking and housework to enable me to sit at my laptop day in and day out. He was also one of my trusted readers and his feedback was invaluable. I couldn't have knitted a better husband if I'd tried! I know that he is delighted to be getting his wife back and we are looking forward to hitting the open road together in our campervan now that lockdown is easing off.

Finally, a huge thanks to you, dear reader, for buying this book. Stay safe.

ABOUT THE AUTHOR

Marion Macdonald

Marion developed an interest in creative writing when she retired from her job as Director of a Housing Association and enrolled on a course with the Open University. She found that she loved writing and began with short stories and poetry. She then decided to try her hand at a novel. The result was One Year which she self-published in 2017. One Year was awarded second place in the Scottish Association of Writers' competition for a self-published novel in March 2020. The judge said, 'The idea of this book grabbed me from the outset and I found myself staying up late wanting to read just one more chapter - the sign of a well-written page turner.'

Her second novel, The Circle, will be published in August 2020. She describes it as 'An intriquing psychological novel with a twist.' As usual, contemporary issues provide the backdrop to the story. Last time it was the financial crash and the refugee crisis, now it is coercive control and the #MeToo Movement.

In the meantime she has continued to write short stories and was delighted recently to receive a runner up prize from Write Time for 'I Promise' and acceptance by the Weekly News of 'Always on my Mind.'

Marion was born and educated in Scotland. She lives in Glasgow with her husband, Charlie. Her interests include reading, travelling, scrabble, singing in a choir, knitting, learning to play the ukulele and, of course, writing.

BOOKS BY THIS AUTHOR

One Year

When Suzie's husband, Andy, is killed while delivering aid in Syria, she is left devastated and virtually homeless. He had remortgaged their home to buy twenty properties in El Paraiso, an almost deserted golf resort in Spain, and she can't afford the repayments.

While in Spain trying to decide what to do with her legacy, she meets and is attracted to the mysterious Josh who appears to be living illegally in one of the apartments that Andy bought. To complicate matters, Andy's friend Ewan delivers a suitcase to Suzie and the contents suggest that Andy may have been involved in refugee smuggling.

Determined to uncover the truth, Suzie embarks on a journey of discovery, but what will the truth reveal?

An intriguing and emotional page-turner that keeps the reader guessing right up until the final chapter.

Printed in Poland
by Amazon Fulfillment
Poland Sp. z o.o., Wrocław